THE REVEREND'S WIFE

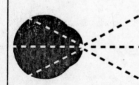

This Large Print Book carries the
Seal of Approval of N.A.V.H.

THE REVEREND'S WIFE

KIMBERLA LAWSON ROBY

THORNDIKE PRESS

A part of Gale, Cengage Learning

Detroit • New York • San Francisco • New Haven, Conn • Waterville, Maine • London

GALE
CENGAGE Learning®

LIBRARY OF CONGRESS CATALOGING-IN-PUBLICATION DATA

Roby, Kimberla Lawson.
    The reverend's wife / by Kimberla Lawson Roby.
        pages ; cm. — (Thorndike Press large print
    African-American) (A Reverend Curtis Black novel)
    ISBN 978-1-4104-4984-9 (hardcover) — ISBN 1-4104-4984-X (hardcover)
    1. Spouses of clergy—Fiction. 2. African American clergy—Fiction.
    3. Black, Curtis (Fictitious character)—Fiction. 4. Adultery—Fiction.
    5. Chicago (Ill.)—Fiction. 6. Domestic fiction. 7. Large type books. I. Title.
    PS3568.O3189R48 2012b
    813'.54—dc22   2012019729

Published in 2012 by arrangement with Grand Central Publishing, a division of Hachette Book Group, Inc.

Printed in Mexico
1 2 3 4 5 6 7 16 15 14 13 12

To all of my readers everywhere —
thank you
for just being you.

Thank you for everything.

CHAPTER 1

Charlotte smiled at Curtina, the stepdaughter she once hated, and could hardly wait for her birthday guests to arrive. Curtina had turned three shortly after they'd moved into the new church, and today, here it was a whole year later in the middle of May, and her little princess was actually turning four already. Curtina was a big girl now, and Charlotte was glad she'd chosen the most adorable bright pink jean outfit, with cute little rhinestones forming a heart across the back of the jacket, for her to wear. She was picture-perfect and more beautiful than any child Charlotte could think of. She was as sweet as anyone could imagine and a joy to be around — she was the daughter Charlotte couldn't and wouldn't ever want to live without, no matter the circumstances.

Charlotte scanned the pink-, lavender-, and white-decorated family room in the lower level of the house and was satisfied with the way everything had turned out. The area was filled with tables adorned with festive tablecloths and a plethora of balloons, some held down by weights and others touching the high ceiling. The setting was just right, and there was no mistaking that Charlotte had spent weeks planning the biggest party Curtina had ever been given and that Charlotte had enjoyed doing what she thought would make her daughter happy.

"So, are you excited, sweetheart?" Curtis asked Curtina.

"Yep. And I can't wait for all my friends to get here."

"I'm sure," he said, hugging her at his waist side.

Charlotte studied her husband from head to toe. After all these years of being married to him — nearly eleven that is — Curtis was still as gorgeous as ever and, truthfully, was even better-looking than when she'd met him. His skin remained flawless, his hair still held a soft wave, and even a person with poor eyesight could see how religiously he worked out. He was still the man of her dreams, the man she loved with all her heart, the man she was finally completely committed to — even if he refused to believe it. Yes, she'd made tons of mistakes, the most recent being last year when she'd slept with two different men, but she couldn't have been sorrier for her actions. She'd allowed her ill feelings toward Curtina, the child Curtis had conceived outside of their marriage and brought to live with them permanently, to get the best of her, but now she felt differently. Today, she had forgiven Curtis, and since Curtina's mother had passed away, she was honored to fill that role. It was true that for a while, she'd treated Curtina horribly and had wished she could move elsewhere, but soon Charlotte's heart had softened and she'd slowly become close to her. As time had continued, she'd come to love and cherish Curtina as if she were her own.

Nonetheless, her new feelings toward Curtina hadn't made much of a difference to Curtis, and his plans hadn't changed. He was cordial and polite enough whenever he was around her, but he'd made his intentions very clear: He was still divorcing Charlotte as soon as Matthew headed to Harvard three months from now. He seemed so sure about it, like there was no way anything could change his mind, and this saddened Charlotte. It terrified her because she didn't know what she'd do without her husband. She had no idea how he could possibly expect her to go on, when as far as she was

9

concerned, there was no life for her at all if it wasn't with him.

But no matter what she said, no matter how hard she pleaded her case, he didn't seem to care one way or the other. He was quite set on his decision, content with it even, and all Charlotte could do now was pray for some sort of a miracle. She was hopeful that God would soon intervene and bring them back together again.

Then there was her semistrained relationship with Matthew, her handsome six-foot-two and highly intelligent eighteen-year-old son who had always been a very caring and forgiving child but now couldn't seem to fully forgive his mother for the way she'd hurt him. Just thinking about that Tom character and how he'd forced her to meet him at a motel made her cringe, not to mention the sneaky way he'd tricked Matthew into driving miles to witness it. Matthew had even knocked on the door and caught her trying to get dressed. While this had all been Charlotte's fault — her sleeping with Tom, a man she'd never met, right after drinking too many Long Island iced teas at a jazz club outside of Chicago and then being blackmailed by him — Tom's actions had still been downright dirty. They'd been deplorable at best, and it had taken her months to try to forget about him — months before she'd finally stopped toying with the idea of getting revenge.

"Agnes, thank you so much for all your help," Charlotte said to their longtime housekeeper. "Thank you for everything."

"Of course. I was glad to do it. Especially for my little pumpkin," she said, smiling at Curtina.

"Thank you, Miss Agnes."

"You're quite welcome, sweetie."

"I'll bet you're going to get a lot of gifts, Curtina," Alicia said, standing close to her ex-husband, Phillip, and Charlotte wished that witch hadn't even bothered coming. There was a time when Charlotte had loved her stepdaughter, Curtis's eldest child and the one he'd had with his first wife, but now Charlotte couldn't stand her. Although, it wasn't like it was Alicia's fault that things had turned ugly between them; it was Curtis's. Their falling-out had occurred right after Curtis had given Alicia total control over his estate, should something happen to him, and just before Curtis had transferred all of his money into new accounts that didn't bear Charlotte's name. Some were now being jointly held with Alicia and some were listed in his name only, and this angered Charlotte to no end.

The only problem was, there wasn't a whole lot she could do about it — not when Curtis had told her right from the beginning that if she caused any difficulties for him financially, he would have no problem releasing a few of those degrading photos of her that Tom had sent him. She also didn't complain because in all fairness to Curtis, he wrote her a five-figure check on the first of every month and had promised to do right by her when it was time for the divorce settlement. He'd told her how he didn't expect her normal way of living to change and that he would always honor the fact that she was his son's mother.

"We should take a couple of family photos," Matthew suggested.

Curtis looked for a spot they could all stand in. "I agree."

"How about outside?" Richard said, pointing toward the sliding glass door.

Richard was the hired photographer who had come highly recommended by multiple parents at Curtina's school, and Charlotte was glad she'd contacted him.

"Sounds good to me," Curtis said.

Everyone, including Agnes, paraded through the lower level and out to the patio, and Richard positioned each of them.

"I'm the smallest, so that's why I have to

be in the front," Curtina announced proudly.

"Maybe I should kneel down in front of you," Matthew said, teasing her.

"No, Matt, then no one will be able to see me, and it's my birthday, remember?"

"Whatever, little girl," he said.

Everyone laughed but all Charlotte focused on was Curtis and how she wished she could do more than just stand beside him. What she longed for was his touch and the way he'd once held her — all the time. She wanted this and so much more, and she was willing to do whatever it took to win him back. She would do anything to make him love and trust her again, and she prayed the opportunity would present itself — before it was too late.

CHAPTER 2

Curtis drove his black luxury SUV into the church parking lot, eased into his designated spot, and sat for a few minutes. They'd moved into the new building about a year ago, but Curtis was still in awe of all that God had blessed him and his congregation with. So much so, the thought of it all got him emotional. It sometimes made him cry like a baby with gladness. It was true that years ago, Curtis had been senior pastor of two very large congregations in the Chicago area — two churches he'd been ousted from because he hadn't been living the way God wanted him to — but having the first two-thousand-seat sanctuary in a smaller city like Mitchell, Illinois, was a major accomplishment. Everyone in the area was impressed by Deliverance Outreach and with how quickly its membership had grown, and Curtis was excited about the number of people who lived as much as an hour away but still had no problem driving over to worship with them every Sunday. This kind of ministry and support was all that Curtis had prayed for, and he thanked God every day for all He'd done.

Curtis left his vehicle and started toward the church. Once inside, he strolled down two different plush, carpeted hallways and into his office. Lately, he'd been arriving earlier than normal on Sunday mornings, and while he'd told himself he was only doing it because he needed a bit of quiet time before delivering his sermon, deep down, he knew the real reason was because he didn't want to ride in the same car as Charlotte. When he'd first begun doing this a few months ago, Charlotte had highly objected to it, but Curtis had insisted this was best for everyone involved. He hadn't elaborated, although his thinking had been that it was better to drive separately since they'd be doing so permanently not very long from now.

Curtis removed his navy blue suit jacket and sat down at his desk. He'd certainly loved the office he'd resided in at the old building, too, but this one was on a whole other level. It was twice the size, it had a sitting area larger than some living rooms, and it was decorated with the most tasteful charcoal-gray leather furniture. There was also a spacious bathroom connected to the office that housed a huge shower and double sinks, and on the opposite side of the office was an attached conference room with multiple bookcases, a projection screen, and a classy mahogany table that seated twenty. His suite had everything he could possibly want and he was thankful.

He thumbed through a few sermon documents and then glanced at his latest book, *God's Favor and How to Accept It,* which had just been released in January. He was elated to know it had made number one on the *New York Times, USA Today,* and *Publishers Weekly* bestsellers lists, but he was glad all the traveling to promote it was over. He'd been out for five weeks straight, visiting seventeen cities and spending two days in each of them so he could do all sorts of media interviews and book-signing events — where in some cases, nearly a thousand people had attended and he'd sometimes signed for eight hours. It was all a blessing, of course, but the entire tour had proven to be physically taxing, and it had taken him a full week to recover from it.

Now, he looked at the beautiful photo of his three children and soon swiveled around in his chair, staring out the massive picture window, and sighed. Gosh. In only a matter of months, four to be exact, he'd be filing for divorce from his third wife. Even more surprising, this would be the first time he'd be the one initiating the process. His first two wives had left him and rightfully so, but this was different. Yes, he'd taken Tanya and Mariah through a lot, but when it came to Charlotte, she'd dished out a lot more than she'd ever taken. She'd done things he hadn't expected, and while he'd had an affair on her, too, she'd had three, and he just couldn't get beyond it. He had forgiven her, but his feelings had waned so much that he couldn't see himself staying with her — not even for Curtina's sake, and that's who he worried about because interestingly enough, Charlotte and Curtina held a special bond. They loved each other the way any mother and daughter should, and Curtis worried how negatively the divorce would affect his child. He'd thought about that a lot, but in the end, he'd decided he just couldn't be married to Charlotte any longer. He worried about Matthew, too, but the good news there was that Matthew had made it very clear that he understood Curtis's decision and that he was fine with it. Although, Curtis did wonder if the reason Matthew felt that way was because he still hadn't fully

forgiven his mother for the two affairs she'd
had last year. He'd been terribly hurt by
them, and in many ways, he hadn't been as
close to her since.

Curtis reminisced about his past a little
while longer and finally turned around and
reviewed his sermon notes. At the same
time, however, he thought about Sharon
Green, the woman he'd almost slipped and
had an affair with. *But* who he'd also been
thinking about a lot more than usual was
his first wife, Tanya, and how over the last
few months, he hadn't been able to stop
reflecting on the love they'd once shared,
how perfect they'd been for each other, and
how horribly he'd treated her. He could kick
himself a thousand times for sleeping
around with so many women behind Tanya's
back. It had been eighteen years since the
day Tanya had taken little Alicia and walked
out on him, but there were times when he
felt like it had happened yesterday, and Curtis wished things had turned out differently.
He wished he'd been completely faithful to
his first wife, the woman he'd loved with all
his heart — God forgive him, the woman
he'd never fully stopped loving in the first
place. He knew it was wrong, not to mention he did have the greatest respect for her
second husband, James, the man she'd been

18

married to for years, but he couldn't help how he felt. He couldn't change the fact that Tanya had been his soul mate ever since college or that even to this day, no one, not Charlotte or anyone else, compared to her. No woman was classier or kinder, and he'd made a grave mistake having lost her. He would regret it from now on, and it bothered him.

Greta, the church announcement clerk, gave details about an upcoming breakfast, and Curtis locked eyes with Charlotte. Only for a second, though, because soon he noticed Sharon, staring at him in her normal beguiling manner. He looked at her for a bit longer than he should have, but he had to admit that while she was extremely attractive and there was undeniable chemistry between them, he was pleased he hadn't given in to sinful desires and slept with her. Of course, she had offered herself to him regularly for well over a year, and though at times it had been tough telling her no, his fighting nature had ultimately prevailed. Still, he longed for the day when Sharon would give up and join another church. If she did, he wouldn't have to struggle with temptation or concern himself with what that temptation might lead to. He also wished he didn't have this great need to talk to her by phone as much as he did, because there were times when they chatted for hours.

Then there was Charlotte who had gone out of her way, too, trying to get him into bed, but he had refused her also — something that was completely out of his character. As a matter of fact, it had been hard for a man like him to go more than twelve months — twelve extremely long and very stressful months — with no intimate relations. Absolutely none. In the past, it would have been unheard of for him to as much as consider the idea of celibacy, but he was trying his best to live by God's Word. His goal was to do right by his children and not do anything that would bring additional pain or shame to their lives, and he was proud of himself for hanging in there.

When Greta finished informing the congregation about an upcoming citywide concert featuring Deliverance Outreach's choir, she said, "I think that's all I have, but at this time, I'd like to turn the podium over to our beautiful first lady."

Charlotte, dressed in an off-white, knit skirt suit, walked over to Greta, hugged her, and stood in front of the microphone. "Good morning."

"Good morning," the congregation responded.

"As always, it's such a blessing to be in the house of the Lord."

*Amen*s rang from every direction, and many of the parishioners smiled.

"I won't keep you long, but if you'll allow me, I'd like to tell you a little about the marriage seminar I've been working on for the last few months. It's been a long time coming, and I'm happy to say that the first in the series is scheduled for next month, the third Sunday in June."

"Amen," more people repeated in unison.

"What a great idea," a woman toward the front said.

But Curtis couldn't believe what he was hearing.

"I'm so excited," Charlotte continued, "because this kind of seminar is very much needed. I knew the divorce rate was on the rise, but it wasn't until I did further research that I discovered forty to fifty percent of all marriages now end in divorce."

Members of the congregation chattered amongst themselves, and Curtis could tell by some of their facial expressions that they were stunned.

Charlotte scanned the audience. "I know. Hard to believe, isn't it? But it's very true, and that's what got me thinking — what made me question why this is happening. I thought about it and then realized couples are getting divorced because they simply don't value the sacred institution of holy matrimony anymore, and they've become a lot more comfortable with just living together. Even for me, there was a time when I didn't value my marriage the way I should have, but I certainly do now, and that's why I feel so passionate about this seminar, and I want as many folks as possible to sign up for it. Young married couples just starting out as well as couples who have been married for years. Pastor and I, too," she said, looking over at Curtis, "have definitely had our ups and downs the same as anyone else, but we've both learned some very valuable lessons."

Curtis stared at her, emotionless, and wondered how she of all people felt as though she could offer advice to anyone about the sanctity of marriage. He wondered how any woman who had slept around on her husband the way Charlotte had could ever believe she was qualified to help anyone with their marital issues. The whole idea of it was ludicrous.

"As I said, I don't want to keep you long, but just so you know, flyers will be available at all exits, and if anyone has questions, they can call my office here at the church. I'll be glad to speak with you."

Curtis sat quietly but also thought it was interesting, too, that Charlotte was finally spending more time at the church during the week and that she was so much more involved with church activities, specifically the women's and children's ministries. She was doing all the things she should have been doing for years and was even being a great mother and wife, but unfortunately, Curtis wasn't moved by her newfound commitment to him or the church.

When Charlotte went to her seat, Curtis stood, stepped in front of the glass podium, and quoted his favorite scripture. "This is the day the Lord hath made, so let us rejoice and be glad in it."

He made general comments and offered his standard observations but never as much as acknowledged Charlotte's marital seminar information. He acted as though she hadn't said a word to the congregation and, more important, like she didn't exist. Instead, he continued on with his Sunday morning duties, business as usual, and thought about his future. Funny how it hadn't really dawned on him much before now, not in a serious manner, anyway, but suddenly he wondered who was going to be the next Mrs. Curtis Black. It seemed strange having to think about the idea of finding another wife, but he also knew the last thing any pastor needed was to be single. Especially given the number of women in churches hoping and praying for a pastor and his wife to break up. It was a very sad state of affairs but it was also reality, and Curtis knew he would indeed have to marry again at some point. There was no doubt he would eventually have to choose a new bride for him and a mother for Curtina.

CHAPTER 3

Charlotte hung her St. John suit inside the walk-in closet and for the first time ever, realized name brands didn't mean nearly what they once had to her. Not even the lavish master bedroom suite that housed one of the most expensive bedroom sets money could buy made much difference to her. There had been a time when luxury and owning the finer things in life had meant everything, but not now. Not when she was about to lose the man of her dreams. The man she'd loved for years. The man she still loved with her entire being. What good would any of it do if she couldn't have him? And it was at this very moment that she made a huge discovery: money and material possessions didn't make a person happy.

Charlotte slipped on a T-shirt and a pair of sweatpants, removed her pearl earrings, and pulled her sandy brown hair back into a ponytail. She gazed into the mirror, thinking what seemed a million thoughts, and while she'd been about to head down to the kitchen to warm up the lasagna dish she'd prepared yesterday for dinner, she decided to go chat with Curtis first. She knew the children were already downstairs in the family room because she'd helped Curtina change into her play clothes right after they'd gotten home, and she'd heard Matthew yelling up to his dad, letting him know he'd better hurry if he didn't want to miss some NBA play-off game that was about to come on.

Charlotte strode down to the opposite end of the hallway toward the guest bedroom Curtis had moved into and knocked a couple of times.

"Come in."

Charlotte opened the door, walked inside, and closed it behind her. "Can I talk to you?"

"What about?" he said, slipping on his house shoes and leaning against the dresser.

"When you stood before the congregation this morning, I noticed you didn't say anything about the marriage seminar I'm hosting."

"What do you think I should've said?"

"I don't know. That it was a great idea? That you completely support my efforts?

Something."

Curtis just looked at her, obviously not wanting to answer.

"Okay, this is the thing, baby," she said. "I'm not sure what else I can say or do, but Curtis, I'm so sorry. I'm sorry about everything, and I'm begging you not to leave me. Please don't end things like this. Not when I'm still completely in love with you."

Curtis settled onto the edge of the bed. "Sit down for a minute."

Charlotte sat next to him but made sure there was enough space between them so she could face him.

"I know this is hard on you and that maybe you truly are sorry for what you did, but things just aren't going to work out for us. I wish I felt differently, but too much has happened, and we can't change that."

"I hear what you're saying, baby, but all married couples have problems. You have to know that."

"I do, but how many major problems can a person stand? I've done my dirt, I admit that, but you've done way too much, Charlotte."

"But if you'd just give us another chance, I know things would be better. If you'd just let me show you how serious I am. I mean, why do you think I'm hosting the marital seminar I spoke about earlier?"

"To be honest, I really don't know."

"I'm doing it because I finally value the sanctity of marriage. After all these years, I finally know how important it is."

Curtis sighed. "Look . . . there's a part of me that will always love and care about you, but I could never stay married to a woman I will never trust again. I can't spend the rest of my life with a woman who has no problem sleeping around whenever she doesn't get her way or when things don't go exactly the way she wants them to."

"But I promise things are very different with me now," she expressed genuinely from her heart. "I'm a much better person than I was before, and I know how wrong I was. So, please, just let me make things up to you. Please give me one more chance, Curtis."

"I'm sorry. I know this is tough, but you and I have to move on now."

"Well, maybe if you could pray about this a little more."

"I have prayed," he said, sounding irritated. "And since we're on the subject, I may as well tell you that I've already had my attorney draw up the initial divorce papers."

Charlotte swallowed hard, her heart beating quickly. "You what? Why?"

"So that everything's ready to go."

"I thought you said you weren't doing this until after Matt left."

"I'm not, but I wanted to make sure everything was in order. That way, I'll be able to file right after he's gone."

"You've found someone else, haven't you?" she asked, dreading his answer.

Curtis squinted. "No. And just for the record, I'm not sleeping with anyone else either."

"Yeah, right."

"Think what you want, but I'm not."

"Whatever, Curtis."

"I'm sorry," he said, rising from the bed. "But going our separate ways is the right thing for everyone involved."

"No, it isn't. It's not good for you, me, or Matthew, and it certainly isn't good for Curtina. Have you even thought about that little girl and how she'll be losing a second mother in less than two years?"

"Of course I have. I've thought about it a lot, but she'll be fine."

"How can you say that?"

"Because she will."

"She won't, Curtis. She'll be miserable, and I think you know that."

"What I know is that our marriage is over

and that I've made my decision."

Charlotte's heart beat faster. "But what about all we've been through? What about the vows we took? What about forgiveness?"

"That's just it . . . I have forgiven you. I forgave you months ago."

"Well, if that's true, then how can you simply walk away, acting as though I never meant anything to you?"

His body language changed, and he was visibly annoyed. "Okay, look, Charlotte. I do respect you as the mother of my son —"

Charlotte interrupted him. "So, what are you saying? That I'm not a mother to Curtina, too? That I'm lying every time I say how much I love her?"

"No, but it wasn't all that long ago when you hated her. You literally couldn't stand the sight of her, and you wanted nothing to do with her."

"That was then, Curtis."

"Yeah, but it's still the truth."

Charlotte stood up. "I now love Curtina no differently than if she were my own, and I'm offended that you keep trying to insinuate otherwise."

Curtis shook his head. "I'm going downstairs."

"Just like that. You're just going to leave me standing here?"

30

"There's nothing else to talk about, Charlotte, and I definitely don't feel like arguing. My mind is made up, and I wish you'd just accept that."

Curtis moved past her and left. Charlotte waited a few seconds, blinking away tears and wondering how he could expect her to accept anything of the sort. Especially since there was no way she ever would — not today or even four months from now in a courtroom.

CHAPTER 4

It was Tuesday, Curtis sat reading the *Chicago Tribune* and drinking a cup of a coffee, the children were eating their breakfast, and Charlotte sipped some of the fresh-squeezed orange juice Agnes had made and just set in front of them. Yesterday was Curtis's usual day off, but since he'd chosen to spend it running errands — at least that's what he'd claimed he'd been doing — Charlotte had spent most of her day at her favorite mall, Oakbrook Center. She'd debated taking the drive, since it was located about eighty miles from Mitchell, but when she'd realized she had nothing else to do and didn't want to spend another day at home alone, she'd gotten dressed and headed on her way. She hadn't bought much of anything, though, something that wasn't the norm for her, so it just went to show how unhappy she was. Some might say she was depressed even, but that was something she refused to believe about herself. She was sad and very worried about the future of her marriage, but she wouldn't say her misery was that extreme.

Curtina bit into a piece of her toast. "We had so much fun at school yesterday, Mommy."

"That's great, sweetie. But what I want to know is if you learned anything."

"Yep. We learned a lot of stuff. And did you know that turtles leave their babies on their own once they're born?"

"No, I didn't," Charlotte said, shocked that a four-year-old was being taught this much about animals.

"Well, they do. We have a turtle in our class, and that's what our teacher read in one of the books. Isn't that sad?"

"It is, honey."

Curtina swung her legs back and forth. "I'm glad regular mommies don't leave their children after they're born, because that would be even sadder."

Charlotte smiled and was glad Curtina had been much too young to remember her own mother's passing. "It would be, sweetie. It would be very sad, and that's why I would never leave you no matter what."

Charlotte looked across the table at Curtis. He cast an eye at her but then looked back at his newspaper.

Matthew drank half of his milk in one gulp. "Turtles aren't the only animals that abandon their young."

"What does 'abandon' mean?" Curtina asked.

"It means to leave something or someone alone," he said.

"Oh."

"Anyway, for example, pandas do it when they give birth to two cubs because they only have enough milk for one. And that's when they choose their favorite and leave the other one behind."

Curtina bugged her eyes. "And does it die?"

"Probably."

"I don't wanna talk about this anymore," she said, dropping her head and eating more of her food.

"Why? Does it scare you?" Matthew teased.

"Stop it, Matt," she said sadly.

"Okay, okay. But you brought it up, and I was just adding to the conversation. Plus, I didn't know you were going to be a baby about it. I thought you were a big girl," he said, kiddie-punching her shoulder.

"I am a big girl. I turned four, remember?"

"You crack me up," he said.

Charlotte smiled at her children but then said, "So, Matt . . . are you ready for your finals?"

"Pretty much, but I can't wait to get them over with."

"I'm sure. And at least you only have two weeks to go."

"I know."

"Gosh . . . I can't believe you're going to be graduating and that you'll be leaving us for good." Charlotte smiled again but now tears streamed down her face.

"You say that almost every day, Mom, but I won't be gone forever. And you know I'll come home whenever I can."

Curtina turned to him. "I don't want you to go away, Matt. I want you to stay here with us."

"I wish I could, but if I don't go, I won't be able to get a good job in a few years. And, anyway, if I go to school and get a good education, I'll be able to buy you anything you want."

Curtina grinned. "Like that doll I showed you on TV last night?"

"Yep."

"What about a car?"

"Little girl, you know you're not old enough to have a car yet."

"Yes, I am. Remember, I already have that

pretty pink truck Daddy got me!" she said, referring to the battery-operated Fisher-Price Cadillac Escalade Curtis had gotten her for her birthday last weekend.

Matthew laughed. "You're funny. That's just a play truck."

"No, it's not. It's just as real as Daddy's. Only smaller."

Curtis smiled at his children, and Charlotte wished he'd smile at her, too, but to her disappointment, he turned another page of the newspaper and kept reading.

Charlotte wished he would say anything to her, but since he didn't, she looked back at Matthew. "So, is Racquel all ready for the prom?"

"I think so, but she won't let me see her dress. Says she wants it to be a surprise."

"Well, at least she told you what color it is so you could get a matching tie."

Matthew rolled his eyes toward the ceiling. "Yeah, don't remind me. It's mango," he said, and Charlotte, Curtis, and Agnes all laughed.

Charlotte still couldn't fathom the idea of Matthew being eighteen and dating on a serious basis. Over the last year, he'd taken a few girls out, but none of them had seemed a big deal until Racquel Anderson had come into the picture. It was clear that he'd liked her from the beginning, but when he'd started talking to her multiple times per day on the phone and spending most of his free time with her — seeing her right after football practices and Friday night games were over instead of hanging with his childhood best friends, Elijah and Jonathan — Charlotte had known her son was completely smitten with his new girlfriend. He was in awe of her, and while she hadn't asked Matthew one way or another, she knew Racquel was probably his first love.

The only thing was, Charlotte wasn't sure how she felt about it. For the most part, she did like Racquel, but she also worried that many of these young girls might run after Matthew for the wrong reasons. They might be overly interested because they knew his parents were wealthy. To be fair, Racquel came from a pretty well-to-do household herself, what with her father being a neurosurgeon and her mother owning a business, and Racquel was also a straight-A student, armed with a number of four-year academic scholarship offers just like Matthew. But Charlotte still worried because when it came to Matthew's father, well, Curtis wasn't just wealthy; he was world-renowned, a highly-sought-after speaker and author, and he earned seven figures annually. So, what Charlotte didn't want was for Matthew to be taken advantage of because of his father's prominence, and she certainly didn't want him making the grave mistake of having sex with Racquel or any other young lady. She didn't want him getting anyone pregnant and becoming trapped — she didn't want anything stopping him from getting the Ivy League education he'd worked so hard preparing for.

As Agnes cleared some of the dishes, Matthew said, "You *are* coming to my graduation, aren't you?"

"I wouldn't miss it for anything. I'm so proud and so excited for you."

"Thanks, Miss Agnes."

"Can you make spaghetti for us today, Miss Agnes?" Curtina added.

"Well, I guess I could — that is, if it's all right with everyone else."

Curtina looked back and forth between her parents. "Can she, Mommy? Can she, Daddy?"

"Of course," Curtis said.

"It's fine with me, too, honey," Charlotte told her.

"Then spaghetti it is," Agnes confirmed.

"Yeeaahhh!"

Matthew scooted his chair back. "Curtina, we'd better get going."

Matthew had been driving for two full years, but Charlotte still wasn't all that comfortable with it. She worried every time he got behind the wheel and even more when Curtina rode with him. Still, every now and then, she allowed him to drop his sister off at her preschool.

"You two be careful," she said.

Curtina hugged her. "We will, Mommy." Then she hugged her father.

Matthew bumped fists with his dad, and he and Curtina hugged Agnes on their way out the door. There was a time when Matthew would never have left the house without embracing Charlotte, too, but ever since that awful night in February of last year, he hadn't treated her the same. He was no longer angry with her, and he seemed to have fully forgiven her, but it was clear he hadn't forgotten what happened. She knew he was well aware that her infidelity was the reason his father was divorcing her. More so, Matthew also blamed her for his father's car accident, the one Curtis had gotten in shortly after hearing the news about her affairs. Matthew had been so disappointed in Charlotte, and she often wondered if they'd ever be close again. She knew Matthew loved her, but she longed for the exceptional mother-son relationship they'd shared since the day he was born.

Not long after the children left, Curtis folded the newspaper, grabbed his jacket from the back of his chair, and slipped it on. "Breakfast was great as usual, Agnes."

"I'm glad you enjoyed it."

"Oh and, hey, if you get time, I think I have some dry cleaning that needs picking up."

"You do. I was planning to go there this afternoon."

"Thanks, Agnes." Then he glanced over at Charlotte. "You have a good day."

"You, too," she said.

When he left, though, Charlotte wanted to burst into tears. He was so cordial, polite, and pleasant toward her, and the more he behaved this way, the more nervous she became. She was bothered because these noticeable niceties of his meant that he couldn't care less about her being his wife anymore and that he was looking forward to moving on and finding someone else. He hadn't stated those words exactly, but his actions screamed his future intentions — loudly and clearly — and his calm demeanor and straightforward conversation told her she needed to act fast if she wanted to keep her husband.

Although, sadly, she was starting to feel

that the idea of saving her marriage was slipping further and further out of her reach and that not even the most desperate attempt at sustaining it would make a difference. It was the reason she'd never felt more troubled.

CHAPTER 5

The morning had zipped by pretty quickly, and now Curtis sat in his conference room, preparing for their weekly staff meeting to begin. There were a total of fifteen people in attendance, but those sitting closest to him carried the most responsibility. To his immediate right was his longtime executive assistant, Lana Jenkins, and to his left were his two lead officers, Elder Jamison and Elder Dixon, who were now paid full-time salaries as a result of all the added duties they'd taken on since moving to the larger facility. Also in attendance were his first and second assistant pastors, Nicholas Simmons, a thirtysomething minister who was a truly dynamic speaker, and Sam Morgan, a wonderfully kind man who'd just turned fifty-five and had retired from corporate America about a year ago. Then there was the new CFO, Kendra Smith, who'd replaced the former CFO Raven Jones — the woman who'd been caught embezzling money from the church and was now serving time for it. Finally, there was Riley Davison, senior director of broadcasting.

Everyone filed into the room, and soon the meeting was called to order.

Lana gently swept her salt-n-pepper bangs to the side of her face. "The first thing on the agenda is a review of the goals we've met so far this year and those we still need to accomplish before the end of December."

"Let's start with the former," Curtis said.

"Gladly," she said, smiling. "First, we successfully moved into the new church in a seamless fashion and without any major inconveniences to the members. Second, the membership has already increased twenty percent, even though we were only expecting fifteen."

Everyone applauded.

"God is good," Curtis beamed.

"That He is," Lana said. "Third, our children's ministry is up and running at full capacity. Not only do we finally have enough adult volunteers to run it, but we now also have a few who have been placed on a waiting list."

"You can't beat that, sweetheart, now, can you?" Elder Dixon said, laughing. "You can't beat that at all."

"Number four . . . ," Lana said, blushing and trying not to look at him.

Curtis wondered why after all these years, Lana still pretended she and Elder Dixon weren't an item. Everyone knew they were, though.

"The television commercials are working in high capacity, and there are more visitors attending because of it. And finally, goal number five, Deliverance Outreach has officially been nominated for Church of the Year by the newspaper."

Everyone clapped and spoke loudly. They were all very excited.

"That's what I'm talking about," Elder Jamison said, reaching across Elder Dixon and high-fiving Riley Davison.

Curtis relaxed farther into his chair. "Wow. We've certainly come a long way in a very short period of time, haven't we?"

"That's for sure," Lana said. "And this is only the beginning, Pastor."

"You know . . . I really believe that. And I'm trusting and depending on God to do even more."

Elder Dixon leaned forward. "He will, Pastor. You just wait and see. He's gon' bless this church in every way 'maginable."

They discussed remaining goals and a few other items, and then Curtis brought up a problem that was sort of troubling him. "Before we move on to broadcasting, there is something I would like us to improve on."

"What's that, Pastor?" Elder Dixon asked.

"Visiting the sick and shut-in members. We're not getting out nearly enough to see them in a timely fashion, and it's unacceptable."

"Did someone complain?" Elder Jamison asked.

Elder Dixon pursed his lips. "Probably that ole Vera Jean Cox woman."

Everyone snickered, and Curtis knew why. "Come on now, Elder Dixon."

"What? Everybody in here knows that woman is a hypochondra or whatever you call it."

"Hypochondriac," Curtis said, "but we knew what you meant." Elder Dixon didn't have the keenest vocabulary in the world, but he also wasn't ashamed of it and was one of the sharpest men Curtis knew. He was also dependable, and Curtis admired that more than anything.

"Is that how you pronounce it?" Elder Dixon said. "Anyway, every time we turn around, that woman is ailin' with somethin', and I just don't think it's right for us to have to run over to her house every time she get the sniffles. I mean, even babies don't demand that kind of unnecessary attention."

Everyone laughed and Curtis said, "She did call the church a few times, saying she'd been sick for an entire week and no one came to see her."

Elder Dixon looked at Elder Jamison and then back at Curtis. "And when was that?" he asked, frowning.

"Last week."

"Last week? Wasn't she here at church on Sunday?"

"Yep," one of the younger administrative assistants down at the other end of the table said, and she and another young woman from accounting laughed.

Elder Dixon threw his hands in the air. "I rest my case."

"Still, though," Curtis said, "now that we have a lot more members, we need to create a better system and figure out a better way to schedule everyone in."

"Well, Pastor," Lana said, "you're busy enough, and you already cover members and their loved ones who are gravely ill."

"True, but even if someone breaks a hip, I want someone to visit them. I want us to make sure they're okay and that they aren't in need of anything. That's what we're here for."

"I'll sit down and take a closer look at how we're handling things now," Elder Jamison said, "and then I'll present a new plan next week."

Curtis nodded. "Sounds good. I appreciate that." Then he looked at Riley, his broadcasting director. "So how's everything with our radio and TV ministry?"

"Everything's going great. I still think we can perfect a few things, and while we're up and running pretty smoothly here locally, I'm hoping we can begin rolling out our services on a regional basis by early next year. Then, of course, after that, we'll start moving toward the idea of going national. It's a big step, but with the way things are going, I have no doubt it'll happen."

"Glad to hear it," Curtis said. "That's been a dream of mine for a very long time."

After they followed through on a couple of other agenda items, Curtis was shocked when Charlotte knocked on the door and opened it. He wondered why she was all of a sudden attending staff meetings again. She'd been doing so for nearly a year, but prior to his decision to divorce her, she'd stopped coming to the meetings entirely. He hoped she wasn't thinking her participation would influence him in some way, because if she did, she was sadly wasting

47

her time.

"Hey, Charlotte," Lana said, greeting her.

"Hey, Lana. Hi, everyone."

They all spoke to her, and interestingly enough, many of them were clearly glad to see her. They'd grown to love Charlotte over the last year, once she'd begun showing up more often, but they also didn't know what she'd done. They had no clue she'd betrayed their pastor with outside men.

"I'm so sorry for arriving late."

Lana passed her a copy of the agenda. "Don't worry about it. We're just happy you're here."

"Is there anything else?" Curtis asked everyone, glad the meeting was almost over now that Charlotte was there.

"I have something," Charlotte said. "If it's okay."

"Of course," Lana said.

Curtis wanted to object, but he didn't want anyone thinking something was wrong. He would have to make an announcement to the congregation about their marriage soon enough, but he didn't want anyone suspecting anything beforehand.

Charlotte rested her elbows on the shiny table. "First of all, I'd really like to take our women's ministry to a whole new level, so I wondered if I might be able to hire another assistant. Someone who would be dedicated just to the women's ministry."

Curtis looked at her and then around the room. To his dismay, everyone looked at *him,* waiting for a response — he guessed because Charlotte was his wife. Truth was, he couldn't understand why she was asking for anything when in a matter of months, she would no longer hold the position of first lady. They'd be divorced, and even if she decided to remain a member of Deliverance Outreach — she was the cofounder, after all — he would see that her responsibilities with the women's ministry were transferred to someone else. He also couldn't imagine any ex-wife wanting to be in the presence of her ex-husband's new wife once he remarried. But then, when it came to Charlotte, there was no telling what she might do.

"I think we should revisit that topic another time," he finally said.

Charlotte didn't look too happy but nodded.

"So, if there's nothing else, meeting dismissed," Curtis said, sliding back his chair.

Charlotte got up from the other end and walked over to him. "I need to talk to you about something."

All the staff members left the room, and

as Lana walked out she said, "Don't forget you have a conference call in twenty minutes, Pastor."

"Thanks, Lana," he said, and she closed the door behind her.

"What is it, Charlotte?"

She took a seat adjacent to him. "Us."

She was starting to get on his nerves, but he kept his mouth shut and listened.

"I've been thinking about our conversation on Sunday. I've also thought about all the infidelity that we're both guilty of, but no matter how I try to accept the idea of divorce, I can't. You see, Curtis, I love you more than I have ever loved anyone, and now I realize I can't live without you."

Curtis repositioned his body, making himself more comfortable. "Look, I hear you. Believe me I do, because there was a time when I felt the same way. But not anymore. It's like I told you the other day — too much has happened. Too much betrayal and deceit. Too many lies and far too much pain, and I can't do this with you anymore. You and I have had enough drama to last a lifetime."

Charlotte grabbed one of his hands with tears flowing down her face. "But I love you, Curtis. I love you so much I can't even explain it."

"Maybe. But you'll get over me soon enough. You'll eventually find the man of your dreams, someone you truly want to be faithful to."

"But, baby, I don't want someone else. I want you," she said, sniffling.

"I'm sorry," he said, slipping his hand away from hers. "I know this isn't easy, but, Charlotte, I just don't want to be married to you."

"Maybe if we went away for a long vacation, just the two of us. Maybe we could hash out everything, and you'd finally be able to forgive me. I know I really hurt you last year, but I'm willing to do anything you want. Anything it takes to make things up to you."

"I keep telling you that I *have* forgiven you."

"Then what's the problem? Why are you doing this to us?"

"I'm filing for divorce because whenever I look at you, I don't feel anything. I feel like you're someone I don't even know."

"You don't mean that," she said, obviously stunned by his words. "Not after all the years we've been together."

"I wish I didn't, but it's the truth. There's a part of me that does still love you, but I'm not *in* love with you. I haven't been for months now, and it really is over between us."

"Baby, please," she said, touching his hand again. "Please just give this a little more time. Let me make this right."

"You're going to be well taken care of," he said. "You'll never have to worry about anything. But you do need to start looking for your own place."

Charlotte's stomach churned. "What about Curtina? What about how sad that little girl is going to be once she realizes she won't see me anymore?"

Curtis could tell he wasn't getting through to Charlotte and decided the best thing to do was end the conversation. "I have to get going," he said, standing up.

Charlotte got up, too, moved closer to him, and quickly wrapped her arms around him. "Baby, I'm begging you," she said in a hurry. "Please don't throw our marriage away like this. Please don't break up our family. Please, Curtis. Please don't do this."

He grabbed her arms from his neck and backed away from her. "Charlotte, please pull yourself together. And then go home."

"Dear God, please, please, please, don't do this," she declared, frantically reaching toward him again.

But Curtis only stared at her and soon

left the conference room. He headed down the hallway and wondered when Charlotte would finally realize their divorce was practically a done deal. He hoped it would be sooner rather than later. For his sake and hers.

CHAPTER 6

Charlotte drove in front of Curtina's school as if she were on autopilot. She couldn't stop thinking about Curtis and part of what he'd said to her: *"Whenever I look at you, I don't feel anything."* His words had been noticeably cold and far too forthright, and they'd cut her straight to the bone. What hurt her more, though, was that she now thought back over the years before their marriage when she'd slept with her first cousin's husband. Then she'd slept with Aaron, Curtis's best friend, and had gotten pregnant. She'd done so many awful things throughout her adult life, and they'd all come back to haunt her. She was reaping what seemed ten times more than what she had sown, and she knew these consequences were a result of her actions — her sleeping around on Curtis like some whore. Back then, she hadn't looked at things quite the way she did now, and she was so embarrassed. She was terribly ashamed of the way she'd betrayed Curtis, especially since he'd kept his promise and commitment to her. He'd made mistakes, too, but over the last four years, he'd remained consistently true to her and couldn't have been a better husband.

Charlotte watched as all the teachers, aides, and children exited the building and soon saw Curtina running toward the car. Other children did the same, and they all seemed relieved to be out of school and going home.

"So how was your day, sweetie?" Charlotte asked, hugging Curtina and waiting for her to slide into her booster seat, which she was nearly too tall for, but legally she had no choice but to sit in.

"Good."

"I'm glad," she said, securing Curtina's seat belt and going around to the driver's side and getting in.

"Guess what, Mommy?"

"What's that?"

"You know my friend Jada?"

"Yes."

"Well, she told me her parents are getting something called a divorce and that her dad won't be living with them anymore."

Charlotte drove away from the school but

could barely fathom how ironic this was. Here she'd just had her own divorce discussion with Curtis less than an hour ago and now Curtina was disclosing bad news about her little friend's parents.

"I'm really sorry to hear that, honey."

"So, does divorce mean mommies and daddies don't love their kids anymore and that's why they don't want to be together?"

"No, honey, of course not. It doesn't mean that at all."

"Does it mean Jada won't ever get to see her dad again?"

"No, it doesn't mean that either. I'm sure Jada's dad loves her very much, and she'll still see him all the time."

"I hope so, Mommy, because Jada was very sad. She was even crying, and I'm glad you and Daddy won't ever get a divorce because that would make me sad, too."

Charlotte stopped at the red light, looked at her daughter in the rearview mirror, and fought back tears. Thankfully, Curtina wasn't paying much attention and said, "Mommy, can you turn on the DVD player?"

"Sure."

"Thank you," she said, already singing along with one of her favorite cartoon characters.

Charlotte continued driving but it wasn't long before she realized something. Maybe this unfortunate situation with Jada's parents had happened for a reason. Maybe it was divine intervention, because Charlotte now had the perfect plan. She'd come up with a sure way to bring Curtis to his senses.

She glanced at Curtina in the rearview mirror again. "Sweetie, you know what?"

Curtina had on headphones, though, and couldn't hear her. So Charlotte waved her hand toward the backseat and Curtina removed them. "Yes, Mommy?"

"You know what?"

"What?"

"I was just thinking. Maybe you should tell your daddy about Jada's parents so he can pray for them."

"Okay," she said, slipping her headphones back on.

Charlotte knew it was dead wrong, using their daughter for her own benefit, but she had to do whatever it took to get Curtis's attention. As it was, he'd already made up his mind about them and wasn't listening to a thing she said, but he would never ignore his daughter — not when she would certainly tell him the same thing she'd told her, that she would be sad if her own parents ever split up. He would hear her,

57

sympathize with her, and realize divorce wasn't their best option.

So, Charlotte exhaled and knew everything was going to be all right. It had to be.

CHAPTER 7

Before Agnes had left for the day, she'd graciously prepared her famous baked spaghetti dish, generously saturated with ground turkey and covered with melted cheese, and now Charlotte and Curtina were setting the dining room table.

"Spaghetti is my favorite," Curtina said, smiling, "and I'm so glad Miss Agnes made it for me. I asked her this morning before I went to school."

"I remember," Charlotte said, smiling back at her. "I'm glad she made it, too."

Charlotte glanced at her watch and knew Curtis would be home any minute now. About a half hour ago, he'd sent her a text message, saying he'd be there in about thirty minutes or so, but she didn't like the fact that *texting* was the method of communication he primarily used when he needed to contact her — she guessed so he wouldn't have to speak to her directly. Still, she couldn't wait for him to get there. She was also looking forward to hearing the wonderful conversation he and Curtina were going to have about Jada's parents, and most of all, she couldn't wait to hear his response . . . or see the guilt-ridden look on his face.

Just then, however, Matthew strolled in and pulled his sister's ponytails. "Hey, little girl."

"Hey, Matt," she said, hugging him. "How was school today?"

Charlotte shook her head because there were times when Curtina sounded more like an adult than a four-year-old.

"It was good. How was your day?"

"I had a good day, too."

"Hey, Mom," he said.

"Hey," she said, but was saddened because he still wouldn't hug or acknowledge her the way he used to. It was if he never even thought about it.

"I'm going upstairs to wash up for dinner," he said. "Oh, and guess what, Mom? Racquel received another four-year scholarship offer. So that makes five."

"Really? From where?"

"Northwestern."

"Good for her. That's a great school, too. Is she considering it?"

"No, of course not. She's going to MIT so she can be close to me at Harvard. Remember, I told you, we'll only have like maybe a fifteen-minute walk and only five minutes by car to see each other."

"Oh, that's right." Charlotte did remember, but she'd also been hoping and praying Racquel would change her mind about MIT. She'd wanted Racquel to take one of the other scholarship offers so Matthew would be free to focus on his schoolwork and not her. Clearly that wasn't going to happen.

Matthew ran upstairs, and about ten minutes later, Curtis dropped his keys onto the island and removed his blazer. Curtina didn't bother waiting for him to come into the dining room and rushed into the kitchen to see him. Charlotte followed her and saw Curtis picking her up.

"Boy, sweetheart, you're getting big."

"I know, but not too big for you, Daddy."

"Yes, you are. You're getting heavy."

"No, I'm not," she said.

Curtis hugged her and put her down. "So, what's new?"

"Jada says her parents are getting a divorce. And a divorce means her dad won't be living with her and her mommy anymore. Isn't that sad?"

"It is sad, sweetheart, and I'm very sorry to hear that."

"Will you pray for them, please?"

"Of course I will."

"I told Mommy that I'm glad you and her won't ever get a divorce because I don't ever want to be sad like Jada."

Charlotte watched how uneasy Curtis was. He tried focusing on the mail he'd just picked up, but she could tell he was lost for words. There was no getting out of this one, though, so she waited for him to tell Curtina what she wanted to hear. That her mommy and daddy *wouldn't* ever separate.

"No," he finally said. "I don't ever want you to be sad about anything. But even if anything ever made you sad, the one thing you know is that Daddy will always be here for you, right?"

"Right," she said. "Can we eat now?"

Charlotte wanted to scream. This whole scenario hadn't gone nearly the way she'd planned, and if she could rewind back to a couple of hours ago, she would coach Curtina a lot better than she had. She would give her a specific script, the one she needed her to recite, and she would help her practice her lines. She would help her get ready for her grand performance.

But it was too late for that now. She'd

been hoping this part of her strategy would run a bit more smoothly, making Curtis a lot more vulnerable and open to new ideas, but as it was, she would just have to move on to the next phase of things. She would keep her head up, remain positive, and pray for the best.

It was half past midnight, and Charlotte walked out of the bathroom, down the hallway, and over to the king-size bed. She pulled out a bottle of vanilla-scented body mist, sprayed it across her chest, arms, and legs, and slipped on a brand-new, lace-trimmed lavender nightie. It was the one thing she had purchased yesterday from Nordstrom, and it would now come in handy for this evening. She'd chosen what she thought was the perfect piece, the one that accentuated her complexion, and she hoped Curtis would agree. Especially since they hadn't made love in such a long while, and just thinking about the way she would feel got her excited. There was no question Curtis had always known how to satisfy her, and she looked forward to experiencing that same sort of pleasure again. What she wanted was to be close to her husband and make him happy. What she wanted more than anything else was to please him in more ways than one and, at last, convince him that leaving her, not to mention divorcing her, was a huge mistake. She wanted him to see that not only would she never be able to live without him, but he would never be content without her either.

She left the master suite and made her way toward the guest bedroom. She eased the door open, shut it softly behind her, and tiptoed over to the bed. The lights were out, but the clock on the nightstand shone brightly, so she could see Curtis was resting peacefully. She could also hear him breathing quietly yet deeply enough to know he wasn't awake, so she gently slid under the covers right next to him. At first, he nestled his head farther into his pillow, but then he slightly turned his body from his side to his back. Charlotte moved closer, caressed his face and kissed his neck. She continued until he finally woke up and realized what was going on.

"Charlotte? What are you doing?"

Instead of answering, however, she rested her body on top of his and kissed him on the lips. Surprisingly, Curtis didn't argue or resist, and he kissed her back. Charlotte's heart thumped harder than usual, and soon, Curtis eased her body to the side of him and removed his pajama bottom. She half-expected him to say something, she wasn't sure what, but he didn't. He said not a word, neither did she, and they kissed again. Now, Charlotte was doubly thrilled about making the decision to approach him without warning. Initially, she'd debated the idea, wondering if this was the right time, but shortly after dinner, she'd decided that what she wanted and needed more than anything was to reconnect with her husband physically. In fact, she'd been trying tirelessly to do so for months, doing all she could to make it happen, but no matter what, Curtis had repeatedly rejected her. He'd acted as though he couldn't care less about sex anymore, and this worried Charlotte — particularly since they'd always been so good together. They'd always been so flawlessly in sync and completely compatible, and they had never, not since the day they were married, missed many days of being intimate. It hadn't mattered whether they'd been relaxing at home, traveling on one of Curtis's business trips, or vacationing on some tropical island, making love had always been a priority. And it would be again if Charlotte had anything to do with it. All she had to do now was make him see what he was missing. Although, maybe that wouldn't be as difficult as she'd thought, because at the moment, they were enjoying each other as husband and wife in every way possible. They were joined as one — mind, body, and soul — the same as they used to be, and Charlotte couldn't imagine Curtis reverting back to divorce mode. Not after experiencing this kind of rekindling of emotions — there was just no way.

CHAPTER 8

Charlotte stretched her arms toward the headboard and glimpsed over at her wonderful husband. She hadn't been this relaxed or happy in months, and she was glad Curtis had finally given in and hadn't rejected her. He'd seemed so receptive to her advances, and their lovemaking had felt like old times — like they hadn't had a single problem in the world. It was as if Curtis had decided to let bygones be bygones and was ready to get back to the wonderful life they'd once had. It had taken a lot of begging and pleading on her part, that was for sure, but it had all been worth it. She was elated to say her many prayers had thankfully been answered.

She watched Curtis sleeping, but it wasn't long before he moved his body from side to side, stretched, and opened his eyes. He lay there for a few seconds, looking at her. Charlotte smiled, but when he didn't say anything or return the gesture, she got nervous and said, "Good morning."

"Hey," he said and Charlotte leaned over and pecked him on the lips. Then, she tried kissing him more intensely, but he gently pushed her away and sat up on the side of the bed with his back to her.

Charlotte wondered why he was being distant and couldn't help worrying. "Baby, what's wrong?"

"Nothing."

"Didn't you enjoy making love to me?"

"I guess."

"You guess?"

"No, truthfully, I did enjoy it. But, Charlotte . . . that still doesn't change anything."

Her heart sank. "What do you mean?"

He turned and looked at her. "I'm still filing for a divorce."

"Why?"

"Because no matter how hard I try, I can't get past the idea of you sleeping with those two men last year. I wish I could, but I can't. And I don't trust you."

"Then why do you keep saying you've forgiven me?"

"Because I have. I'm not angry with you, but I also can't stop thinking about those photos Tom sent me of you and him in bed together. As a matter of fact, I still pull them

68

up on my computer from time to time because I just can't believe you did that."

"But you know Tom was blackmailing me."

"*Eventually* he blackmailed you, but in the beginning you slept with him because you wanted to. You did it because you were upset about my allowing Curtina to come live with us."

"I know, I know, I know, baby, but I was confused back then. I was hurt, and I wasn't thinking clearly. I made a huge mistake the same as you've made mistakes in the past, but as God is my witness, I promise I won't ever sleep with anyone else again."

"I've heard those promises before."

"I know, but this time, you can believe it. This time I'm dead serious."

"Doesn't matter. I still can't stay married to you."

Charlotte didn't know what else to say, and soon Curtis stood up and grabbed his robe from the chair. "I've thought about this long and hard, and while I do still love you, Charlotte, I won't spend the rest of my life wondering what you're going to do next. I haven't been some perfect angel myself, but when I told you I was done messing around with other women and that I was fully committed to you, I meant it. And I kept my word."

Charlotte got up and rushed toward him. "Baby, can't you see that I've learned my lesson? Haven't you noticed how committed I've been this whole last year? I've been a good wife to you, even though you've insisted you're still divorcing me, and I've been a wonderful mother to Curtina. I've also become much more active with the church. But most importantly, I still love you from the bottom of my soul."

"That's all fine and well, but I can't help the way I feel. Too much has happened, and you know the saying . . . sometimes love just isn't enough. Sometimes you have to know when to let go and move on."

Charlotte rested the palms of her hands onto his chest, tears streaming down her face. "Curtis, I'm begging you. Please just give me another chance. Please don't break up our family like this. And didn't you hear Curtina last night when she talked about how sad she would be if you and I separated?"

Curtis took both of her hands with tears welling up in his eyes, too. "I've thought about that, and the last thing I want is to cause my little girl any pain, but I'll be here for her. Our divorce will be hard on her in the beginning, but she'll be fine."

"So you're really going to end almost eleven years of marriage?"

"I'm sorry, but yes. I have my children to worry about along with the ministry, and I can't be the best father or pastor if I'm constantly worrying about you and what you might be up to. When you had a baby with Aaron behind my back, it was beyond painful. Then this whole fiasco last year completely knocked the wind out of me. I mean, Charlotte, you slept with two different men like it was normal and like you had the right to do whatever you wanted. So, there's no way I'm setting myself up for that kind of disappointment again."

Curtis released Charlotte's hands, and she fell to her knees, weeping like a child. She cried loudly and while Curtis tried comforting her, it didn't help, and soon there was a knock at the bedroom door. Charlotte never looked up, but the next thing she knew, she heard Curtina saying, "Daddy, is Mommy crying? Can I come in?"

"We'll be out in a minute, sweetheart," he said.

But Charlotte needed her daughter and said, "Yes, sweetie, you can."

Curtina walked inside, strolled over to Charlotte, and fell into her arms. "Mommy, what's wrong?"

Charlotte couldn't speak, but she held on to Curtina as tightly as she could.

"Please don't cry, Mommy," she said, and then looked at her father. "Daddy, why is Mommy crying?"

"She'll be fine, sweetheart."

Charlotte heard his lame response but held on to Curtina for dear life. She held her like it was her last opportunity and prayed she would never have to be separated from her. Although, with the way Curtis was acting, her hopes and wishes seemed completely out of the question.

CHAPTER 9

Curtis responded to an e-mail Lana had
sent him regarding his schedule for next
week and tried pushing Charlotte out of his
mind. All morning, he'd attempted doing
everything he could, anything so he
wouldn't have to focus on his wife and what
had happened between them. The killing
part was that while he couldn't forget about
the way she'd hurt him, he'd still enjoyed
his time with her — and realized he had
more feelings for her than he'd been willing
to confess. They weren't as strong as, say,
two years ago, but he cared about her a lot
more than he'd been acknowledging. He'd
even realized that to a certain extent he
missed the closeness they'd once shared and
that their recent occasion of unbridled passion had caused old feelings to surface.

But who was Curtis fooling? Certainly not
himself because the truth was clear and
there was no changing it. There was no

pretending they could make a fresh start and go on as though nothing had happened. It just wasn't possible, and Curtis knew he had to accept that. He had to stick with his plan of moving on without Charlotte. With this in mind, he picked up his phone and dialed Sharon. Not because he was dying to speak to her but because conversing with Sharon would serve as a much-needed diversion, and he wouldn't have to think about his situation with Charlotte.

"Hey, you," she said in a welcoming tone of voice.

"Hey, yourself. So, how's it going?"

"Everything's good now that I'm talking to you. You know it's been a while, though, right?"

"Only a few days."

"Well, to me that's a long time."

"I've been busy. Plus, my daughter's birthday party was last weekend."

"Did she have a good time?"

"A great time. She was thrilled."

"I'm glad."

He leaned back in his chair. "So what's new?"

"Not a lot. So why don't you come see me?"

Curtis chuckled. "Are you ever going to stop asking me that?"

"No."

"Well, I really wish you would."

"Why, because you know you want to?"

"No, because I know it's wrong."

"Yeah, yeah, yeah, I know. You're married."

"Well, I am."

"Maybe, but if you ask me, that's only a technicality."

Curtis couldn't believe her sometimes. She was so self-confident and aggressive. "You're too much."

"No, I'm just being real, and whether you're ever planning to admit the truth to me or not, I know for a fact that you and your wife aren't happy. I've been saying that for months and months, and I know I'm right."

"No comment."

"You don't have to. And, anyway, if you're so happy, why are you calling *me?*"

"For good conversation."

"Yeah, okay."

"I'm serious."

"I'm sure you are, but our relationship is much more than that. You and I have undeniable chemistry, we can talk about anything, and you feel comfortable with me. You have ever since the one time you came to visit."

Curtis casually rolled an ink pen back and forth across his desk. "Yeah, but that never should have happened."

"Why? It wasn't like we did anything."

"I realize that, but we came pretty close, and I'm glad my son called before things went too far."

"Things only go as far as people want them to. And the reason you're afraid of being alone with me is because you know what's going to happen. You know you won't be able to fight all those feelings you have."

Curtis hated this. Hated how she was so sure of herself and how she saw right through him. She'd been this way all along, and it was becoming more and more difficult to refuse her invitations.

"What's wrong?" she said when he didn't comment.

"Nothing."

"You're quiet because you know I'm right."

He still didn't respond.

"Come on, Curtis, why don't you come by? Just for a little while."

"I can't do that, Sharon."

"You know, I have to say, you certainly have a lot more willpower than I'd been counting on."

"Yeah, well, to be honest, it has nothing to do with willpower. Turning you down has taken a ton of prayer."

They both laughed.

"Nonetheless," she said, "I still wanna see you."

"Not gonna happen. Plus, I have a busy day today. I have two more meetings and then Bible study this evening."

"That's right. I guess I'll see you there, then. Especially if that's the only way I'll get a chance to connect with you in person."

"That's fine, but you shouldn't be coming just for that. You should be coming because you want to learn the Word."

"I'm coming for that, too, but I won't lie — I'm mainly coming for the reason I said."

Curtis laughed quietly. "Good-bye, Sharon."

"See you soon."

Curtis laid his phone down, glad he'd ended his call with a woman he clearly had no business communicating with, but then picked it back up when he thought about Tanya. He'd been wondering how his ex-wife was doing and dialed her office.

"This is Tanya speaking."

"Hey," he said.

"Hey, how are you?" she asked in her usual pleasant manner.

"I'm well. You?"

"Fine. And how are Charlotte and the kids?"

"They're doing well, too, but I'm still counting down the months before my marriage is over."

"Are you really sure about that? I know I've asked you this several different times, but are you positive you guys can't work things out?"

"Yes. I'm as sure as can be."

"And Charlotte finally feels the same way?"

"No, she's still apologizing and pleading with me, and now she's trying to use Curtina."

"How?"

"By saying the divorce will devastate her."

"Well, actually, Curtis, I tend to agree with her. It might be extremely traumatic for Curtina if she loses another mother."

"She was only two when Tabitha died and doesn't even remember her."

"But it can still be damaging. This will also mean she'll be losing the only mother she has ever really known. Plus, you've said yourself how close Charlotte and Curtina are now."

Tanya had been a counselor for years, and clearly her professional skills were kicking in, but he really didn't want to hear this. "Curtina will be fine."

"Maybe, but I think you should consider this some more."

"My mind is made up."

Tanya paused and then said, "And what about Matthew? Have you thought about how all this will affect him while he's in college?"

"Matt is a very strong, independent, intelligent young man, and he completely understands."

"So you've told him you're divorcing his mom?"

"In so many words, and he's known for a while that our relationship isn't the same. Actually, he still isn't very happy with his mom for his own reasons, too. He loves her, but I can tell he doesn't have the same respect for her. They're not nearly as close."

"I'm sorry to hear that."

"I am, too, but Charlotte should have thought about that when she slept with those men."

Curtis was livid. He wasn't sure what had come over him, but suddenly those photos of Charlotte and Tom flashed through his mind, followed by images of her naked and in bed with that Michael character during her trip to Florida — a trip Curtis had thought she'd gone on alone until he'd learned otherwise. At the moment, he despised Charlotte for the way she'd hurt him. He resented how she'd gone out whoring around like some high-priced call girl and then had come home to him, smiling and pretending to be a loving wife.

"Curtis? Are you still there?"

"Yes," he said, realizing he'd been so caught up in his thoughts, he'd forgotten Tanya was on the phone.

"Did you hear me?"

"No, I'm sorry. I drifted off for a second."

"I asked you a question. I wanted to know if years ago, you'd thought about Alicia and how she would be affected when you were having affairs on me?"

Curtis felt like a heel. He knew Tanya was right, but he tried his best not to think back to those days because they were too hard to accept. He'd cheated on Tanya regularly, and no, he hadn't contemplated the idea that Tanya would finally leave him or that any of what he had done with other women would indirectly hurt Alicia. Back then, he'd been too selfish and careless to even consider it.

"No, I didn't, and I'm sorry for that. I'll regret what I did to you and Alicia for the rest of my life, and you know that."

"I do, but I'm making a point."

"Which is?"

"Charlotte may have been wrong for sleeping around on you, but I'm sure she never meant to hurt Matthew."

"Well, that's between her and him."

"Maybe. But as his father, you should explain to him that we all make mistakes, ones we deeply regret, and that what he should focus on is the fact that his mother loves him and would never hurt him on purpose."

Curtis wasn't sure how they'd gotten on this subject, but what he did know was that his conversation with Tanya wasn't going nearly the way he wanted it to. She was sounding just as logical and understanding as always, and while he admired that about her, his hope had been to talk about something else. What he'd wanted was for her to side with him and tell him he was right on all accounts when it came to his relationship with Charlotte.

"Okay, so you know I didn't call you for all this, right?" he said, and they both laughed.

"I'm sure you didn't, but, Curtis, you know I'm making some pretty valid points."

"But the bottom line is that I simply don't want to be with Charlotte any longer, and I don't think anything or anyone can change that. Not even you."

"You need to pray about this."

"I have prayed. Last year, I did little else and while I know we took vows, I just think I need a fresh start. I want to start over with someone I love, someone who will love me back. I want to be with a woman who wants only one person."

"And you don't think that woman is Charlotte? You don't think the two of you can make a final try?"

"No, I don't. I think we'll get along much better as friends. And that'll mainly be for Matthew's sake."

"And you don't see where you'll have any regrets?"

"Not when it comes to Charlotte. Maybe when it comes to my children because I know the kind of shame divorce can bring. But that's it . . . and since we're on the subject, you wanna know what my primary regret is? The one thing I have the greatest remorse about?"

"What's that?"

"Losing you."

Tanya didn't say anything.

"I'm serious," he continued. "I know you're happily married, but if you weren't, I would spend the rest of my life trying to win you back."

"Curtis, where is this coming from?"

"You know it's true, Tanya. You've always known. And yes, I realize we've become good friends over the years and that it's partly because we have so much history and we have a child together, but for me it's always been about so much more than that. For me, it's been because I will always love you."

"Curtis, you and I divorced a very long time ago, and I've been with James ever since."

"I know that, but I've been doing a lot of thinking and reflecting, and I can't hide the way I feel anymore."

"So, are you saying you don't love Charlotte?"

"No, I'm not saying that at all. But I definitely don't love her as much as I used to. Even last night, we made love for the first time since before my accident, but by this morning, it meant nothing to me."

"And why do you think that is?"

"Because as soon as we finished, all I could do was think about those other men she was with."

"Have you considered counseling?"

"We're beyond that."

"But how can you be so sure?"

"I just am."

"Well, I think you should give it a try."

"And I think you're trying to change the subject."

"You're right."

"Why?"

"Because it's like you said — I'm happily married."

"Maybe it's because the feeling is mutual. Maybe you've never stopped loving me either, but you just don't want to tell me."

"I have to go, Curtis."

"I'm right, aren't I?"

"You're wrong for doing this," she said.

"I know. And I'm sorry. But my feelings are what they are and so are yours."

"I really have to go, Curtis. You take care."

Curtis set his office phone onto its base and leaned back in his chair. He knew he *was* as wrong as Tanya said he was for confessing his feelings to her, but once he'd started, he hadn't been able to stop himself. The truth: He didn't want to stop, because he was tired of being miserable and wanted to be a hundred percent happy again. He wanted to know what it was like to genuinely live happily ever after. He no longer wanted to pretend the way he'd been doing with Charlotte, and he no longer wanted to settle. Of course, there was a huge chance

Tanya would never admit her real feelings for him and that she might never leave her husband, James, but he was glad he'd told her how he felt. He'd been honest, and if things still didn't work out the way he wanted, he would accept it and go on. He would be a man about it and wait for the next Mrs. Curtis Black to come along. He would exercise great patience until God brought his new wife to him.

CHAPTER 10

Charlotte was a nervous wreck, and as the day had gone on, she'd slipped further and further into panic mode. She'd been so sure that making love to Curtis would open his eyes to what he'd been missing and to what he didn't want to lose for good. But her plan of seducing him and bringing them closer together hadn't worked. They'd made beautiful, passionate love and had fallen asleep holding each other, but Curtis had awakened with the same frame of mind he'd been in for months. He was still divorcing her.

She just didn't understand how they'd arrived at this point in their lives. Yes, they'd had problem after problem. Yes, there had been scandal after scandal, and yes, they had both committed adultery. But what about "for better or worse" or "till death do us part"? Had Curtis forgotten those words? Words they'd told each other more than a decade ago in the presence of witnesses and, more importantly, before God?

He seemed so through, and while she'd been trying to stay positive, it wasn't until this morning that she finally realized he truly didn't want her. She'd seen it in his teary eyes when he'd held her hands. He'd spoken a few words, but his eyes had revealed the full story: He was genuinely sorry; he hated that things had turned out so terribly, but he would never trust her again. Trust, or the lack thereof, that's what this whole scenario had boiled down to, and Charlotte knew she was to blame for it. She'd wanted to believe Curtis was just as guilty as she was, but she could no longer deny what he kept saying: She'd been the first to have an affair, it was only then that he'd had his affair with Tabitha, and then she'd had two additional affairs last year. The score: Three to one, and even in baseball, three strikes always meant you were out. You didn't get do-overs or second chances; the game simply continued on with the next player. In Curtis's case, she knew he would continue, too, with the next love of his life, whoever that was going to be.

Charlotte wiped her eyes with bare hands, but more tears rolled down her face. She wanted to die, and it was all she could do not to kill herself. She was pitiful, helpless, and felt like a failure, but what kept her halfway sane was Matthew and Curtina. She knew they needed their mother, even if Curtis didn't think so, and she couldn't let them down. She wouldn't cause them even more pain than they were already going to endure when the divorce was final. There was no doubt it would be traumatic for everyone involved, and she just wished Curtis could see that. She wished he would listen to what she kept trying to tell him. She also wished she'd been smart enough to stop taking her birth control pills, because if she had, maybe she would've gotten pregnant last night. Maybe the anticipation of having a newborn baby would have made a difference to Curtis, because surely he wouldn't leave a wife who was expecting his child. But that was neither here nor there; even if she stopped taking her pills today, there was no guarantee she could get Curtis into bed again. Or was there?

Charlotte got herself up and went into the bathroom. She looked a complete mess, but maybe if she took a shower, combed her hair, got dressed, and went out for some fresh air, she'd feel a lot better. Yes, that's exactly what she would do. She would also call her mother and her best friend, Janine, neither of whom she had spoken to in a while — at least not for more than a few minutes. She'd wanted to have longer conversations with them, but it was just that she'd been so preoccupied and focused on Curtis. Trying to make things right with him had become her daily agenda, and she hadn't had time.

It was now shortly after one, and Charlotte went downstairs to the kitchen.

"Hey, Agnes, I was planning to pick up Curtina from school today so we could run by the bookstore, but if you don't mind, can you do it for me?"

"Of course, Miss Charlotte. No problem."

"Thank you so much. I know you've been doing that a lot more often lately, and I really appreciate it."

"I don't mind at all. You just take care of you."

Charlotte smiled. "It's no secret that I have a lot on my mind, and I know you're not blind. You can see and hear all that's been going on around here."

"I can, and I pray all the time that you and Mr. Curtis are able to work things out. The last thing I want is for the two of you to break up."

Charlotte hugged her. "Thanks, Agnes.

You're always so kind, and I love you very much."

"I love you, too. I love all of you."

Charlotte entered her car and backed out of the garage, then drove her silver Mercedes down the winding driveway and through the electric, wrought-iron gate. She drove onto the street and thought back to Curtis and how this was the exact spot where he'd had his accident, the night he'd found out about Michael and Tom and how she'd slept with both of them. He'd been so upset when he'd rushed into the house and confronted her about her unfortunate indiscretions, and when he'd stormed back out and gotten into his SUV, he'd driven into traffic and crashed into another vehicle. Thank God he'd survived and had only had to stay in the hospital a few days, but ever since then he'd been indifferent toward her. He'd been angry, hurt, disappointed, and disturbed by her actions, and she would do anything to erase them. But it was like she'd been thinking earlier — there were no do-overs or second chances when a person had struck out.

Charlotte drove into Chelsey's parking lot and was glad she'd decided to take herself out to lunch. Chelsey's was a popular restaurant and sports bar that a number of people in Mitchell frequented. They served great food and made some of the best sandwiches in town, and she and Janine occasionally met there for lunch.

She got out of her vehicle and went inside, where the hostess escorted her to a booth near a window and gave her a menu. It felt like the restaurant was already running the air-conditioning, which was strange since the temperature was only in the upper sixties. Charlotte was thankful she'd worn a black blazer over her white, button-down, long-sleeve shirt and a pair of jeans.

"Hello, my name is Amber, and I'll be taking care of you today," the chipper, twenty-something woman with blond hair said.

"Hello."

"Our specials for today consist of a grilled chicken fillet sandwich, a gourmet turkey burger, a fried catfish fillet sandwich, or a Philly beef sandwich. Of course, fries come with each of those. We also have a huge Cobb salad special as well. But first, what can I get you to drink?"

"I'll have a strawberry margarita with a little extra tequila."

"Sounds good. I'll be back shortly."

Charlotte relaxed against the back of the seat, looked around at the various folks who were already eating, and then thought about the last time she'd gone out and had a drink. It was fifteen months ago when she'd driven over to Covington Park, the suburb where her parents still lived, and where she'd spent an evening at her favorite club, Jazzy's. The night had started out fine, but sadly, it had ended on a humiliating note when she'd gotten drunk and then gone to a motel with a man she'd met only hours before. This man had turned out to be Tom, the jerk who'd eventually threatened her with blackmail. *What was I thinking? I must have been out of my mind to do something so crazy.*

She sat looking out the window for a few more minutes until Amber returned with her drink. "Here you go. Now, what can I get you for lunch?"

"I think I'll have the fried catfish fillet."

"Excellent. You'll really like that. Can I get you anything else?"

"No, I think that'll be it."

"One catfish fillet special coming right up."

"Thanks," Charlotte said, and heard her phone ringing. She was glad the place was slightly noisy and laid-back and that she was sitting in a corner, because she'd forgotten to place her BlackBerry on silent before walking in. When she pulled it out of her purse, she saw it was Janine calling.

"Hey, girl," Charlotte said, sipping her drink. "I was just thinking about you earlier."

"So, how are you?"

"I've been better, but I'm hanging in there."

"You don't sound so great. Are things okay?"

"Truthfully? They're not good at all."

"Where are you?"

"At Chelsey's."

"Well, why didn't you call so I could've met you? We're in the midst of final exams this week, but I had a two-hour break between classes." Janine was a professor at the local university.

"I don't know. Now I wish I had, though."

"You know I love that place."

"We'll have to plan on coming here next week maybe."

"Sounds good. But you sound like you need someone to talk to now."

"I'll be fine, girl," Charlotte said, sipping a huge gulp of her margarita and then closing her eyes because of how cold it felt sliding down her throat.

"I'll be leaving campus around three-thirty, so call me then, okay?"

"I will."

"Talk to you later."

"Thanks, J."

Charlotte placed her phone back inside her purse and sucked up the rest of her drink. Just then Amber walked by.

"Wow. I guess that margarita was pretty good, huh?"

"I guess it was."

"Can I get you another?"

"No, actually, I'll have a glass of red wine."

"We have a great Cabernet. Would you like to try that?"

"That'll be great."

"I'll be right back with it."

Now Charlotte wondered if she'd drank her margarita much too quickly, because suddenly she felt a few physical effects. Her head was a little woozy, but at the same time, she felt a lot better emotionally. She felt relief from some of the stress she'd been under, and this was a good thing.

She sat waiting for her wine, and soon Amber brought it to the table. She also brought her food shortly thereafter, and it was very tasty. Charlotte ate half of her sandwich and a few of her fries, but once she'd finished her glass of wine, she ordered another one. This time, she sipped it slowly, savoring the flavor and enjoying the way it made her feel, and she wanted to laugh out loud for no reason. Yes, getting away this afternoon all by her lonesome was definitely what she'd needed, and if she got the chance, she would do it again tomorrow.

Charlotte looked at her watch, realizing it was almost time to pick up Curtina but then remembered Agnes was doing it for her. So, she relaxed back in her seat again and beckoned her waitress to the table.

"Check?" the young woman said.

"Noooo," Charlotte sang. "But what I will have is another glass of wine."

"Of course."

Charlotte smiled, watched Amber walk away, and waited for her fourth drink to be delivered.

CHAPTER 11

Charlotte shoved the door open, staggered into the kitchen, and tossed her handbag onto the counter. Curtis frowned and Matthew raised his eyebrows. Curtina said, "Hi, Mommy," and hugged her.

"Hi, sweetie . . . how was school today?" Charlotte asked, slurring her words and obviously trying to pretend she wasn't intoxicated.

But Curtis knew she was as drunk as could be.

"It was good," Curtina said. "How was your day, Mommy?"

"It was the best I've had in months, sweetheart. I tell you, it was just peachy."

Matthew laughed. "Peachy?"

"Yep," Charlotte said, "just peachy."

Curtis was speechless. She couldn't be serious. It was already after five, so had she literally spent the entire afternoon out drinking? And then driven home under the influence?

"Mom, were you drinking and driving?" Matthew asked, and Curtis wondered if his son had been reading his mind.

"I had a couple glasses of wine and then drove home. So, it's not like I've committed some crime, Matt."

"It looks like you had a lot more than that," he said matter-of-factly.

Charlotte's smile vanished. "Well, I haven't! And, anyway, don't you have some homework or something you need to be doing?"

Matthew raised his eyebrows again, then looked at his sister. "Curtina, let's go upstairs."

"But I wanna show Mommy what we did in art class today."

"You can show her later. Let's go."

Matthew led his sister out of the kitchen and up to the second floor, and Curtis tore right into Charlotte. "Have you lost your mind? And how dare you yell at Matt for no reason."

"Excuse me?" she said, opening the refrigerator, pulling out a bottle of water, and letting him know she couldn't care less about what he was saying.

"You heard me. What's wrong with you?"

Charlotte plopped down into one of the

chairs. "Nothing's wrong with me. What's wrong with *you*?"

"Why were you out drinking?"

"Because I wanted to."

"And you don't see a problem with getting drunk and driving?"

"Nope . . . because I'm not drunk. I had a couple of drinks and that's all."

"You're such a liar."

"Were you with me? If you weren't with me, you don't know how many drinks I had."

"I know you had more than two. Any fool can see that."

"Why do you care, anyway? You're divorcin' me, remember?"

"I care because I don't want you setting a bad example for my children, and I certainly don't want you driving around putting other people's lives in danger."

"Whatever," she said, sipping her water.

"You need prayer."

"No, what I need is a husband who will do what he says. Someone who will stand by his word. You know, like when you and I took vows, and you said you would be with me until death. Remember that, Curtis?"

"So, because our marriage is over, you've turned into this?"

"I've decided to do whatever makes me

feel good, and right now, I feel great!" she said much too loudly, and Curtis couldn't stand the sight of her.

"Suit yourself, Charlotte," he said, and left her sitting there.

"I hate the ground you walk on," she yelled back at him, but Curtis continued down the hallway to his study, went inside, and closed the door.

When he sat at his desk, he blew out a sigh of frustration and relief. Frustration because he couldn't understand why Charlotte had decided to get drunk, and relief because he was glad he no longer had to look at her. She was pathetic, reckless, and irresponsible, and he couldn't imagine what had gotten into her. Yes, he knew she wasn't happy about their divorce, but drinking wasn't the answer. She'd done the same thing when she'd been upset about Curtina coming to live with them, and he'd been shocked about her getting drunk back then, too. But thankfully, that had been the only time.

Maybe he shouldn't have slept with her last night. Maybe this was the reason she was acting so irrationally. In reality, he'd known it probably wasn't the best idea and that their making love might get her hopes up or convey the wrong message, but to be honest, he'd *needed* to be with her. He'd gone without for far too long, and since he wasn't planning on having sex outside of his marriage, he'd given in to Charlotte right when she'd approached him. She'd tried to lure him into bed many other times, too, ever since he'd cut her off, but for some reason, last night he hadn't resisted her. He'd done so willingly and selfishly, and now he was sorry for it.

Curtis brought his hands toward his mouth, formed them in a praying position, and closed his eyes. *Lord, please give Charlotte strength and understanding. Help her to accept that our marriage is over, and please keep her from destructive behavior. Guide her and give her the kind of peace she's looking for.*

He rested his hands on his desk and eventually gathered his Bible and lesson for the evening. Bible study would begin in an hour, but after witnessing Charlotte's condition, he wondered if maybe he should ask one of the associate ministers or elders to fill in for him so he could stay home. Just then, though, Charlotte burst into his office.

"Why you got your door closed? Tryin' to hide somethin', are you?"

"Charlotte, please."

"Please, nothin'! I know you're probably sneakin' around talkin' to your little girl-friend, whoever the whore is."

Curtis got up, walked over, and took her by her arm. "That's enough, Charlotte, and I want you out of here."

"Let me go!" she spat, snatching away from him. "Don't you ever put your hands on me."

"You need to calm down."

"No, *you* need to calm down. What you also need to do is man up and do the right thing."

"You're drunk."

"Why do you keep saying that?"

"Because you are, and it's ridiculous."

"Awww," she said, smiling, losing her balance and wrapping her arms around him. "Don't be that way. Don't you love me anymore?"

Curtis pushed her arms away and stepped backward.

Charlotte laughed like a crazy woman, but in a matter of seconds, she stopped, held her stomach, and vomited all over the carpet. She heaved multiple times and finally rested her body against the wall. When she saw the mess she'd made, she glanced over at Curtis and burst into tears. But Curtis didn't budge. He just stood there, staring and wondering how much more of her he'd be able to take.

CHAPTER 12

Hangover wasn't even the word, Charlotte thought as she lay in bed, as sick as ten flu patients. Her head throbbed like she'd been clobbered with a bat, she could barely lift it off the pillow, and she struggled to open her eyes. When she did, she blinked a few times, trying to bring them into focus, and saw a hint of sunlight beaming through a tiny slit between the draperies. She opened her eyes a bit farther, looked over at the clock, and saw that it was ten twenty-five. Good. This meant the children were already at school, and Curtis was already at the church, and she wouldn't have to face any of them. However, she was sure that Agnes was downstairs somewhere, but that didn't bother her because Agnes would never say anything negative or condescending. Even if she didn't agree with what Charlotte did or said from time to time, she never let on. She was always as nice as usual.

Charlotte swung her legs to the side of the bed and placed her feet on the floor. She was extremely nauseated and wanted a drink of water, but she didn't have the energy to walk down to the kitchen. However, right when she pulled her legs back onto the bed, preparing to lie down, there was a knock at her door.

"Miss Charlotte? You awake?"

"I am."

"Do you need anything?"

"Some water if you don't mind."

"I'll be back in a minute."

Charlotte stayed sitting up, and soon Agnes returned and came into the room. She turned on the light, and Charlotte squinted.

"Here you go," she said, passing her a glass of ice water. "I also brought your purse up. You must have forgotten it downstairs last night."

"Thank you so much for bringing it," she said, not remembering where she'd actually left it.

"Can I get you anything else?"

Charlotte gazed at her with sad eyes. "Can you get me my husband back?"

Agnes sat down on the bed, sighing. "I wish I could. But he really seems to have his mind made up. I've tried talking to him several times since his accident, but all he says is that your marriage is over."

"I know I've done a lot, Agnes, but Curtis means everything to me. He's been my whole world for a very long time, and I don't know what I'm going to do without him."

"I understand."

"I just wish I knew what I could say or do to make him hear me. Make him love me again the way he used to."

"All we can do at this point is keep our faith strong and stay prayerful. You're going to have to trust God more than ever before and just wait for Him to fix things."

"But what if He doesn't? What if God doesn't feel I deserve a second chance?"

"The God we serve believes in second, third, fourth, and even one hundredth chances, and don't you ever forget that."

Charlotte smiled. "I wish I could be as optimistic as you are, but Curtis has never seemed more serious about anything. He just doesn't want me anymore."

"Mostly it's his pride and all the pain he's been through, but I'm still praying he'll come around."

"I know I hurt him pretty badly, but we've been here before, and we've always been able to work out our issues."

"Unfortunately, I think it's different this time. At least for Mr. Curtis."

Charlotte wanted to cry, but she refused to shed more tears. "I feel so lost and powerless, and it's driving me insane."

Agnes rested her hand on Charlotte's. "I can imagine. But please try to hang in there, and just keep praying. The Bible says to pray without ceasing, and that's what you're going to have to do."

Charlotte hugged Agnes. "Thank you for listening."

"Anytime. Now, you lie back down and get some rest. And just holler if you need me."

"I will."

Charlotte lay there for a few minutes, thinking about one thing after another and finally drifted off to sleep.

The phone startled her, but since her handbag was across the room in the chair where Agnes had left it, Charlotte ignored it. Seconds after it stopped ringing, however, it rang again.

"What?" she said out loud, and went over to see who was calling. She calmed down, though, when she saw it was her mother and got back in bed. "Hey, Mom."

"Hey yourself. How are you?"

"I'm fine."

"It sounds like you just woke up."

"I did."

"Are you sick? Is everything okay?"

"Not really."

"What's wrong?"

"I had a pretty rough day yesterday."

"I'm sorry to hear that, honey. What happened?"

"Curtis and I sort of had it out," she said, not planning to mention anything about her afternoon of drinking.

"I'm really worried about both of you."

"I'm worried, too, Mom, because I thought by now things would be better between us. But he's not budging. He's really filing for a divorce, and now he's saying I need to start looking for my own place."

"What?"

"He wants me to have something lined up by the time Matthew leaves."

"You have to do something," Noreen said, sounding horrified. "You have to make him see how sorry you are."

"I've been doing that for a whole year now, Mom, and it's not working. He's done, and there's nothing I can do about it."

"Are you praying?"

Charlotte exhaled forcefully. She was so

tired of hearing the same old thing, over and over. First Agnes and now her mother. She knew they both meant well, and she loved them with all her heart, but prayer wasn't doing a single thing for her. She'd prayed daily right after Curtis's accident, and while God had answered her prayer about Curtis's health being restored, He hadn't done a thing about her marriage. He hadn't fixed any aspect of her problems with Curtis, so she didn't see where praying was worth her while anymore. She didn't see a reason to keep harping on something that was proving to be a massive waste of time.

"Did you hear me, honey?" Noreen said. "Are you praying about this?"

"Yes," she said, lying, because if she told her mother the truth, she'd have a lot of explaining to do, and she wasn't in the mood for that. Her mother wasn't perfect and not as much of a Christian as say her mother's sister, Emma, but she fully believed in God and that He was everyone's protector. She believed it wholeheartedly, but Charlotte didn't necessarily feel the same. At least not now.

"Well, I'm going to keep praying, too," Noreen insisted. "We're going to pray until Curtis comes to his God-given senses."

Charlotte didn't know what she was supposed to say to that, so she said nothing.

"Do you want your dad and me to drive over to talk to Curtis?"

"No."

"Are you sure? Because you know I'm willing to do anything when it comes to keeping you happy. I know how much you love Curtis."

That was true, Charlotte thought, but she also knew how much her mother loved telling people that *the* Reverend Curtis Black was her son-in-law. It had always been that way, so Charlotte knew her mother's unyielding support wasn't just about her daughter's long-term happiness; it was about her own wants and desires, too.

"I do love him, Mom, but I can't force him to stay with me if he doesn't want to."

"Everything is going to be fine. It has to be."

"But what if it's not?"

"It will be, and if he doesn't give up this divorce business soon, you're going to have to do something drastic."

"Like what, Mom?" Charlotte was tired of talking, and suddenly she didn't feel well again.

"I don't know, but as Curtis's wife, it's your job to do whatever you have to to keep him."

"I thought the same thing, but not after yesterday morning. Not after the way he looked at me with calm eyes. He wasn't even angry. He was just done with me."

"But you have to keep fighting. You have to fight for your marriage until you get the upper hand."

"Mom, I thought I could, but to be honest, I just don't have the energy anymore."

"Then you'd better *find* the energy. You'd better figure out a way to make this divorce thing go away."

"Mom, can I talk to you later?"

"What's wrong with you, Charlotte? You sound so downtrodden. So defeated."

"I'm just tired, Mom, okay?"

"I'm really worried about you."

"I'll be fine. I'll call you tomorrow."

"I love you, honey."

"I love you, too."

Charlotte set her phone on the nightstand, curled her body into the fetal position, and pulled the Egyptian cotton sheet over her head. It wasn't long before she dropped off to sleep again.

CHAPTER 13

"I tell you, Lana, I'm this close to filing right now," Curtis ranted, "because I'm not sure I can deal with Charlotte." He and his assistant were in his office, going over a few church details, but Curtis hadn't been able to focus on that.

"I hear what you're saying, Pastor, and I know this is a very tough time, but for Matthew's sake I hope you'll hang in there."

"I've been trying my best to be patient, but I'm not sure I can deal with all this new drinking drama."

"Maybe this was a one-time thing. Maybe she simply got a little carried away because of how upset she's been."

"I hope that's the case, but she was completely lit by the time she got home. And she was rude to Matt."

"Really?"

"Yes. He questioned her about how many drinks she'd had, and she went off."

Lana shook her head, her face full of empathy. "That poor child. He's been through so much, and now this."

"I know, and I'll be doggoned if I let Charlotte ruin the rest of his senior year. I'm just not having it."

"Do you want me to talk to her?"

"You can if you want, but I'm not sure it'll do any good. She's so thoughtless and rash these days and not like herself."

"If she comes in today or tomorrow, I'll chat with her then."

"Well, I can tell you right now she won't be in today because she's too hungover."

"So, it's that bad."

"Unfortunately."

"Maybe tomorrow."

"We'll see."

"Well, worst-case scenario, I'll catch her early next week."

"I appreciate you doing that."

"Also, I know you don't want to hear this, especially since I've brought it up way too many times to count, but is there any possible way you'd be willing to reconsider?"

"The divorce you mean?"

"Yes. Because, Pastor, I have to say, I'm really worried about little Curtina, and I think Matthew is going to be hurt by this as well. I know you said he understands, but

I've yet to meet one child who's excited about their parents separating. Maybe in some instances, such as when a child has watched his mother being mentally or physically abused for too long, but for the most part, children want their parents together."

"I realize that, and believe me, I wish there was another way, but . . ."

"There is another way. You could call your father in the ministry, Pastor Abernathy, and have him sit down with you and Charlotte. You could talk everything out and then go away on one of those marriage retreats we get brochures on. We receive them all the time."

Curtis didn't want to disrespect the woman he looked up to like a mother, so it was best to keep quiet. He didn't have harsh words for her, but he also didn't want to tell her that counseling with anyone, even Pastor Abernathy, was out of the question. He didn't want her to know that his heart had taken a monstrous beating last year and that he'd built a concrete wall between him and Charlotte. Yes, he'd given in to her the other night, but regardless of how wonderful she'd made him feel, that rock-solid wall he'd erected was still in place and wasn't going anywhere.

"I think we should move on to my travel

agenda," he said, slightly smiling.

Lana smiled, too. "So, in other words, you want me to mind my own business."

Curtis laughed. "No, of course not. You know I value your opinion."

"Yeah, okay, but I hope things turn around, and soon."

"So," he said, changing the subject and wanting to confirm a few items for the trip he'd be taking a little over a week from now, "am I all set for Detroit?"

"Pretty much. You don't have to arrive at the COBO center until around three, and you'll walk onstage at four. So, we scheduled you a very early morning flight out of O'Hare, because I know you like to rest a few hours before speaking. Lisa," she said, referring to his personal publicist, "will meet you in the lobby of the hotel before you head over to the conference, though."

"Perfect. And then I'm flying back early Sunday morning? I'm also taking the day off from Deliverance so I can spend the rest of Memorial Day weekend with the kids."

"Yes, you arrive back at ten."

"Sounds good. I'm really looking forward to speaking again this year. The Women of God conference is one of the most awesome events I've done."

"I remember how much you enjoyed it last time."

"It's amazing, and I'm honored to be their keynote speaker. You really ought to go sometime."

"Maybe I will. My niece, Tracey, loves those kinds of conventions, so maybe I'll talk her into going with me next year."

"Why wait?"

"Well, it's a little too late for this one."

"Not really. Am I staying at my usual hotel in Dearborn?"

"Yes."

"Well, why don't you see if you can get a room there for you and your niece? As a matter of fact, I think you should go late Thursday so you can enjoy the conference all day Friday as well."

"You know," she said, standing up, "maybe I will."

"Great. And by the way, you can also go ahead and book first-class tickets for both of you. Not on the church, but on my personal card."

"Are you sure, Pastor?"

"Of course. Consider it a thank-you for everything you do for me."

"You never cease to amaze me," she said as Curtis's cell rang.

"This is Alicia calling. But anyway, you

deserve a weekend away, and I'm glad you're going."

Lana waved good-bye and left his office.

"Hey, baby girl, how are you?"

"I'm fine, Daddy. How are you?"

"Okay, I guess," he said, wanting to tell her about the latest Charlotte episode but deciding not to.

"Is something wrong?"

"No, just busy."

"I know the feeling. I've been working feverishly trying to finish up the ghostwriting project I've been working on for my actress friend so I can get back to my own novel. Then, of course, it's almost tour time for my second book."

"You have a lot on your plate."

"I know, but it's all good. I will say, though, that I'm glad this book was moved from June to October, because now I'll be able to enjoy the summer at home. Last year, I traveled June through August and before I knew it, fall was here."

"You really were out for a long time, but I think it was worth it so you could get your name out there."

"True. And don't get me wrong, I'm not complaining at all. I'm very, very grateful to my publisher."

"We've both been very blessed in that

respect, and I'm thankful, too," he said, standing and walking over to his window. "But on a different note, how's my son-in-law?"

"You mean ex-son-in-law."

"No, I mean my son-in-law. He's my ex because you guys got divorced, but he'll always be just like a son to me."

"You crack me up, Daddy, but I'm glad you feel that way."

"Phillip is as good as it gets, young lady."

"That he is, and I hope he'll eventually ask me to marry him again."

"He will, but please be patient, because I know how he feels. I know what it's like to lose trust in someone you love."

"I know, and, Daddy, I'm still sorry about Charlotte and what she did to you."

"I appreciate it, but that's all in the past." He paused for a couple of seconds and then said, "Hey . . . how's your mom doing?" He purposely didn't let on that he'd already spoken to her this week.

"She's good, but James hasn't been doing too well."

"No? Is he sick?"

"Kind of. He has some sort of an infection, and his doctors can't seem to find the right antibiotic for it. He cut his finger with a weed wacker a couple of weeks ago and didn't get it checked out for a few days."

Curtis wondered why Tanya hadn't mentioned anything to him but said, "I'm sorry to hear that."

"I wish he'd gone to the emergency room when Mom told him to, but for some reason he didn't think it was that serious."

"Well, I'll be praying for him," he said, feeling a bit guilty about his last conversation with Tanya.

"Thanks, Daddy. I'll make sure to tell him that when I go by there today. Oh, and I'll see you this Saturday. Phillip and I told Matt we'd drive over to see him and Racquel before they go to dinner. They must be so excited about the prom."

"They are," Curtis said, but his mind wandered to Tanya and whether he should call her. But then he decided against it when he realized he would mostly be calling to hear her voice versus checking to see how her husband was doing. He knew his thinking was inappropriate, so he quickly resumed his conversation with his daughter. He did whatever he could not to think about his first wife.

CHAPTER 14

The big day had finally arrived, and Curtis couldn't have been prouder. Matthew was all decked out in the most elegant black tux they could find, and yes, against his will, he was sporting the mango-colored tie that perfectly matched Racquel's exquisite, free-flowing evening gown. She was a beautiful girl, resembling a royal princess, and Curtis wasn't sure he'd seen Matthew happier. His son couldn't stop smiling, and now that Curtis thought about it, he acted as though he were getting married instead of heading to prom. But Curtis knew this was an extremely special day for him, and he understood.

"Let's take one more in front of the gazebo," Curtis said, focusing the digital camera and preparing to take another photo. It was a gorgeous, sunny, seventy-degree day outside, and the setting in their backyard was flawless.

Matthew held Racquel around her waist, and Curtis pressed the button. "That was a good one."

"Now let me take a picture," Curtina said, even though Curtis had already shot no less than ten photos of her and her brother before he'd left to go pick up his girlfriend. "I wanna take a picture with Matt and Racquel."

"Well, you'd better hurry up," Matthew said, "because we're gonna have to get goin' pretty soon."

"I'm coming," she said, running in their direction and standing between them. "Okay, we're ready, Daddy."

Curtis shook his head, laughing. "Well, we should probably make sure Matthew and Racquel are ready, too."

"Oh," she said, looking at both of them. "They look ready to me, Daddy."

Now Racquel laughed. "Yep, we're all ready."

Curtis snapped the button again, and Curtina rushed back toward her father. "Let me see, let me see."

Curtis turned the back of the camera toward her, and Curtina nodded with approval.

"Wow," Alicia said, walking out through the patio doors and down the steps leading to the pool. "Take a look at my handsome baby brother."

"Handsome indeed," Phillip said, walking alongside her, and then they each hugged Matthew.

"Thanks, sis. Thanks, brother-in-law, and thanks for driving over."

"We wouldn't have missed seeing you two for the world," Alicia said, hugging Racquel. "And you, my dear, look absolutely gorgeous. Where'd you get that dress?"

"My mom and I bought it from a bridal shop in downtown Chicago."

"Well, it was a great choice. It's fabulous."

"Thanks! I'm so glad you like it."

"You two will be the best-looking and the best-dressed couple there tonight," Alicia said, and then leaned down and hugged her little sister. "Hey, Miss Curtina."

"Hey, Licia," she said.

Curtis remembered how when Curtina had been younger, the most she could say was Lee Lee, and it made him realize how quickly time was passing and how much Curtina had grown up over the last two years.

"So, where are you guys going for dinner?" Phillip asked Matthew.

"The Tuxon."

"Great choice. That's still my favorite

restaurant here in Mitchell. Alicia and I went there all the time when we lived here."

"I know," she said, "and we'll have to make reservations for the next time we're in town."

"Or maybe you'll both eventually move back here for good," Curtis hinted. "That way I can have my favorite son-in-law added back to our pastor roster."

"We'll see," Phillip said, and Alicia smiled.

"Where's Charlotte?" she asked.

"She's not feeling well," was all Curtis said, trying not to think about his wife at all. He tried not to let his anger get the best of him.

"Oh, I'm sorry to hear that."

Just then, though, they heard conversation up toward the house and turned around. It was Agnes, trying to discourage Charlotte from coming outside. She was trying to talk some sense into Charlotte's hungover behind, but she clearly wasn't listening. Curtis could only imagine how embarrassed Matthew must have been, and when he finally found the nerve to look at his son, his suspicion was confirmed.

Sadly, Charlotte hadn't stumbled in until sometime after two a.m., waking the entire household with all her laughter and chitter chatter, and she and Curtis had gotten into a huge argument. Eventually, however, he'd seen her as a lost cause and had left the master bedroom, and Charlotte hadn't caused any more commotion. He'd known that she'd likely passed out across the bed, though, and when he'd gotten up a few hours later and checked on her, he'd seen exactly that. She hadn't even bothered removing her shoes or clothing, and while he certainly hadn't planned on doing it for her, when Agnes had arrived, she'd gone into the room, woken her up, and helped her into a nightgown.

Now, here she was looking like a crazy woman with her hair scattered all over her head and black eye makeup smudged under her eyes. Curtis was furious. This was supposed to be a joyful day for Matthew, and he couldn't imagine why Charlotte would want to humiliate her own child like this.

"I just want to see my baby is all," they heard her tell Agnes.

"But, Miss Charlotte, maybe you should lie down for a little while longer."

"I will, but I have to see my baby before he leaves."

Agnes held her arm, doing all she could to keep her inside, but Charlotte wrestled away and staggered onto the grass.

"Awww," she said, walking directly in

front of Matthew and grabbing both sides of his face. "You look like a million bucks . . . and I'm so, so proud of you, sweetie. You hear me? I'm proud of you, Matt."

Matthew seemed uneasy but didn't say anything. Racquel didn't flinch.

"I love you so much," Charlotte continued. "And I don't know what I'm going to do without you when you're gone," she said with tears rolling down her face. "I'm going to miss you so much."

Curtis looked on in silence, and it was all he could do to not snatch her away from Matthew and drag her back up to the house.

Alicia must have been thinking the same thing and said, "Charlotte, why don't we go back inside so Matt and Racquel can get going. They have dinner reservations, and I know you don't want them to be late."

Charlotte jerked her arm away, staring straight into Alicia's eyes and slurring her words. "I'll go . . . inside when I get good and . . . ready. You got that? And anyway . . . shouldn't you be locked away somewhere counting all your father's money? Miss Power of Attorney."

Alicia folded her arms. "You know what, Charlotte —"

"Alicia," Curtis said, defusing what was

sure to be a huge blowup between his daughter and wife. "It's not even worth it."

Thankfully, Alicia backed down, but something dawned on Curtis. When Charlotte had first come outside, he had assumed she was still suffering from a hangover, but now it appeared she was loaded again. Although, as far as he knew, she hadn't left the house yet today, so that could mean only one thing. She'd brought liquor into their household.

"Matt, why don't you guys get going," he told his son.

"Okay, Dad. You ready, Racquel?"

"Whenever you are."

The kids took a couple of steps, but Charlotte pulled Matthew backward. "Aren't you going to give me a hug?"

Matthew gazed at her. "No, Mom, I'm not. You've been drinking, and I really don't want that smell on me."

Charlotte bugged her eyes. "Why, you ungrateful little . . . I'm your mother and you've got the nerve to speak to me that way?"

Curtis grabbed her arm. "Just stop it, Charlotte! Matt, you and Racquel go on."

Charlotte struggled to get loose, unsuccessfully. "You make me sick, Curtis. You all make me sick," she said, looking around at everyone, and it was then that Curtis smelled liquor on her breath. Fresh liquor. Which meant his theory about her drinking in the house had been right.

"It's okay, Matt, go ahead," Curtis said. "Don't you worry about anything. Just have a great time."

"Not too good of a time," Charlotte yelled. "You hear me, Racquel? You make sure you keep those long legs of yours closed up tonight, because I'm not ready for any grandbabies. You hear me? I don't want you or any other little skank tryin' to trap my son."

Tears flowed down each side of Matthew's face, and tears filled Curtis's eyes, too. His heart ached for his child, and he knew Matthew would never forget what should have been one of the best days of his life. He wouldn't forget how ignorant his mother had acted.

"Mommy, you're hurting Matt's feelings," Curtina screamed, crying. "Mommy, please don't do that."

Charlotte glanced down at Curtina, and although Curtis held his breath, waiting for some other indignant comment, all Charlotte did was drop to the ground. "Oh my God, sweetie. Oh my God. I'm so sorry, Curtina. Come to Mommy."

Curtina fell into her mother's arms, and everyone else strolled toward the house.

"Matt, please forgive me," Charlotte said. "Honey, I'm so sorry. I didn't mean what I said."

But they all kept walking and never looked back. They went into the house, and Curtis stood watching his wife and little daughter. He gaped at the woman he'd been married to for years and wondered how and when she'd discovered this new love for alcohol. It was so unlike her, but he was already growing tired of it. He was tired of *her,* and as his mom used to say, his patience was wearing very thin. He didn't want to ask Charlotte to leave before the divorce, but if she kept pushing him, he wouldn't have a choice. He would do whatever necessary to protect his children.

CHAPTER 15

"You really embarrassed him, Charlotte," Curtis said. "You scolded him in front of everyone, and it was totally uncalled for."

"I know," she said, clasping her hands together under her chin. "And I'm so sorry, baby. I don't know what came over me."

"You don't know?"

"I really don't. I'm starting to feel like I'm losing my mind, Curtis."

"You're not losing anything. You're acting this way because you're drinking."

It was five after eleven. Curtis had taken Curtina over to Charlotte's aunt Emma's to spend the night, and now he was standing in his home office, listening to Charlotte's sob story. She'd finally slept a few hours, and while she still wasn't completely sober, she wasn't nearly as drunk as she'd been this afternoon when Matthew had left.

"I promise I won't do that anymore. But, Curtis, you have to help me. You have to be there for me."

"What are you talking about?"

"I need you to love me again. Tell me that we're going to be all right and that you're not going to leave me. Tell me you don't want anyone else."

"Charlotte, why do you keep harping on the same old thing? Our marriage has been over for a full year now."

"Baby, please. I mean, I hear what you're saying, and I know you don't think you can trust me, but I've really changed. I'm a brand-new woman, and I've learned my lesson."

"That's good to hear, but my decision stands."

Charlotte glared at him. "I'm not giving up on you, Curtis. I can't."

"Well, you might as well because if you don't, you'll be wasting a lot of precious time."

"Why are you being so cruel?"

"Because you won't stop bothering me about this. You won't accept the inevitable."

"So, you're saying you want me to find someone else? You want me to look for a new husband?"

"What I want is for you to be happy. With whoever that might be with."

Charlotte's face turned grim. "You don't

mean that."

"I do mean it. I've felt that way for a long while. There was a time when I struggled with the idea of not being with you. But then I realized that separating is the only way you and I will ever truly be free of each other. It's the only way either of us will finally have peace."

Charlotte opened her mouth to respond, but when she did, Matthew stuck his head inside the door. They hadn't even heard him walk in.

"Hey, Dad," he said, ignoring his mother.

Curtis forced a smile on his face. "So, how was the prom?"

"It was good. I dropped Racquel off at home so she could change for the after party, and now I'm gonna run upstairs and do the same."

"I'm glad you enjoyed yourself."

Matthew started to walk away. "I'll see you later."

Charlotte stopped him. "Matt, wait. Let me talk to you for a minute."

"What is it, Mom?" he said, refusing to look at her.

"I'm so ashamed of the way I acted this afternoon, but you have to know that wasn't me talking."

"Then who was it, Mom?"

"It was the liquor. I know that doesn't make it better, but, baby, I was completely under the influence, and I'm sorry."

"But, Mom, you yelled at me and then you told Racquel she needed to keep her legs shut. You said some horrible things to both of us, and it's going to be a long time before I forgive you for that."

"I know I was wrong, but I couldn't help it. And, Matt, it's not all my fault because the only reason I've been drinking is because I'm hurting so badly. I'm trying to do everything I can to cover up all the pain I'm feeling."

"What pain, Mom?"

"The pain I'm feeling because of your dad."

"You know what, Charlotte, just stop it, okay?" Curtis said.

"No, I want Matt to hear this. I want him to know the truth."

Matthew folded his arms. "What truth? You mean about you and Dad and how he's filing for a divorce?"

"Yes. That's exactly what I'm talking about. And he's serious, Matt. He's really going to break up our family."

Matthew pushed the door all the way open and walked farther into the room. "No, Mom. You broke up our family. You're the one I found at a motel with that Tom guy, and then you went to Florida with some other man all in the same month. What was his name?"

Charlotte closed her eyes, and although Curtis knew he shouldn't feel sorry for her, he did because he couldn't imagine what it must have felt like having your own son remind you of your infidelity. Matthew was very aware of Curtis's affair with Tabitha, too, but for some reason, physically seeing his mother with another man had been too much.

"I'm sorry, Mom, but you brought this all on yourself, and I don't blame Dad. I mean, I would love nothing more than to see my parents stay together forever, but if I found out Racquel was sleeping with other guys, I'd leave her alone in a heartbeat."

"But you're not married to her, Matt," she said. "You're only dating her, and dating is very different. You and Racquel don't have the same kind of commitment as people who have taken vows before God. It's not the same, and you're way too young to understand any of this."

"I understand perfectly," he said. "I understand why Dad can't be with you anymore, and like I said, I don't blame him."

"I can't believe you feel this way," she said.

"Well, I do. And I'll tell you something else, Mom. When you said, 'you little ungrateful . . .' and then you stopped mid-sentence, the first thing that entered my mind was 'you little ungrateful bastard.' "

"What? What are you talking about?"

"I think you wanted to call me a bastard, and all I could think about was how if you did, you'd actually be telling the truth. Because it wasn't like you were married to Dad when I was born, anyway. You were sleeping with him when he was married to Alicia's mom."

"Oh my God, Matt . . . ," she said, moving closer to him. "You know I would never call you that."

Matthew held his hand up. "Please don't, Mom. There's nothing you can say, so let's just end this conversation." He turned back toward the door but not before Curtis saw his eyes watering the same as this afternoon.

"Matt, I'm so, so sorry . . . and I promise you nothing like this will ever happen again," she said.

Matthew ignored her. "I'll see you later, Dad."

"Enjoy yourself, son. And you be safe out there, okay?"

"I will."

When Matthew left, Curtis walked around

his desk and sat in his seat. "You're too much."

"So everything's all my fault, I guess."

"Nobody's saying that, but you have done a lot, and now you've hurt Matthew even more. You should have kept your drunk behind in the house like Agnes told you. But no, you had to come outside and humiliate him in front of everybody."

"How many times do I have to say I'm sorry? Huh? What is it going to take to get through to you people?"

"No one wants to hear your apologies, Charlotte. And if you don't mind, I'd like to be alone now."

"You know, I'm really getting tired of begging you, Curtis. Begging you to forgive me for something that happened over a year ago."

"Then don't."

"You're such a jerk."

Curtis flipped through his sermon notes.

"And you call yourself a pastor. A true man of God. But yet, you can't forgive your own wife?"

Curtis turned through more pages, marking a couple of lines with his highlighter.

"So now you're going to give me the silent treatment?"

Curtis never looked up, and when she

finally walked out and slammed the door behind her, he leaned back in his chair and called Sharon.

CHAPTER 16

"I thought talking about your wife was off-limits," Sharon said.

"Not tonight. Not after the way she talked to my son."

"I'm really sorry she hurt him."

Curtis hadn't wanted to call Sharon with all his problems, and like she'd just said, he also didn't want to discuss anything about Charlotte with another woman. He'd never thought that was the right thing to do, and until now, he hadn't — well, maybe with the exception of when he spoke to Tanya about Charlotte, that is. But this whole drinking fiasco of hers and the idea that Matthew believed she'd almost called him a bastard had been too much for him to stomach, and for some reason he'd wanted to hear Sharon's voice. He'd needed someone to talk to, someone who would listen to his every word, someone who truly cared about him as a man. Yes, he could easily call his long time mentor, Pastor Abernathy, the way Lana had suggested, but he just couldn't bring himself to dial his number. As a matter of fact, he hadn't even bothered telling him about his impending divorce because he knew Pastor Abernathy wouldn't understand. Pastor Abernathy was one of the truest men of God Curtis had ever met, and he would never favor a breakup. He would suggest that Curtis and Charlotte fix things and stay together no matter what.

"I just don't get where all this craziness is coming from," he said.

"Maybe there's something going on that you don't know about."

"That's an understatement."

"Meaning?"

"There's a whole lot going on. Still, though, I don't know why she's turned to the bottle."

"Have you talked to her?"

"To be honest, I'm done talking. I'm done with Charlotte, period," he said, immediately wishing he could take his words back.

"Wow. You sound really, really upset. Are you leaving her?"

"I think we should talk about something else."

"Why?"

"Because."

"Well, it sounds to me like you have a lot to get off your chest, and you know I'm here for you. I've made that clear since the beginning, and I've been very patient. I've also known from the beginning that things weren't right between you and your wife. Anybody could see that just by watching the two of you on Sundays. When she's up speaking, you always seem so uninterested and like you can't wait for her to sit back down. And when you're delivering your sermon, she barely nods her head and mostly sits staring at you with no expression on her face. It's almost as if she can't wait for you to finish or like she has something more important on her mind."

"It's that noticeable, huh?"

"Very."

"That's really too bad because the last thing I want is for our congregation to get wind of my marital problems."

"Well, it's not like you haven't had them before. I mean, no offense, but I told you last year, even before I moved to Mitchell, I'd read about a couple of scandals."

"I realize that, but no one really knows about what's been going on lately."

"Are you going to answer my question?"

"What question?"

"About whether you're leaving her or not."

"No."

"No, you're not leaving her or no, you're not answering my question?"

"I'm not answering your question."

Sharon chuckled a little. "Then that pretty much tells me everything I need to know."

"Like I said, I think we should talk about something else."

"Well, if you change your mind, I'm all ears."

"I'm sure."

"So why are you up so late? Aren't you giving the message in the morning?"

"Yeah, but I've got way too much on my mind to go to sleep."

"Then why don't you come over?"

"I don't think so."

"You know you want to."

Curtis opened his mouth to insist he didn't, but since he knew he'd be lying, he said nothing.

"I don't hear anything," she teased. "Cat got your tongue maybe?"

"You're funny."

"I know. But I'm also serious."

She had no idea how badly he actually did want to jump into his SUV and speed over to her place. Especially since she lived far out in the country, and it wasn't like anyone would see him. But he couldn't shake how wrong it would be if he did. Yes, he knew he was finished with Charlotte, however, there was no denying that he was still married to her, and if he slept with Sharon or any other woman, he would still be committing adultery. In the past, he wouldn't have cared one way or the other, but this was a new day, and things were different. *He* was different. And he was trying with all his might not to revert back to his old ways. It was the reason he read the book of Romans regularly and, lately, the reason he recited the King James version of Romans 12:2 daily: *"And be not conformed to this world: but be ye transformed by the renewing of your mind, that ye may prove what is that good, and acceptable, and perfect, will of God."* There were times, though, when he read from his New Living Translation version of the Bible, because every now and then, this version seemed to speak more plainly to his psyche: *"Don't copy the behavior and customs of this world, but let God transform you into a new person by changing the way you think. Then you will learn to know God's will for you, which is good and pleasing and perfect."*

"Are you coming?" she said.

Now, Curtis realized she'd probably said much more but he hadn't heard her. "No, I don't think so."

"Pretty please."

"Can't do it."

"With sugar on top."

They both laughed. "Now you're just being silly," he said.

"Well, at least your spirit is a lot brighter than when you first called me."

"Yeah, I guess you're right, but the truth of the matter is, Sharon, I'm married."

"Uh-huh, and what do I always say every time you remind me of that?"

"That I'm not *happily* married."

"Exactly. Because if you were, you wouldn't talk to me as often as you do. You'd be spending time with your wife."

"So you think you've got everything all figured out."

"No, but I know more than you're willing to admit. Not to mention, I think it's a shame when anyone stays in a miserable relationship. It just doesn't make a lot of sense to me."

"That's because you've never been married. And you don't have children."

"Still."

"I know you don't understand it, but having children changes everything. You have an obligation to them. As it is, my first wife and I divorced, and I've always felt like I let my oldest daughter down because of it. The divorce was very hard on her."

"I'm sorry to hear that, but do you think it would have been better for her to be in a house with two parents who no longer loved each other?"

Curtis chose his words carefully because he didn't see a reason to tell Sharon or anyone else how much he did in fact still love Tanya. "At the time, that wasn't the case."

"I don't get what you mean."

"We didn't separate because we stopped loving each other. We separated because I wasn't being faithful to her."

"Oh. But nonetheless, I don't think it would have been good for your daughter if you'd stayed together just because."

"Maybe not. But I regret not being there for her as a full-time dad, and if I had it to do over again, I would."

"What about now?"

"What about it?"

"Your marriage to Charlotte. Are you staying in it because of your two younger children?"

"You just won't give up, will you?"

"You know what they say, inquiring minds wanna know."

"Well, I'm sorry to disappoint you, but I'd better get going."

"I really wish you'd come see me. Just for a little while. You wouldn't even have to stay very long."

"I don't think so. Plus, it's already late, and I have to get at least a few hours of rest before heading to church."

"Okay," she whined. "I guess I'll just have to see you there, then."

"I guess so," he said, laughing, but looked up when Charlotte burst back into his office.

"Who are you talking to, Curtis?" she yelled. "I know you thought I'd gone upstairs, but I've been standing outside your door the entire time. So what whore are you sleeping around with now?"

"I'll talk to you later," he said, then ended his call.

"Who is she, Curtis?"

"Nobody."

"So, you were on the phone with *nobody* all this time?"

"I'm not doing this with you, Charlotte."

"And you have the audacity to discuss our problems with some trick? How could you do that?"

Curtis stared at her for a couple of seconds. "How could you do the things *you* did?"

"Don't even try it. Don't try to turn this

back on me when you're the one sitting in here talking to another woman. Some whore who's trying to get you into bed."

"Nobody's trying to do anything."

"Then why did you tell her it was too late? Was she asking you to come see her?"

"This discussion is over," he said, standing up.

She stepped closer to him. "No, don't leave now. As a matter of fact, why don't you call her back and tell her the *rest* of our business. You already told her you were done with me and that you didn't know why I'd turned to the bottle. So why not tell her everything else?"

Curtis had been hoping Charlotte was bluffing when she'd said she'd heard all of his conversation, but now he knew she had.

"You make me sick."

"I know," he said. "You told me that earlier, remember?"

"You think this is a joke? You think I'm going to sit around, listening to you talk to other women on the phone about me?"

"I don't expect you to do anything. Except find a new place to live."

"You're sleeping with her, aren't you? And that's why you're so in a hurry to divorce me."

"Not that it's any of your business, but

I'm not sleeping with anybody."

"You must think I'm a fool."

"You know what, Charlotte, this conversation is over," he said, moving past her and over to the doorway.

"Don't walk away from me, Curtis," she exclaimed, but Curtis continued down the hallway and up to his bedroom. He shut the door and kneeled at the side of his bed, praying for his days with Charlotte to be over.

CHAPTER 17

Charlotte squirmed against the back of the pew, wishing morning service would end. To be honest, she wasn't even sure why she'd come, what with all the arguing she and Curtis had done. Worse, she still felt hungover. But she was here now and there was no sense complaining about it. It was better just to smile and pretend she was elated. Plus, she didn't want Janine or her husband, Carl; her aunt Emma; or her cousin Anise suspecting anything was wrong. They were all sitting next to her in the second row, in that order, and Charlotte saw no reason to alarm them.

She listened to the choir belting out one of her favorite songs, but suddenly she wanted to cry. She would do anything if she could take back the words she'd rattled off to Matthew yesterday afternoon, and she wondered if he would ever forgive her. He'd seemed so disgusted prior to leaving for his postprom activities, and he hadn't bothered speaking to her before she'd left for church a couple of hours ago. Charlotte knew this was all her fault, but she'd still been hoping her son might have a little more compassion this morning. She'd been praying he would realize she wasn't planning to call him a bastard because she hadn't. She wasn't even sure what name she'd wanted to call him, but it certainly hadn't been that.

Curtis slowly strutted across the pulpit and glanced at Charlotte. "My sermon for today is 'Obsession, Temptation, and Dire Consequences.' "

Members nodded in approval and many said, "Amen."

"Of course, it is no secret that no man or woman is perfect," Curtis continued, "and that at some point we all find ourselves dealing with some sort of obsession, but I think when it causes us to act recklessly and we end up hurting innocent people, it's time to take a closer look at ourselves."

"You got that right, Pastor," Elder Dixon replied.

"So so true," a woman toward the back added.

"I say this," Curtis said, "because when we act selfishly and don't check ourselves, there are usually tons of consequences to deal with. We reap what we have sown, and as many of you know, I'm not just talking for the sake of talking. I'm speaking from experience."

Charlotte wondered where this little message of his was going, but already she didn't like the sound of it.

"You see," he said, "what happens is that we become tempted by something, we give in to it, we soon become obsessed with it, and the next thing you know, we're completely addicted. We find ourselves caught up in ways we never thought imaginable, and we have no idea how to overcome it. We find ourselves caring more about our sinful desires than we do about the people who love us, and that's when things get messy. The whole scenario ends up becoming a total shame for everyone involved."

Members shouted, "Amen," and Curtis stepped in front of the podium. "The other thing I should add, too, is that human beings can become addicted to almost anything. Alcohol, drugs, sex, shopping, Facebook," he said, and laughter could be heard throughout the sanctuary. "Y'all know I'm telling the truth, though, right? These days, some of y'all can't live without the Internet. And, of course, let's not forget about food and how some of us just can't make it through the day sometimes if we don't get our sugar fix. Some of us become downright mean if we don't get that monkey off our backs."

There was more laughter, but Charlotte sat stone-faced and didn't see anything funny. She also didn't like how he'd made it a point to mention alcohol first, because she knew he'd done it on purpose. He'd gotten his jab in on the sly without anyone else realizing it, and it was all she could do not to stand up, march toward him, and confront him in front of everyone. But instead, she grabbed her purse, stepped into the aisle, and went over to one of the side doors. She never looked back and was glad she'd driven separately from her jerk of a husband.

She raced out of the parking lot and couldn't wait to get home, change into something comfortable, and spend the afternoon with herself. It would have been nice to enjoy some family time with Curtina, especially since Aunt Emma had invited all of them over for dinner, but she would just have to do that another day. If she was truthful, she'd have to admit how she really didn't want to be around her cousin, Anise, anyway, so it was probably good she wasn't joining them. It was best she went to her new favorite spot without anyone.

The atmosphere at Chelsey's was as relaxing as always, and Charlotte didn't mind how noisy all of the men were, those who were consistently rooting and yelling whenever their favorite basketball team scored. It was actually pretty exciting, and Charlotte now considered Chelsey's the place to be. She saw it as a safe haven so to speak, and it was the kind of spot that cheered her up pretty quickly.

She drank the rest of her wine and pulled out her phone when she heard it ringing. It was Janine, and as she pressed the Ignore button, she told her usual waitress, Amber, who was passing by her, "If it's okay, I'm going to step outside to make a call."

"No problem. Your table will be right here waiting for you."

Charlotte passed by a row of men sitting at the bar, and one of them smiled at her. However, all she did was smile back and keep going. When she got outside where it was quieter, she called Janine back.

Her best friend yelled at her as soon as she answered. "Girl, where are you? And why did you leave without saying anything?

I just figured you were going to the rest-room."

"I'm sorry I didn't say good-bye, but I needed to get out of there."

"And you didn't think we'd all be worried sick about you when you never came back?"

"No, I guess I didn't, and I apologize."

"Charlotte, what's wrong? I mean, you never called me back on Thursday when you left Chelsey's, you never returned any of my phone calls from the weekend, and you really didn't say much to me before service started this morning."

"I know, but it's all very complicated, J. I'm going through a lot right now, and I have a ton of stuff on my mind."

"Like what?"

"It's nothing for you to worry about or nothing you can help me with. Just something I need to work out on my own."

"Girl, this is me you're talking to. Your best friend, remember?"

"I know, but I'll be fine."

"You don't sound fine, and now that we're on the subject, you didn't look fine when I saw you earlier. You looked exhausted and upset about something."

"Wow, thanks a lot," Charlotte said, not realizing she looked so terrible.

"I don't mean that in a nasty way. I'm just

saying I know something's wrong. I know you're troubled about something, and I wanna help you."

"I'll be fine, J. I know you don't believe that, but I will."

"Where are you?"

Charlotte had hoped she wouldn't ask that again because she hadn't wanted to lie to her. "I'm outside of Chelsey's about to get in my car."

"So you already ate?"

"I did."

"Do you want to meet at Starbucks or something? Carl is already watching a game and isn't planning to go out, and Bethany's napping."

"That would have been great, but I have a few errands I need to run, and then I'm heading home."

"Errands on a Sunday? And why are you heading home when your family is over at your aunt Emma's?"

Charlotte hated being questioned like this and wished Janine would take no for answer and leave it at that. "I'm getting some things done today so I won't have so much to do next week." Janine didn't say anything, so Charlotte said, "I'll call you tomorrow, okay?"

"Fine."

"Talk to you later."

Charlotte dropped her BlackBerry in her tote and walked back into the restaurant. She truly was sorry for lying to her best friend and for being short with her, but right now, she didn't want to be bothered with anyone. She just wanted to be left alone for the rest of the afternoon.

She slid back into her booth, and Amber walked over. "So, can I get you anything else? One of our sandwich or salad specials maybe?"

"No, I've already eaten," she lied. "But I will have a mango margarita, please."

"I love those, too. I'll be right back."

Charlotte looked up at the large flat-screen television and saw that it was half-time. Just then, the guy who'd smiled at her strolled over.

"Mind if I join you for a few minutes? Just until the game comes back on?"

"Why?"

The tall, broad-shouldered man chuckled, and Charlotte couldn't ignore how hand-some he was if she wanted to. "You were sitting here all alone, so I figured maybe you wanted some company."

"No, I think I'm good."

"Oh," he said, glancing at her left hand. "I see you're married."

"Very."

The man took a couple of steps back. "I'm sorry I bothered you, then, and please know I meant no disrespect."

"No problem," she said. "It was an easy mistake. I guess."

"What? You thought I saw your ring up front but still tried talking to you?"

"You tell me."

"Okay," he said, smiling. "You're right, I admit it. I saw that monstrous rock as soon as I came over here."

Charlotte shook her head, smiling.

"So, please accept my apology. Although, I will say this, your husband is a very lucky man."

"You think so, huh?"

"For sure. He's also a little naïve."

Charlotte's heart skipped a beat, and she wondered if he recognized her or knew Curtis. Chelsey's was local, but since she'd been coming there, she hadn't seen anyone familiar and hadn't thought anyone knew her either. This wasn't the kind of place a lot of Christians would prefer spending time at, and it was one of the reasons she loved it. "Why do you say that?"

"Shoot, a beautiful woman like you and he's letting you come out to sports bars without him?"

Charlotte exhaled. "Well, first of all, I've always come here mainly for the food and not for the setting."

"Really?" he said as Amber walked up and set her drink on the table. "Then that must be virgin."

Charlotte smiled at her waitress. "Thank you."

"You're quite welcome."

"So, is it?" the man continued.

"Do you have a name?" Charlotte asked, sort of teasing him.

"Greg Parker, but you still haven't answered my question."

"Why are you so worried about it?"

"I'm not."

"Sounds like it to me."

"You're funny."

Charlotte held the straw and sipped some of her drink.

"Oh well," he said. "I guess I'll head back over to my boys. But it was nice meeting you . . . although, I still don't know your name."

"Maybe that's a good thing."

"You take care," he said, looking her up and down and walking away.

Charlotte watched him and was glad he hadn't insisted on taking a seat, because deep down, she'd wanted some company.

She hadn't thought so when she'd first arrived or when she'd spoken to Janine, but now she was lonely. She felt good thanks to the very tasty spirits she'd been drinking, but it would have been nice laughing and talking with someone, too. It was the reason she got Greg's attention and summoned him back to her booth with her forefinger. He obliged and sat down in front of her in seconds.

Chapter 18

Curtis hadn't bothered calling Charlotte, because his gut told him exactly where she was. Not specifically mind you, but he knew she was somewhere getting toasted. Fortunately, Curtina had ridden home with Aunt Emma, and though he was on his way there, too, he'd just answered a call from Janine.

"What's wrong with her, Curtis?"

"She's drinking."

"What? Liquor?"

"Yep. And it's excessive. She's come home drunk twice now, and that was just in the last three days."

"No."

"Yep, and my guess is she'll be arriving the same way tonight."

"I'm stunned."

"So am I. You should have seen the way she clowned yesterday, right before Matt left for his prom. It was ridiculous."

"Oh my God. What happened?"

Curtis told her the details.

"This is too unreal. She actually said those things?"

"Every one of them."

"But why?"

"She was drunk, and she didn't care how she addressed any of us."

"But why is she drinking so heavily?"

"I'm sure it's because I won't change my mind about divorcing her. She hasn't told you about it?"

"No, she told me things weren't good, but I had no idea you'd made a final decision."

"I did that a long time ago."

"I'm really sorry to hear that, Curtis. I was so sure things would be okay. Are you positive? Are you sure you can't reconsider?"

Curtis wished everyone would stop asking him that. "I am."

"I'm not saying I don't understand your reasons, but I also don't want to see your marriage come to an end. I don't wish that on anyone."

"Neither do I, but if I stay with Charlotte, things will only get worse, and the next thing you know, we'll end up hating each other."

"You do know how much she loves you, though, right? I know she's done a lot of horrible things, but that's the one thing that's never changed with her."

"Doesn't matter. And it's like I told her, sometimes love isn't enough."

"Curtis, you know I love you like a brother, and Charlotte is the best friend I've ever had, so this really breaks my heart."

"It breaks mine, too, but it is what it is. These problems between Charlotte and me have gone on for years. Almost our entire marriage, and it's time we ended it."

"I disagree, and regardless of what final decision you feel like you've made, I'm going to keep praying for something different. I'm going to do what I've heard you say for years."

"I appreciate your concern, Janine, but put yourself in my shoes. What if Carl slept with another woman, had a child with her, and then in return, you went out and had an affair and had a child with another man?"

"I'd say we both made two huge mistakes but that we're also even. I'd expect us to work things out and go on with our lives."

"Exactly. But what if after all the time you spent reconciling and forgiving each other, Carl went out and had two additional affairs? What would you do then?"

"I don't know. I'd like to believe I'd have a forgiving heart and that I'd still be able to honor our vows. I'd like to think we could get past anything, even if just for Bethany's sake."

"That's easy to say when you haven't actually experienced what I just described."

"I agree, but, Curtis, I know you still love Charlotte."

"That's true. I won't deny that, but we'll get along so much better once we separate."

"Maybe that's all you need to do. Maybe if you separate from her, you'll realize how much you miss her."

"I wish it were that simple. I wish I had better news, because I know you really care about us, but . . ."

"What about the children? What is Matt saying? And what about poor little Curtina?"

"Matt knows what's going on, and he'll be fine. Curtina will be, too."

"Gosh, Curtis, I wish there was something I could say."

"I know. It's not a pretty situation, and I'm hoping things don't turn even uglier, but if Charlotte continues on her drinking binges, it will."

Janine didn't comment.

"Well, I guess I'd better go. I just drove into Aunt Emma's driveway, and I'm sure they're waiting for me."

"You take care of yourself, Curtis."

"You, too, and please give Carl my best."

Curtis ended the call, parked his SUV, and went to the front door. He rang the doorbell twice, and Anise let him in.

She held the door open, waiting for him to walk past. "Mom and I are almost finished warming everything up and setting it on the table, and Curtina's in the den watching a DVD."

"Figures, and thanks so much for looking after her."

"Of course. You know she's more like Mom's granddaughter than she is her great-niece. The two of them are like twins."

"Isn't that the truth."

Aunt Emma set the yams onto an iron trivet. "Hey, Curtis."

"Hey, and thanks for having us over."

"Of course. Where's that wife of yours? And why did she leave church so early?"

Curtis scanned the smorgasbord Aunt Emma had prepared — macaroni and cheese, baked ham, mustard greens, sweet corn, fried chicken, home-baked dinner rolls, and banana pudding. "Who knows? She could be just about anywhere."

Aunt Emma placed her hand on her hip. "Meaning?"

"It's a long story, but Charlotte has been going out drinking. A lot."

Anise frowned. "Why?"

Curtis filled them in about everything that had happened, and Anise said, "How pathetic."

"Now, Anise, don't you be like that," Aunt Emma said.

"I'm sorry, Mom, but the truth is the truth. And, Curtis, you're a good one, because I'm surprised you've stayed with her this long."

Aunt Emma started back into the kitchen but said, "I wish you didn't feel that way about your cousin, Anise."

"Mom, you know I've felt like this for years. Ever since Charlotte slept with my husband."

"I realize that, but that was a long time ago, and you and David have been divorced forever."

"Still, I know who Charlotte is and what she's capable of. I know she can't be trusted."

"She's still family, and as a Christian woman, you have an obligation to forgive her."

"I have forgiven her . . . to a certain extent. But every time I think about my own first cousin, my own flesh and blood sleeping with the man I loved, it makes me sick. Especially since I loved Charlotte like a sister. I did everything with her and for her, and this was the thanks I got?"

Curtina ran into the room, and Curtis was sort of glad because he didn't want to talk about Charlotte anymore.

"Daddyyyy!"

"Hey, sweetie. How's Daddy's girl?"

"I'm good," she said, looking around the room. "Where's Mommy?"

"She had someplace to go."

"Where?"

"Just something she had to do. She'll be home later, though."

"Will she be there before us?"

"I hope so."

Thankfully, Anise changed the subject. "So, where was Matthew's picnic?"

"Mitchell Forest Preserve."

"Oh wow, they have all kinds of water activities and some great barbecuing locations."

"Yeah, he was pretty excited about going."

Anise set extra napkins on the table. "I'll bet he and Racquel looked fabulous last night, didn't they?"

"They did. We'll make sure you and Aunt Emma get copies of the photos."

"That would be great."

Curtina ran back into the den, and Curtis pulled out his vibrating phone to see who was texting him. He got a little nervous when he saw it was from Sharon, because the last thing he wanted was for Anise or Aunt Emma to know he was communicating with another woman. Still, he scrolled through and read what she'd sent him.

C, I just saw your wife at Chelsey's so I know you're alone. Please call me.

Curtis slipped his phone back into the leather case attached to his belt and wished Sharon hadn't confirmed what he already knew. Charlotte was out drinking — at a sports bar no less — and the last thing he wanted was to deal with her madness. He also didn't want Curtina witnessing Charlotte in a drunken state, so he decided right then he would ask Aunt Emma to keep Curtina overnight again. That way, he could confront Charlotte about her drinking once and for all.

CHAPTER 19

Curtis waited impatiently, contemplating everything he would say to Charlotte. It was six p.m. and he'd already taken clothing over to Curtina for school tomorrow. Finally Charlotte dragged herself into the house. Drunk as all get-out. Looking worse than some street person. Acting as though she barely knew where she was.

"You just don't plan to stop, do you?" he said.

"Stop what, Curtis? Doing what I want? You're just mad . . . because . . . you . . . can't control . . . me."

"I'm pissed off because I'm tired of dealing with this. I'm tired of dealing with you, and if you can't end this, then you need to leave."

She held on to the island, squeezing her eyes shut and opening them like she was dizzy. "I'll do whatever I feel like doin'."

"You need help."

Charlotte laughed like a wild woman and pointed at him. "You're the one with the problem, misterrr."

"Look, either you stop this or I'm putting you out of here."

Charlotte laughed louder than before. "I'm not goin' anywhere. I'm stayin' right here with my babies."

"Keep it up and see what happens."

Charlotte's smile faded. She looked as though she'd sobered up for just a few seconds. "You're not the boss of me, Curtis. You got that? I'm a grown woman, and how dare you threaten to kick me out."

"Like I said, keep it up."

"I will," she said, letting go of the island and struggling to make her way through the kitchen and family room and over to the staircase.

"I also better not catch you driving around with Curtina, or you'll find yourself in jail. I don't want her in the car with you from now on."

"Yeah, yeah, yeah."

Curtis watched her disappear and grabbed his keys. There was nothing worse than being around a drunk anybody, but being around a drunk woman was atrocious. So unladylike and downright repulsive, and Curtis needed to get as far away from Charlotte as possible. He needed to clear his head and settle his nerves, and he knew the perfect place to do that — the one place where he'd be welcomed with open arms. He knew he was exposing himself to unnecessary temptation, but he was tired. Tired of Charlotte and the drama she brought to their marriage every single day now. So, as far as he was concerned, he deserved a night out — he deserved an evening of total serenity, and he would get it.

Sharon shut the door behind Curtis. "This really is a wonderful surprise. When you didn't text me back, I wasn't sure what to think, so I'm glad you called."

"I was at dinner and then had other business."

"No problem. I'm just happy you're here. Can I get you anything?"

"Tea maybe?"

"Raspberry?"

"That'll be fine."

"Have a seat," she said, leaving for the kitchen, but Curtis could still see her from the family room.

Curtis sat on the plush, purple sofa and stretched out his legs. He was so worn out, mentally and physically, and he was already enjoying his escape — his time away from reality. He gazed at his surroundings, admiring Sharon's elegant décor but soon noticed a Louis Vuitton handbag lying on one of the lavender armless chairs. Strangely enough, it was the exact same style Charlotte had purchased a few months ago and now carried to church quite regularly. It was interesting how similar some women's tastes were.

After a while, Sharon came back into the room, handed him his drink, and set a coaster on the oversized, square ottoman in front of them. Finally, she took a seat next to him.

"It's hard to believe this is only your second time visiting me. After more than a year. And I'm shocked you came this evening."

"I needed a place of refuge."

"Well, you'll always have that here. But did something happen? Is there a reason I saw Charlotte hanging out the way she was? I mean, I run in there all the time to pick up carryout and sometimes I go there for lunch with colleagues, but it's not the sort of place most women tend to frequent alone. Unless, of course, they're looking for men."

"Her drinking has gotten worse, and it's

starting to be a regular thing. Then, tonight, she was so wasted she couldn't even drive her car up the driveway. When I left, I saw it sitting on the street in front of our house."

"I'm so sorry."

"Not as sorry as I am. But it'll all be over soon."

"I'm not sure I get what you mean?"

"I'm talking about our marriage and how I'm ending it."

Sharon turned her body slightly toward him. "I'm not surprised."

"I'm sure you're not." Curtis sighed. "This has been a long, tough road, and while I've tried keeping things private, I'm relieved to finally be telling someone other than family."

"Releasing pain is good for the soul, and talking about it makes all the difference."

"I know. I've always known that, but you have to realize, this whole ordeal isn't going to affect just my wife and me. It's going to involve my children, and to a certain extent, it'll affect our congregation."

"I agree, but you'll be okay. It'll be hard in the beginning, but before you know it, time will pass, everyone will adjust, and you'll be living a new normal. You'll realize you made the right decision for everyone."

Curtis wanted to believe her, and he

guessed he did for the most part, but he still wasn't looking forward to the overall process. He didn't want to think about the tears Curtina would likely shed or the internal pain Matthew would pretend he wasn't feeling. He also dreaded having to tell the members of the church that their senior pastor, the man they loyally supported, was getting a divorce — again. Not once or twice, but for the third time. He'd been married to Charlotte ever since they'd founded Deliverance Outreach, but everyone still knew his history. They knew he'd been the cause of his other two marriages falling apart, so he feared they might wonder if this particular split was his fault, too. There was no pretending he was completely innocent, not even in a miniscule sort of way, but he also wasn't the one who'd caused the grand finale.

Sharon flipped on the DVD player, and they watched some love story Curtis had never seen before, but mostly he thought about his problems, the future, and possible repercussions. He worried about the potential aftermath, because he couldn't imagine Charlotte leaving quietly — regardless of what any judge had to say about it. She would fight until the very end, and Curtis knew he was in for a spectacle.

Sharon turned her entire body toward him, moved closer, and bent her leg onto the sofa. She rested her elbow on the back of it. "So what are you going to do once you divorce her?"

Curtis would have much preferred she'd kept her distance, so he kept his eyes on the TV screen. "I haven't thought that far."

"Will you and I finally be able to spend more time together?"

"Can't say."

"Why?"

"Because publicly I don't want to bring any more shame to my children than I have to."

"Well, what if we were discreet?"

He finally looked at her. "Why can't we just enjoy the friendship we have now?"

"We are, but I also wanna know where we'll stand later on."

"Wish I could say."

Curtis didn't think there was any room left between them, but Sharon moved even closer. She gazed into his eyes and smoothed the hair on the back of his head. Curtis drank some of his tea, purposely not looking at her again.

"You must be the most handsome man I've ever seen, and I'm not sure how much longer I can continue fighting these urges

— how long I can keep going without."

Curtis glanced at her in shock.

"What? Did you think I'd been seeing other men?"

"Well, actually, yes. I mean, why wouldn't you?"

Sharon gently rubbed the back of his head again. "Curtis, Curtis, Curtis. You really don't get it, do you?"

"What?"

"That I want only you and no one else."

"I guess I understand now," he admitted. "But I really wish you would date other guys."

"Why?"

"Because I can't guarantee I'll ever be able to commit to you or see you on an exclusive basis."

"Are you saying there's someone else or that there's no possibility for us?"

Curtis thought about Tanya, but said, "No, I'm not saying anything like that."

"Then if it's okay with you, I'll take my chances. I'll wait for as long as I need to."

Curtis gazed into her light brown eyes but quickly regretted it because they were more mesmerizing than ever.

"Let me show you how much I love you, Curtis."

"*Love* is a very strong word. Especially for

two people who haven't shared much more than phone conversation."

"Lots of phone conversation. Many times, every week over the last year. Enough for me to know I'm in love with you. So come on."

"You know I can't do that."

"Come on, baby. Please don't keep denying me. Don't make me suffer the way you have been," she said, caressing both sides of his face.

Chills trickled through his body. Then she slid her hand across his chest and onto his lap.

Curtis slowly pushed it away. "This is wrong."

"If you didn't want me, baby, you wouldn't be here."

"That's just it — I *do* want you," he said, slightly laughing and standing up.

"Then stop fighting me. Stop trying to delay our fate."

Curtis thought about all the scriptures he'd been reading, those that had prevented him from committing adultery, but tonight, he felt weak and like he couldn't control himself. Like he couldn't restrain the sinful desires of his heart. Lust consumed the forefront of his thinking, and he was frightened by it. For four straight years, he'd been faithful and free of a cheating spirit, but now he found himself at a crossroads, and he was confused.

Sharon left the sofa and grabbed him around the neck. "Baby, this is our destiny. You and I were meant to be, so let's not try to change that. Let's do what you know you came here to do in the first place."

Curtis fixed his eyes on her and knew he had to make a choice — and then he'd have to live with it.

Sharon held him tighter and said, "Plus, it's not like your wife was alone when I saw her. She was sitting with some guy."

Curtis swallowed hard, not knowing how he should feel about this latest newsflash. For months, he'd told Charlotte their marriage was over, but now that he was hearing about another man, it didn't feel so good. Not because he was planning to change his mind about divorcing her, but maybe it was because they had so much history. They had children, they'd lived a full life together, and truth was, he'd gotten used to what he'd gotten used to. With Charlotte, there had always been a certain sense of security and comfort through good times and bad, and this was the first time he'd seriously thought about the end result — what life would be like as a single man with no companion.

Over the next couple of minutes, he replayed Sharon's words but knew this had been bound to happen. He'd been sure Charlotte would ultimately give up on him, because after all, he'd been repeatedly encouraging her to do so. But he couldn't deny that this news about her and some other man had caught him off guard.

"Baby, come on. Let's go in my bedroom," Sharon said, clasping her hands inside his, and Curtis realized he still had a choice to make. Clearly, there were only two viable options, though: escaping this place as quickly as possible or sleeping with a woman who craved him.

So what was a man to do?

CHAPTER 20

Yesterday had certainly been a close call, but Charlotte was glad she hadn't slept with Greg — even though she'd sort of wanted to. She knew it was a disgrace even admitting something like this, even to herself, but it was true: She had seriously considered accepting an invitation over to his place and had fantasized about what it would be like making love to him. She'd almost told him yes, because she'd wanted to be close to someone — she'd needed a strong, handsome man to love, appreciate, and make her happy. She'd longed for intimacy and attention, something she no longer received from Curtis.

Charlotte peered into the bathroom mirror and couldn't remember ever looking so run-down. Well, maybe she had that one time when she'd caught some nasty, two-week virus, but that was it. Today, however, she looked exhausted, unsightly and pale, and she knew it was because of how drunk she'd gotten. She'd already downed a couple of drinks by the time Greg had joined her, and he'd bought her three more. Soon she'd become a lot more than tipsy. In fact, she'd consumed so much it hadn't been until this morning that she'd sort of remembered it was Greg who'd driven her home. He'd insisted she was too intoxicated to get behind the wheel, and Charlotte had agreed. Although, now she was mortified about her decision because what if Curtis had seen another man driving the Mercedes he'd given her as a gift two years ago and parking it in front of their house? What if he'd seen Greg helping her out of the car and then waiting for her to make it safely up the driveway before taking off in another vehicle with his friend? Worse, had she actually been careless enough to allow a stranger access to their security gate remote controller? She wouldn't have. Would she? But if she hadn't, how had she been able to enter the driveway and walk up it? Sadly, she couldn't recall one way or the other but prayed that maybe the gate had somehow already been open, and Greg hadn't had to use it. She prayed the controller would still be in her car when she went outside, and now she was sorry she hadn't programmed the signal into one

of the buttons on the overhead console of
her car the same as she had for the garage.

She left the bedroom and went downstairs,
and as she strolled closer to the kitchen, she
heard Curtis, Matthew, and Agnes laughing. However, as soon as she entered, there
was complete silence until Agnes said,
"Good morning, Miss Charlotte."

"Good morning."

Matthew scooped up some of his grits and
never looked at her. Curtis did his usual
reading-the-newspaper thing so he wouldn't
have to acknowledge her either.

Still, Charlotte sat down and said, "Good
morning, Matt."

He looked straight ahead but at least
mumbled, "Mornin'."

"Can I get you something, Miss Charlotte?" Agnes asked.

"Maybe some juice."

"Of course."

"And where's Curtina? Up in her room? I
thought she'd be down here already."

Curtis ignored her question and so did
Matthew, so Agnes said, "She spent the
night with Miss Emma, and she's going to
drop her off at school today."

"Really?" Charlotte said, feeling embarrassed and realizing she'd been too drunk
last night to even notice her little girl wasn't

home. She was also sure Curtis had told Aunt Emma and that cousin of hers way too much of their business.

Curtis shook his head, clearly incensed, and Charlotte wanted to cry. He and Matthew treated her like a nonentity, and now she wished she'd stayed up in her bedroom.

Agnes set a glass of apple juice in front of Charlotte and then looked at Matthew. "So, it sounds like you had a great time at your prom."

"I did. Racquel and I had a blast, and it was great hanging out with my boys and their dates, too."

"I'm so glad. And what about yesterday? How was the picnic?"

"That was a blast, too. There was a ton of food, and Elijah, Jonathan, and I completely stuffed ourselves."

Agnes chuckled. "Shameful."

"Yeah, but you know that's how we roll, Miss Agnes. We love to eat more than anything else."

"You don't have to tell me," she said, laughing.

"So, did Racquel enjoy the picnic, too?" Charlotte asked, hoping Matthew would chat with her also.

But all he said was, "Yep," and still didn't look at her.

"So, is that all you're going to say? You're not gonna elaborate?"

"For what, Mom? You don't even like Racquel."

"I do like her, Matt. Why are you saying that?"

He looked away again and flipped through some magazine lying in front of his plate.

"Matt, did you hear me?" she asked.

He sighed. "Yep. But, Mom, let's not talk about Racquel. Let's not talk about anything."

"Why?"

Her son looked away again.

"Matt, I already told you how sorry I am, so why are you acting this way?"

"Because you said some terrible things to Racquel. You said terrible things to both of us."

"I know, but, honey, I didn't mean them."

"Well, I've always heard that when people get drunk, they blurt out whatever they want. They say exactly what they mean."

Charlotte wondered what had gotten into him. She knew she'd said some hurtful words on Saturday, but being disrespectful was so unlike him. In the past, he never would have spoken to her in such a curt manner, and she hoped this new attitude of his was only temporary.

"I'm going to call Racquel and apologize to her," she said, "because I really am very sorry."

Matthew glanced at his watch and pushed away from the table. "I'm outta here, Dad."

"See you later, son. Have a good day."

Charlotte was shocked Curtis was even alive since for the last few minutes, he'd said nothing. He hadn't looked at her or Matthew the entire time they'd been conversing, and he acted as though he didn't have a single problem with the way their son had addressed her.

Matthew grabbed his duffel bag. "See you, Miss Agnes."

"See ya. Enjoy your day."

"I will. Although, I'm not really looking forward to spending whole class hours reviewing all the stuff we learned this semester. We're doing that every day this week."

"Well, at least your finals are just around the corner, and you'll be free."

"Yep, and graduation is only two weeks from today."

Charlotte wanted to tell him how proud she was of him, but since he wasn't talking to her, she decided against it. He was speaking directly to Agnes and making it a point to keep his back to his own mother.

When Matthew went out the door, Agnes went to change the sheets on everyone's beds and Curtis left the kitchen only minutes thereafter. Charlotte sat for a few seconds but then ran upstairs, searched through her cell phone contact list, and dialed Racquel.

"Hello?"

"Uh, Racquel, this is Mrs. Black, Matthew's mom."

"Oh . . . hi."

Her voice was uneasy, so Charlotte quickly said, "I just want to say how sorry I am about Saturday. My words were totally uncalled for, and I hope you can forgive me."

"It's fine, Mrs. Black."

"Are you sure?"

"Uh-huh."

"I was completely out of line, and I'll never insult you like that again."

"It's no problem."

"Okay, well, I know you have to get going for school, so have a great day."

"You, too, Mrs. Black."

Charlotte thought about jumping in the shower, but then she thought about Curtis leaving the house last evening. So she went back downstairs to his study.

"So where'd you go last night?" she asked.

He frowned at her. "Excuse me?"

"Where were you? I remember you leaving right after I got home."

"It's a wonder you remember anything."

"Well, I do."

"I was out."

"Where?"

"It's not important. I'll tell you what is, though."

"What?"

"You and the fact that you were hanging out with some guy."

Charlotte stared at him, paralyzed. Had he seen Greg driving her up to the gate but hadn't said anything until now? Had he been waiting to see if she would tell him about it on her own? Had someone seen her at Chelsey's and she hadn't noticed them? She would never admit anything, though, until she heard additional details, because she didn't want to say any more than she had to. She would be much more careful this time so she wouldn't make the mistake of telling on herself the way she had with that Michael situation last year. "What are you talking about?"

"Humph. So now you're gonna play innocent."

"Who told you that?"

"That's beside the point. Who was he?

Who were you sitting with at Chelsey's?"

She exhaled, happy he must not have known anything more than the fact that she'd been at a sports bar.

"Nobody."

"You sat by yourself the entire time?"

"I did."

"You're such a liar, Charlotte. And not even a good one at that."

"What?" she said, realizing it might be best to just tell the truth. Part of it anyway. "There were all kinds of people in there watching the game, and there was this one guy who came over for a few minutes. But that was it."

"Who was he?"

"How should I know?" she said, lying again.

"Yeah, right."

"It sounds to me like you're jealous."

"Have you found a house yet?" he asked, changing the subject.

"No."

"Have you even been looking?"

"No."

"Well, your time is running out."

"Why? Because you're in a hurry to move in some other woman? And anyway, who were you talking to on the phone the other night?"

"Nobody you need to worry about."

"Well, I am worried, and I have a problem with it."

"What you need to do is find a new house, because if you don't, I'm filing for a legal separation and forcing you out."

Charlotte was taken aback. "What's wrong with you? And what decent man would treat the mother of his children so viciously?"

Curtis grabbed his nylon sweat jacket, slipped it over his snow-white Polo shirt, and strode past her.

"Where are you going?"

Curtis never turned back and kept on his way through the house and out to his truck. Charlotte went upstairs, fuming. The nerve of him, she thought, and she was getting tired of his ice-cold demeanor. She loved him with all her heart, but she wouldn't go on being a fool. She also wouldn't play second string to some mistress. She'd done that a few years ago when he'd traipsed around the country with Tabitha, traveling to a number of his speaking engagements, but she'd eventually forgiven him. She wouldn't stand for it again, though. She was sure he thought he had the right to do whatever he wanted because of the way she'd betrayed him, but she wouldn't tolerate any philandering. She wouldn't continue kissing his behind like some child the way she had for a full year now, and she could show him much better than she could tell him — if he pushed her.

There was still something that bugged her, though . . . well, actually two things. She wanted to know who'd snitched about her sitting with Greg at Chelsey's and who Curtis had been on the phone with a couple of nights ago when she'd stormed back into his office. She wondered about both situations and knew it was only a matter of time before she discovered the truth. Same as always.

CHAPTER 21

Not long after Curtis left, Janine had called Charlotte and invited her to lunch, and she was only ten minutes away from The Tuxon. But as she approached one of the busiest intersections in town, she slowed and stopped at the red light. When she did, her phone beeped, and she wondered who'd texted her. Surprisingly, it was Greg, asking how she was doing, and now she remembered that they'd exchanged phone numbers at some point in the evening. She thought about texting him back, but she called him instead.

He answered after the third ring. "Hey you."

"How's it goin'?"

"Good, but the question is how are you?"

Charlotte laughed quietly. "Much better."

"Glad to hear it."

"Your husband didn't see me drop you off, did he?"

"No."

"Whew, that's a relief."

"I agree. I really appreciate you bringing me home, though. It was very kind of you."

"It was no problem, and I was glad to do it. I also hope it's okay that I sent you a message."

"Well, I won't lie. My husband certainly wouldn't be happy about it."

"But what about you?"

"I guess it's okay."

"You know, I really enjoyed my time with you yesterday."

"I enjoyed myself, too."

"Can we do it again?"

"You know I'm married."

"Yeah, but it's like you said — your husband is done with you and he's filing for a divorce."

Charlotte almost choked. She didn't recall telling him anything of the sort, but how else would he know? And if she'd somehow carelessly blabbed that particular information, what else had she divulged? For the first time, she wondered if maybe she truly had been drinking too much.

"What else did I tell you?"

"A lot."

Fear swept through her. "For example?"

"That there was a time when you hated

your little stepdaughter, but now you love her with all your heart, and also how you were the one who'd ruined your marriage and that you regretted it. You don't remember saying any of that?"

"Of course I do," she said, but her memory was pretty vague.

"It doesn't sound like it," he said with a smile in his voice.

"So, what do you do for a living?"

"Oh, I get it. You wanna talk about something else. I own a landscaping business."

"How neat."

"Thanks."

"Do you contract for residential or commercial?"

"Both."

"That's great, and with it being May, you must be very busy."

"I am. But I have a lot of employees now, so for the most part, I do more overseeing than anything else."

"Can't beat that."

"No. I've been in business for fifteen years, and it's grown every single year. Mostly through referrals."

"Then that means you do good work. Also, how old are you?" she asked.

"Why? Do I look too old?"

"No, actually, you look too young to have

been in business for so long."

"How old do you think I am?"

"Midthirties maybe."

"Wow, what a compliment. I'm turning forty next month."

"You look good."

"I appreciate that. And you?"

"You're kidding, right?"

"No. You're a gorgeous woman with a fabulous body, so what's wrong with telling your age?"

"Fine. I'm in my thirties, but that's the most you're getting out of me."

They both laughed.

"Oh, okay," he said. "I get it."

Charlotte waited for another light to change and accelerated. "Well, hey, I'd better get going. But thanks for texting to check on me."

"You're welcome, but I really would like to see you. Today if possible."

"Maybe another time."

"What about for lunch?"

"I'm meeting my best friend in a few minutes."

"This early?"

"They open at eleven, and we always like beating the lunch crowd."

"Then what about dinner?"

"I don't think so. But thanks for asking."

"Another day it is, then."

"Thanks again for yesterday."

"Anytime."

Charlotte hugged Janine, the hostess seated them, and now they sat browsing through their menus. Charlotte looked up, though, and said, "Hey, I'm really sorry about the way I've been acting lately, but I just haven't been myself."

"No apology necessary. I know you have a lot on your mind, but I just wish you would let me be here for you. I wish you would let me help you."

"There's not a lot anyone can do when it comes to my problems with Curtis."

Janine seemed a little quiet.

"Is something wrong?"

"No, but I guess I have a confession."

"What is it?"

"Now, don't get mad, but when I hung up with you yesterday, I called Curtis."

Charlotte was a little surprised by this. "Really? What about?"

"How worried I am about you."

"But when I spoke to you, I told you I was fine."

"I know, but, Charlotte, I'm your best friend. We're like sisters, and sisters know when something's wrong."

Charlotte gazed out the window they were sitting at.

"Please don't be upset," Janine said. "I only called him because I didn't know what else to do. You won't tell me anything, and it seems like you've been dodging my phone calls."

Charlotte looked at her. "I'm sorry, and I know you mean well, but I'm dealing with a lot of craziness right now."

"Is that why you've been drinking?"

Charlotte wished Curtis had kept his mouth shut. "I went out for a couple of drinks the other day, and now Curtis thinks I'm an alcoholic."

"He didn't say *that,* but he did say you'd gotten drunk twice over a three-day period."

Charlotte's mouth dropped open. "Girl, please. When have you *ever* known me to get drunk?"

"I haven't."

"Exactly, so Curtis is clearly exaggerating."

"But why are you drinking at all? It's so not like you, and I'm only asking because I love you and because I don't want anything happening to you."

Charlotte's anger softened. "Drinking eases my pain, J. My heart is so broken that there are times when I feel like dying. There are times I just don't want to go on."

"I'm so, so sorry you feel that way."

"Did Curtis tell you he wants me to start looking for my own place?"

"No."

"Well he does. He wants me out, and now he's threatening me with a legal separation."

"This is horrible, and I hate that it's happening."

"I do, too, but there's nothing that can be done."

The fiftysomething male waiter walked over. "So what can I get you ladies to drink?"

"Just water for me," Janine said.

"I'll have a glass of Riesling," Charlotte said, but could sense the disapproving expression on her friend's face without even looking at her.

"Sounds good," he said. "Also, our specials for today are shrimp dejonghe, chicken fettuccine, and grilled salmon. I'll take your order as soon as I return with your beverages."

Janine smiled. "Thanks."

The waiter walked away, and Charlotte said, "Gosh, did you ever think my life would end up like this, J?"

"No, never. Not in a million years."

"We've been through so much, but I guess

it never dawned on me that there would come a time when Curtis and I wouldn't be together. Lord knows we've had our ups and downs, but I never thought our marriage would end."

"Well, I'm not giving up on you guys. I still have hope, and I'm going to keep praying day and night for Curtis to change his mind."

"I appreciate that, but I doubt it'll help."

"Prayer always helps, and it's like we've heard in church all our lives: when prayers go up, blessings come down."

"Humph, there was a time when I used to believe in that, but today, not so much."

Janine leaned back. "So are you saying you've lost faith in God?"

"I don't know about anything anymore."

Janine slowly shook her head, visibly horror-struck. "You can't be serious."

"I'm sorry to disappoint you, but that's just the way I feel."

"Maybe you're depressed."

"Maybe. Who knows?"

"Then why don't you make an appointment to see someone?"

"I don't think so."

"Well, I do. I think you should see a therapist as soon as you can."

Charlotte clasped her hands together.

"You worry too much, girl."

"Yeah, and for good reason."

"Okay, then how about this? If I feel any worse, I'll consider calling a counselor."

"I hope you mean that."

"I do. But enough about me and my problems. How's Carl? And how's my beautiful little goddaughter?"

Janine smiled, but Charlotte could tell she wanted to talk more about her and Curtis. "They're both fine. Bethany is getting bigger all the time, and it's so hard to believe she's already one."

"I know. Time flies, doesn't it?"

"It does, but she's such a blessing to us."

"She's definitely a little sweetheart."

"Yeah, and so is Curtina."

"I know. She's my heart, J, and interestingly enough, I feel closer to her than I do to Matthew these days. He's still so distant toward me."

Janine didn't say anything, and now Charlotte wondered if Curtis had told her about the incident on Saturday right before Matthew had left for his prom. She didn't dare ask, though, because the whole scenario was too embarrassing.

Finally, Janine said, "He'll eventually come around. Children always do."

"I hope so, but I've always thought it was

strange how the one person I despised is now the little angel I love and would give my life for if I had to."

"I knew you'd eventually come to terms with your feelings about her."

The waiter returned with their drinks, took their orders, and left again.

Charlotte immediately sipped some of her wine. "I haven't had shrimp dejonghe in a long time, so I'm really looking forward to it."

"I haven't either, so I'm glad I ordered that, too."

The two of them sat chatting about one thing after another, and Charlotte was happy she'd finally gotten a chance to spend some time with Janine. She'd been a little irritated about her having a conversation with Curtis, but she also knew Janine was the best friend any woman could have and that she was only doing everything she could to help her. She was genuinely worried, and Charlotte was thankful for that. Suddenly, though, Charlotte thought about Curtis again, and her questions from the other night came flooding back: Who'd seen her at Chelsey's and told him about it? And who'd he been talking to on the phone? Both questions drove her curiosity wild, and she wouldn't be satisfied until she had answers. She wouldn't be content until she knew exact names and saw faces.

CHAPTER 22

Less than twenty-four hours ago, God had lovingly saved Curtis from himself, and he was very grateful. He'd come a mighty long way in terms of renewing his relationship with the Man upstairs, but in a matter of seconds, he'd almost ruined everything by sleeping with Sharon. The sad part of it, too, was that he'd wanted her badly. He'd fantasized about her and vividly pictured himself in bed with her, and for a few moments he hadn't felt the least bit of guilt. For a few seconds, he'd told himself that everyone was human, that we all made mistakes, and that it was okay to do what he had to do, as long as it would help alleviate his disappointment and pain. He'd decided there was nothing wrong with sleeping with a gorgeous woman who was dying to satisfy him, even if he wasn't in love with her. He did like Sharon, he enjoyed talking to her, and he was strongly attracted to her, but for some reason, there was no I-want-to-spend-the-rest-of-my-life-with-you connection. At least not on his part, anyway. He wasn't sure why exactly, but he knew he'd never be in love with her. He was sure of this because when he'd originally met Tanya, it had been love at first sight. Then when he'd reconnected with Charlotte, he'd fallen in love with her pretty quickly as well. However, when it came to Sharon, he felt a lot differently, like they could never be more than just friends or, at the most, friends with benefits.

Still, he was glad he hadn't gone against God's Word and that he'd left her house in a hurry and driven home. Sharon had even tried calling him only minutes after he'd backed out of her driveway, but he hadn't answered. Partly because he didn't want to take a chance on her convincing him to change his mind and partly because he honestly didn't want to mess up. He didn't want to commit adultery and then regret it. What he wanted was to do the right thing, end of story.

Curtis went inside one of his favorite sandwich spots and wished he'd come a little before noon because the place was packed. Riverside Deli wasn't in the heart of downtown or on the busiest street in town, but people still patronized the establishment regularly because of how good the food was. Curtis loved their Reuben and fries combo, and since he'd had a taste for it for a while, he decided it was very much worth waiting in line for.

"Hey, Pastor," a woman who looked to be in her thirties said, walking in with another woman and standing directly behind him. He didn't know her name but was pretty sure he'd seen her at church.

"Hey, how are you?"

"I'm good," she said. "And I enjoyed your sermon yesterday."

"Good to hear. Are you a member?"

"Not yet, but I've been attending for a few months now. By the way," she said, extending her hand, "I'm Alexis, and this is my coworker, Katrina."

Curtis shook their hands. "Nice to meet you both."

"I've heard the food here is great," Alexis said.

"It is. They have some of the best sandwiches I've tasted."

Curtis turned back around and moved a bit closer to the counter. There were still three people ahead of him, though, so he turned to Alexis and Katrina again. "So, if I may ask, why haven't you joined the church yet?"

Alexis raised her sunglasses toward the top of her head. "I'm thinking about it, but I guess I'm a little hesitant because of the way things turned out at the last church I went to. When scandals happen and pastors disappoint you, it really shakes your faith."

"Sounds like you had a bad experience."

"It was horrible."

"I'm sorry to hear that, but I hope whatever happened won't stop you from choosing another church family. I also hope you won't allow another person's errors to affect your relationship with God."

"I'm trying not to, but it's hard."

"And what about you?" he asked Katrina. "Do you have a church home?"

"Yes, I attend Zion Chapel AME."

"Of course, Pastor Worthington's church. I know him well, and he's a great pastor."

"My parents are charter members, so I've been going there since I was a child."

Curtis took a few steps forward, seeing that he was almost next in line. Just then, though, D. C. Robinson, the loan shark Curtis's former CFO, Raven, had gotten in trouble with, strolled in. It was interesting how whenever Curtis saw him, the first thing he thought was how polite D.C. was and how, regardless of the street life he lived, he'd once given huge financial support to Deliverance Outreach. Curtis had also always been able to trust him.

"Wow, long time no see, Pastor," D.C. said, shaking Curtis's hand.

"It's definitely been a while. So, how are you?"

"Can't complain."

"Good."

"So, you ladies buying?" D.C. asked Alexis and Katrina.

Curtis laughed because it was just like D.C. to flirt with two beautiful young women. Although, since they were dressed professionally, he doubted D.C. was their type.

"Yeah, right," Alexis said. "Since when do I pay for anything when I'm with you?"

D.C. shook his head. "See what I gotta deal with, Pastor? A sister who uses and abuses me."

"This is your sister?"

"Unfortunately." Alexis hit him playfully, and D.C. laughed. "She's a good little sister, though."

"I'm only two years younger than you, remember?"

"But you're still the baby."

"Whatever."

Curtis chuckled. "I didn't even know you had siblings."

"I guess I never got around to mentioning it."

They chatted a few more minutes. Curtis finally placed his order and moved to the side, and D.C. did the same. When Curtis's food was ready, he found a table and soon D.C. joined him.

"So, you invite us to lunch and then you ditch us, huh?" Alexis said.

"I just wanna visit with Pastor Black for a while. I'll take you ladies to lunch another time."

"I guess," Alexis said. "It was good seeing you, Pastor."

"Same here, and I'll look to see you joining Deliverance Outreach very soon."

Katrina followed Alexis and said, "Take care, Pastor."

"You, too."

D.C. ate a couple of fries. "So, how's everything been goin'?"

"Well, to be honest, man, not all that good."

"Is everything okay with the ministry?"

Curtis took a bite of his Reuben. "Everything's fine with that. The problem I'm dealing with is personal."

"Oh. Well, that's a bummer."

"Yeah, it is, and I may as well tell you, I'm getting a divorce. I haven't told my congregation, but that's the deal."

"Wow, Pastor, I'm sorry to hear that."

"It's been a long time coming, but once my son leaves for school this fall, I'm going ahead with proceedings."

"I don't wanna get too personal, but did somethin' specific happen or is it that things just ain't workin' anymore?"

"Long story short, my wife chose to sleep around again."

"You kiddin' me?"

"Wish I was."

"You've really been through it. First you get stiffed by that trick Raven who stole money from the church and now this."

"Yeah, this last year has been the worst, but that's life."

"I guess so, but I hope things get better for you real quick."

"I'm sure they will. But hey, how's Levi?" Levi was one of D.C.'s closest friends, and he was also someone Alicia had had an affair with when she was married to Phillip.

"He's good. Gettin' out next month."

"Is that right?"

"Yeah, he'll finally be free again."

"Good for him," Curtis said. "He hasn't contacted me in a while, but last time I spoke to him, I think he quoted more scriptures than I did."

D.C. laughed. "Don't remind me."

Curtis laughed, too. "I know you'd much rather see him hanging out with you, but I'm thrilled about him turning his life around. I'm glad he knows God and that he plans on doing something different with his life. As a matter of fact, I'm hoping his new way of thinking will rub off on you someday."

"Whoa, now, come on, Pastor, you know I love and respect what you do, but that whole going-to-church-every-Sunday thing ain't me."

"It could be."

"Never."

"Well, I'm not giving up hope, because there comes a point in time in every man's life when he needs God."

"Maybe I should have sat with my sister and her friend," D.C. said, and they both laughed again.

"Maybe you should've because there's no way I'm going to sit here without ministering to you. I'd be less than a pastor if I did."

"I hear you. And don't get me wrong, I do believe in God, but I'd rather love and praise him *outside* of the church."

Curtis shook his head but couldn't deny

how much he liked D.C. "Some things never change."

D.C. grinned. "I guess not, but you know I've got ya back if you ever need me."

"I've always appreciated that."

When they finished eating, Curtis and D.C. went outside and Alexis and Katrina joined them minutes later. They all stood making small talk, but right when Alexis said, "I guess we'd better get back to work," a silver Mercedes pulled into the parking lot, and Curtis wondered what Charlotte wanted. She'd never been in the habit of following him around, so he could only imagine what kind of drama she was planning. But as the car rolled closer, Curtis got a better look and saw that it was Sharon. He was a little shocked because he'd had no idea she even owned a Mercedes, especially the same model and color as Charlotte's. He hadn't seen her wearing her hair in the exact same style as Charlotte's before either, even though the color had always been similar.

D.C., Alexis, and Katrina said their goodbyes, got in their vehicles, and left, and that's when Curtis walked over to Sharon. Her window was already half down, but then she lowered it all the way. Curtis wanted to ask her why she was wearing the same Gucci sunglasses Charlotte had been wearing for months now. It was all very strange, and he'd be lying if he said all these similarities didn't trouble him a little.

"Well, isn't this a coincidence," she said, smiling. "I hope I didn't interrupt anything."

"No, I was just having lunch with an old friend of mine. Haven't seen him in a long time."

"Looked like you were having lunch with more than just him."

"I don't get what you mean."

"The two women who were standing next to you when I pulled up."

"One of them was his sister and the other was her friend."

"I've seen the tall one at church before."

"Yeah, she's been coming for a few months."

Sharon seemed agitated. "I'm sure she has."

"Why do you say it like that?"

"No reason."

Curtis was ready to go. "Okay, well, hey, I'd better get out of here. I have a couple of other stops to make, and then I need to pick up my daughter from school."

"That's fine, but, baby, can I ask you something?"

"What?"

"Why did you walk out on me like that?"

He'd hoped he wouldn't have to have this conversation with Sharon, but no such luck. "I'm sorry, but if I hadn't left, I knew we'd end up doing something we shouldn't."

"But we were having such a wonderful time. We were so connected and in sync with one another. Everything was perfect."

Curtis positioned his sunglasses over his eyes. "Look, Sharon, this is all my fault because I never should have come over in the first place."

"You came because you wanted to make love to me, and there's nothing wrong with that."

"There's a lot wrong with it."

"But we were so close to solidifying our relationship."

Curtis looked around, realizing the last thing he wanted was for anyone to see him having a lengthy conversation with some beautiful woman in a restaurant parking lot, because it wouldn't take long before rumors started. "Hey, I really have to get going."

"Will you call me later?"

"I'll try."

"I love you," she said, but Curtis ignored her and went to his SUV.

He'd never seen Sharon act this way before, and he hoped her seeing him standing in the parking lot of a deli was mere co-incidence and not something that had occurred on purpose. He hoped she wasn't in the habit of following him — more important, he hoped she wasn't obsessed with Charlotte, because while he hadn't wanted to stare at her, he could have sworn the white jean outfit she was wearing was the same one he'd seen Charlotte wearing last summer. But maybe his eyes were playing tricks on him. Maybe it wasn't the same outfit at all. Maybe none of what he'd noticed was any big deal, and it was simply a matter of two women having the same taste in clothing — and in hairdos, sunglasses, purses, and cars. Although, there was something else that crossed his mind. Why had she been at Chelsey's yesterday afternoon at the very same time as Charlotte? If he could recollect, not once had Sharon spoken about Chelsey's before yesterday. In the past, she'd talked about a number of restaurants she enjoyed eating at or getting carryout from, but never Chelsey's.

Although, maybe he was overthinking this whole scenario, and there was no problem at all. Maybe he was just paranoid for no reason. Yes, that had to be it because the alternative was too alarming.

CHAPTER 23

Charlotte couldn't take it anymore. She needed to know who Curtis had been chatting with on the phone, and today was the day she'd find out. It was the reason she'd zoomed home right after having lunch with Janine and had quickly rushed upstairs to her computer. Now she sat perched in front of the screen, creating a user ID and password for Curtis's cell phone account on the Verizon Wireless website. She'd been worried that maybe Curtis had already set them up, but once she'd registered as a new online user and typed in all pertinent information, she discovered he hadn't. They paid their bills through the online bill pay service their bank offered, and knowing Curtis, if there was a discrepancy of some kind or a question he had about his account in general, he would much rather call customer service.

Charlotte accessed the account and saw

that she could select either her cell or his, so she clicked on his number and then clicked View Usage and then View Call Details. She scrolled through today's calls and yesterday's and finally saw Saturday's. Right away, she spotted a call Curtis had made very close to midnight. She knew that had to be the one she was looking for because while she couldn't remember for sure, she knew Matthew had just changed and left for his postprom party around that time.

She pulled her cell phone out of her purse, dialed ⋆67 to block her number, and then dialed the mysterious number on her computer screen. There were two rings before a woman said, "Hello?" But all Charlotte did was sit listening and trying to figure out if she recognized the voice.

"Hello?" the woman said again. "Who is this?"

Charlotte listened intently but still didn't say anything, and finally the woman hung up. So she called her again.

"Hello?"

Charlotte almost asked her who she was but then decided it was best she did more investigating before verbally confronting the woman.

"Hello?" the woman yelled this time. Then

she hung up again.

"I knew it," Charlotte said. She was steaming, but at the same time, she was hurt. Curtis really had been talking to some woman on the phone, and she had to find out who it was. Did she attend Deliverance Outreach? Was she someone from his past? Worse, was she a woman Curtis had fallen hopelessly in love with and was going to marry as soon as possible? Had he already unofficially replaced Charlotte and was simply biding his time?

Charlotte needed to see her little girl, and while Curtis had demanded she not drive Curtina around anymore, she was going to pick her daughter up and spend the rest of the day with her. Since Curtis was off and Curtina had spent the night with Aunt Emma, she knew he was planning to get her from school, but Charlotte missed her, and Curtis would just have to deal with it. Plus, it wasn't like she'd had anything to drink today . . . well, maybe that one glass of wine she'd ordered at the restaurant when she and Janine had lunch, but she certainly wasn't intoxicated. Still, she knew Curtis would have a hissy fit if he saw Curtina getting in the car with her, so she had to leave the house now if she wanted to arrive at the school before him. What she would do was go inside, lie about a dental appointment Curtina had, and pull her out of class thirty minutes early. She hated resorting to this kind of petty deception, but Curtis had left her no choice. She had to do whatever necessary and wouldn't feel bad about it.

Curtina sat in the back of the car, watching a movie and enjoying her McDonald's Happy Meal. She'd been so happy to see Charlotte when she'd picked her up, and she had talked nonstop on their way out of the building and over to the car. She was the light of Charlotte's life, and while Charlotte was still hurt over the idea that Curtis had found someone else, being with Curtina lifted her spirits.

Curtina ate her chicken nuggets and sang to the video, and Charlotte smiled. Then her phone rang. She'd forgotten to connect her Bluetooth, so she couldn't use her earpiece, but when she saw that it was Curtis calling, she broke the law and answered, anyway.

"Where are you?" he shouted.

"Out."

"I thought I made it clear that I didn't want Curtina riding in the car with you."

Charlotte glanced at Curtina in her rearview mirror, making sure her headphones were secure and that she wasn't paying any attention to her conversation. "Look, Curtis, if I want to spend time with Curtina, I will, and there's nothing you can do about it."

"If you're putting my daughter's life in danger, there's a whole lot I *will* do."

"I haven't been drinking, Curtis. Happy?"

"I don't care if you have or haven't. I don't want her in the car with you."

"Well, that's just too bad."

"Bring her home, Charlotte."

"I will. When I'm good and ready."

"You're really trying my patience."

"And you're trying mine, so I guess we're even."

"When are you coming home?"

Charlotte turned into the mall parking lot. "I told you, when I'm good and ready."

"Mommy, is that Daddy?" Curtina said.

Charlotte hadn't counted on her asking any questions. "It sure is, sweetheart."

"Can I speak to him?"

Charlotte said nothing else to Curtis but passed Curtina the phone.

"Hi, Daddy, what are you doing? . . . I'm good . . . Are you going to meet us here at the mall? . . . We're parking right now by Macy's," she said, and Charlotte cringed. "Okay, you wanna speak back to Mommy?"

Charlotte took the phone. "Hello?"

"I'm coming to get my daughter."

"No problem. We'll see you soon, honey," she said in a chipper tone for Curtina's benefit.

Charlotte parked, and the two of them got out and went into the mall as planned. As always, Curtina grabbed her hand, and Charlotte was amazed at how the smallest things she did made her feel special. Made her feel loved and wanted the way she once had with Matthew. They rode down the escalator to the children's department, and as soon as they walked down the aisle, Curtina rushed toward a darling pink short set. "Can I get this?"

"If they have your size." Charlotte picked up a yellow short set and turned it around. "What about this one?"

"I like that one, too."

"Then we'll get both of them. I think you need to try them on, though, but let's take a look at the dresses first."

They strolled down the aisle a bit farther, but just as Charlotte pulled a black-and-white sleeveless dress from the rack, she heard someone call her name, and she turned around. "Oh, hey, Lana," she said, hugging her.

"How are you? And how are you, Miss

215

Curtina?"

"Good."

"So what brings you down to the girls' department?" Charlotte asked.

Lana turned around. "Oh, here she comes now. You remember my niece, Tracey, right?"

Charlotte nodded. "Yes, how are you? I haven't seen you at church in a while, though."

"I know. Lately I've been working a lot of weekends at the hospital, so that's why I haven't been there."

"I understand."

Lana looked across the department. "Tracey has a five-year-old, so we decided to run down here and browse a little before we go up to the shoe section. I need to find some comfortable flats or low wedges for the convention in Detroit this weekend."

"Which one is that?"

"You know, the women's conference Pastor is speaking at," Lana said.

Charlotte wondered why Curtis hadn't had the decency to tell her he was going out of town. On the holiday weekend no less. She was so embarrassed.

She pretended she knew all about it, though. "Oh yeah, I totally forgot about that. I didn't realize you were going."

"I hadn't planned on it, but now I'm glad your husband talked me into it. Still, I wish you were going, too, because I know it'll be a great time."

"Maybe next year," Charlotte said, but knew her chances of ever going were highly unlikely, especially if Curtis kept his word about divorcing her.

Tracey repositioned her purse on her shoulder. "If you'll excuse me, I'm going to take a look around, but it was great seeing you, Charlotte."

"Likewise," she said, but then wheels turned in her head. What if Tracey was the woman Curtis was now interested in and the person he'd been speaking to on the phone? Charlotte had always loved Lana, but she was also extremely loyal to Curtis and treated him like a son, so what if she was covering up an affair between him and her favorite niece? What if Tracey had been the woman who'd answered the phone this afternoon when Charlotte had dialed the number she'd found on the website?

Charlotte snapped back to reality when she heard Lana saying, "Hey, Pastor."

Curtina hugged him. "Hi, Daddy."

"Hi, sweetheart."

"Look what Mommy's getting ready to buy me. I have to try everything on first, though."

"How pretty."

"Okay, well, you all have a good evening," Lana said. "And I'll see you tomorrow morning, Pastor."

"See you then," he said.

Charlotte told her good-bye and wanted to kill Curtis. "Why are you here?"

"To pick up Curtina."

Charlotte rolled her eyes at him, and Curtina went farther down the aisle, looking at T-shirts. "You're taking this thing too far."

Curtis walked away from her and over to their daughter. The nerve of him, driving all the way out to the mall just so Curtina wouldn't be able to ride home with her. He was acting as though she were a bad mother, the kind who would carelessly place her little girl's life in danger, and she was offended. Maybe she had drunk a bit too much last Thursday and then again on Friday night and Saturday — and even yesterday after church, but she hadn't done so today, and that's what mattered. Actually, now that she thought about it, she hadn't even felt as hungover this morning, at least not as much as she had yesterday and the day before, so Curtis was worrying over nothing. He was obsessing over any little thing just to irritate her, but she wasn't going to let him bother her. Not when she had something much more important to concern herself with — figuring out who he was seeing behind her back and how long he'd been doing so. It hadn't dawned on her until now that what she should have done was scroll through the last few months of call details so she could see how often Curtis and his woman chatted. But better late than never, though, because it would be the first thing she did when she got home. It would be her only priority.

CHAPTER 24

Curtis pulled into the driveway, waited for the garage to open, and eased inside. Curtina gathered her bags — those she could carry on her own — and got out. Curtis told her he would get the large one she'd left on the seat. She went inside the house, and Curtis opened the back door of the vehicle. When he did, his phone rang.

"Hello?"

"I thought you were going to call me?"

Curtis wondered why Sharon was contacting him, especially since she knew it was in the evening and he'd likely be at home. Not to mention, he had always pretty much been the one to do all the calling, anyway. "I had a busy afternoon, and now I'm just getting home from the mall with my daughter."

"Can I see you?"

"Not tonight."

"Then when?"

"I don't know."

"I really need to see you, baby."

Curtis wondered what had gotten into her. "I'll try to call you later, but right now I need to go."

"Why?"

"I told you. I just got home."

"Okay, then what time?"

"Can't say."

"Please don't leave me hanging."

Curtis sighed. "I'll call you sometime to-night."

"I'll be waiting, baby."

Curtis pulled the shopping bag from the truck and went inside the house, but he was dumbfounded. He wasn't sure why Sharon had turned into this woman he didn't know, but he didn't like it. First, she'd showed up at the deli earlier and now she was calling him like it was nothing. She acted as though he could talk anytime and as if he weren't married. He knew it had been wrong to chat with her in secret, too, but he also thought they'd had an understanding. He'd been sure she understood the rules, but maybe she didn't. Or maybe she no longer saw a reason to abide by them, now that he'd made the mistake of visiting her again. Worse, she was acting as though they had in fact slept together, because it was usually then that mistresses seemed to lose their minds and suddenly believed they had rights — the right to call a married man whenever they felt like it as well as the right to disrespect the man's wife any way they saw fit. But Sharon had seemed different. For a full year now, she'd been calm and pleasant, and that was part of the reason he enjoyed talking to her. She even made him laugh and offered him the best support and encouragement whenever he needed it. So this new personality of hers was mind-boggling and so out in left field. It didn't make any sense, and if she didn't become her old self, he would have to cut her off completely.

Curtis looked up when Matt walked into the kitchen. "Hey, son."

"What's up, Dad?"

"Not much. You studying?"

"Yep, and Racquel's upstairs doing the same thing, so I just came to get us some sodas. We need caffeine already."

Curtis chuckled. "I remember those days, and as much as I hate telling you, it gets worse in college."

"Ugh."

"It'll be worth it, though. You'll see."

Matthew went back upstairs, but just as Curtis walked down the hallway to his office, Charlotte strutted toward him, and he could tell she was livid.

"I need to talk to you."

He walked in and over to his desk. "About what?"

Charlotte shut the door and tossed a stack of papers onto his desk. They scattered everywhere. "These."

Curtis took one look, and it didn't take a genius to figure out that the number Charlotte had highlighted numerous times was Sharon's.

"Whose number is that, Curtis? I know it belongs to a woman because I dialed it and heard her voice."

Curtis wondered if Charlotte and Sharon had spoken; maybe this was the reason Sharon was acting so boldly. "Charlotte, please. You know Matt has company, so this isn't the time."

"I don't care who's here. I wanna know what whore you've been talking to almost every day for months."

"It's nobody, and before you even try to accuse me, I haven't slept with her."

Charlotte laughed, but Curtis knew this wasn't funny to her. "So you're actually going to stand there lying when I've printed out pages and pages of proof? Do you think I'm that stupid?"

"Look, all I've done is have phone conversations with her. That's it." He knew that wasn't totally true, not when he had gone to Sharon's house twice, but there was no way he was admitting that to Charlotte. Not with his children and Racquel right upstairs. If he did, he knew Charlotte would go ballistic.

"Why do you keep lying, Curtis? You think I'm naïve, don't you? You think just because I've begged and pleaded with you for months not to leave me that you can do whatever you want? You think you can sleep around behind my back and get away with it?"

"Like I said, I haven't slept with her. Sleeping around is your thing, remember? Not mine."

"Yeah, okay, turn this on me the same as always. And, anyway, let's just say you haven't slept with her . . . I mean, I know you have, but just for the sake of conversation. Either way, you've still been having an affair. When any man talks to another woman every day, sometimes for two and three hours, he's having an emotional affair, and to me that's just as bad or worse because that means you'd rather talk to her than to your own wife."

Curtis stared at her in silence, because he knew she was right. He'd been laughing and talking with Sharon regularly and openly sharing with her things that really mattered to him, so there was no denying the definition of his relationship with her.

"You don't even have anything to say, do you?"

"Charlotte, things haven't been right with us for how long now?"

"And? What does that mean?"

"I'm just sayin'."

"You're just sayin' what?"

"Forget it."

"No, Curtis, tell me what you mean."

"All I'm saying is that you did all your dirt last year and now you have the gall to confront me about a few phone calls?"

"I'm still your wife, Curtis. I know you treat me like I'm not, but on paper and in God's eyesight, I'm still Mrs. Curtis Black."

"Really? Then why were you out drinking with some man yesterday?"

"I wasn't out with anybody. He was just a guy who came over to my table, and I already explained that to you."

"Did you sleep with him?"

"Of course not."

Curtis looked at her and while he'd almost convinced himself that he couldn't care less about Charlotte moving on and finding another man, a part of him wanted to believe she was telling the truth. A part of him hoped she hadn't slept with whoever this mystery man was.

"Curtis, I haven't slept with anyone because I still love you. So, the fact that you're seeing another woman . . . that really hurts."

Curtis wasn't sure why, but ever since he'd seen those printouts, his conscience had commenced ripping him apart, and he felt bad about what he'd been doing. There was no doubt that subconsciously he'd known all along that talking to Sharon and ultimately going to visit her was wrong, but until now, he'd always been able to justify his actions because of the way Charlotte had betrayed him. He'd told himself that if Charlotte could sleep with two men, surely he could talk to another woman by phone if he chose to. He'd even decided that he wasn't committing adultery or breaking his vows by doing so. But now he had to admit the truth: He had sort of been having an affair with Sharon — regardless of whether it was simply an emotional one or otherwise — and it wasn't right. He could no longer deny that after all these years of living with high moral standards, after having turned his life completely around, he'd still managed to sin with another woman. He'd still gone against God's Word, and now he regretted it.

Charlotte's eyes watered. "All I wanna know is who she is."

"It's not important, and if it's any consolation, I won't be talking to her anymore."

"But why can't you just tell me?"

"Because it's not necessary."

"Is she a member of the church?"

"Charlotte, let's just leave well enough alone."

"She is, isn't she? Is it Tracey?"

Curtis frowned. "Is it who?"

"Lana's niece."

"You're kidding, right? That woman is married."

"So?"

"It's not her."

"Then who?"

"No one you know."

"Why won't you just tell me?"

Curtis walked around his desk and sat down, but to his great disappointment, his phone rang. He had a feeling it was Sharon, so he ignored it.

"Why aren't you answering your phone?"

"Because you and I are talking."

Charlotte rushed over to him, reaching toward the pocket of his jacket, but Curtis pushed his chair away from her.

"That's her, isn't it?" Charlotte yelled,

227

struggling to grab his cell.

Curtis held her off as best he could. Soon the phone stopped ringing, but Charlotte ranted and raved even louder, and the next thing Curtis knew, there was soft knocking on the door. Charlotte stopped shouting, but Curtina opened the door and walked in.

"Mommy, what's wrong? Why were you screaming at Daddy?"

"I'm a little upset about something, honey, but it's nothing for you to worry about."

"I don't like it when you and Daddy argue, and it sounded like you were arguing."

Charlotte wrapped her arm around Curtina and held her close. "We're fine, sweetie. Now let's go back up to your room so I can check your homework."

Curtina gazed at Curtis with sad eyes, and he could tell she didn't believe a word of Charlotte's explanation, but she left without asking more questions. Curtis was relieved, to say the least, and sat back in his chair. *What a day,* he thought, and then pulled out his phone. Sure enough, it had been Sharon calling, and he knew he had to put a stop to this. He wouldn't take a chance on calling her back now, though, not when Charlotte might burst back into his office at any time, but he would certainly contact her as soon as he arrived at the church in the morning. He would explain that they could no longer speak by phone or in person and that this thing they had, whatever a person wanted to call it, was over. It would be the end of a friendship that never should have happened.

CHAPTER 25

Not every now and then or even every few days, but every *single* day — that's how often Curtis had been conversing with some woman on the phone. When Charlotte had arrived home from the mall yesterday, she'd immediately signed back onto Verizon's website and pulled up their account again. She'd printed page after page, and to her surprise, she'd been able to access the last twelve statements. She'd seen a whole year's worth of usage details, and it was clear that Curtis hadn't missed a beat. He'd chitchatted with this woman like she was the most important person in his life and acted as though he had some great need to talk to her. Now Charlotte wondered even more who she was and what could possibly be so special about her. What did this particular woman have that Charlotte didn't, and how on earth had she seized Curtis's undivided attention? How had she slithered her way into his life, making him feel as though he couldn't go a day without hearing her voice?

If Charlotte hadn't cried herself to sleep last night and could assemble more tears, she would bawl like a baby. But since she couldn't, she pulled herself together and began heading downstairs to breakfast. When she stepped out in the hallway, however, she heard Matthew's TV playing and strolled toward his room. She knocked on his door, which was slightly ajar.

"Yes?" he said

"Sweetie, it's me. Can I come in?"

"It's open."

Charlotte walked inside. "Can you turn that down a little? I wanna talk to you."

Matthew picked up the remote, pressed the Volume button, and dropped it back onto his bed. Then he finished buttoning his starched white long-sleeved shirt and sat down.

"Matt, you know I love you, right?"

He slipped his foot into one of his snow-white gym shoes. "I guess."

"No, I don't want you to guess. I want you to be sure of that. I want you to under-stand that no matter what I've done, no matter how many mistakes I've made, I will always love you."

Matthew slipped on his other shoe and

tied it but never looked up.

Charlotte wasn't sure what else she could say or do to get him to open up to her. To get him to forgive her. "Matt, are you always going to feel this way? Are you always going to hate me for what I did last year?"

He stood with his back to her and went over to his desk. "I don't hate anybody, Mom, so I certainly don't hate you. What I hate is how you keep doing and saying things to hurt people. Last year, you went out of your way to be mean to Curtina, then you hurt Dad, and last weekend you embarrassed me in front of everyone. You got sloppy drunk on my prom day, and I just don't get that. I don't understand you at all anymore."

Charlotte tried finding the right words, but she didn't know what she could possibly say. Matthew had said a mouthful, and there was no room to defend herself. She was guilty as charged. "You're right, Matt. I did everything you said, and I'm sorry. I know I've messed up a lot, but you have to give me another chance."

"You know, Mom, normally it's the child who makes foolish mistakes and then the parent is the one who points them out and helps the child learn from them. But in this house, it seems like things are just the opposite. It seems like you can't help the things you do and that you're never going to stop."

Charlotte moved closer to him. "That's not true. I promise you, it isn't. I promise you I will never hurt you again. I won't ever speak to you or embarrass you the way I did on Saturday."

Matthew grabbed his book bag and keys. "I have to go eat."

"Can I at least have a hug?"

He hesitated but then reached out to her, and Charlotte squeezed him the way she used to when he was a toddler. "Sweetie, you and Curtina are my whole world, so please don't ever forget that. I would die for you if I had to."

Matthew released her and went downstairs, and as Charlotte walked out into the hallway, Curtina came out of her bedroom.

"Can Matt drive me to school today?"

"I suppose. Now, you'd better get downstairs to breakfast so he won't leave you."

"Okay, are you coming, too?"

"I'll be along in a few minutes. You go ahead."

Curtina went on her way, and Charlotte stood thinking about her son and the words he'd said. He'd had such a serious look on his face when he'd spoken to her, but she had also noticed a hint of sadness, and she wished she could somehow erase all her mistakes. She knew that wasn't possible, but she yearned for that nonetheless.

After eating a piece of toast and saying good-bye to the children, Charlotte went back up to her bedroom. Interestingly enough, Curtis had made a tiny bit of small talk with her through his conversation with Agnes about his trip this weekend and how he couldn't wait to get back home to relax for the holiday. Charlotte hadn't said very much to him, though, because she was still riled about those phone calls. She was furious, and during breakfast, she'd begun debating whether she should call this woman up and confront her. But there was one thing that gave her pause. Curtis had built a relationship with this woman of his own free will, so what good would it do talking to her? Would it really make a difference, one way or the other?

Charlotte wondered what her mother would do, so she called her.

She answered on the first ring. "Hey, sweetheart."

"Hey, Mom. How are you?"

"Good, and you?"

"About the same. How's Dad?"

"He's fine. Just left for the golf course about an hour ago."

"I guess it's that time of year."

"That's for sure. So, what's going on in the Black household? Are things better now?"

Charlotte sat on the edge of the tan chaise. "They're worse."

"How?"

"I found out Curtis has been communicating with another woman for a whole year now."

"What? Who is she?"

"I don't know."

"Did you ask him?"

"He won't tell me her name."

"How did you find out about her?"

"I caught him on the phone the other night, and finally yesterday, I pulled the phone records."

"Maybe all he's been doing is talking."

"Yeah, that's what he says, but, Mom, he's been talking to her every day. And sometimes they were on for two or more hours."

"And you don't have any idea who she is?"

"None."

"This is going too far. It was one thing for Curtis to talk about divorcing you, but now that some woman has entered the picture,

235

that changes everything."

Charlotte could only imagine the expression her mother wore, because she spoke fast and her voice was high-pitched.

"You're going to have to squash this whole other-woman thing immediately."

"But, Mom, I don't know who she is."

"Do you think he's been sleeping with her?"

"He says he hasn't. He says all he's done is talk to her on the phone."

"I just don't believe this. Curtis has always loved you, and I never thought it would come to this."

"Well, it has, and if I hadn't pulled those phone records and called the number, he never would have told me."

"You spoke to her?"

"No, when she answered, I just held the phone."

"Well, what you need to do now is call that heifer back and tell her to find her own man and leave your husband alone. You need to get her straight and let her know you mean business."

"I don't know, Mom. I thought about that, but I'm not sure that's the right thing to do."

"Excuse me? You never had any problem

confronting Tabitha, so why is this so different?"

"It's not I guess, but it's Curtis I'm married to, and it's him who should put a stop to this."

"I disagree."

"Why?"

"Because nowadays, these women out here are lonely, desperate, and treacherous. And it doesn't matter if they're single or tied down in a miserable marriage; they have no problem going after another woman's husband."

"I still don't know what a phone call will do to change that."

"It can do a lot if you say the right things. You have to let her know that you're not going to tolerate her talking to your husband or trying to see him and that if she continues, she'll be sorry."

Charlotte sighed. She heard what her mother was saying, but she just didn't feel like calling another woman to argue about her own husband. Or maybe she didn't want to take the chance of hearing more than she could bear.

"You should hang up and call her now," Noreen said.

Charlotte's phone beeped, so she looked at her screen. It was Janine, and Charlotte wanted to talk to her. "Mom, I have another call."

"Fine, but you call me back as soon as you contact that woman."

"I will," she said, not knowing if she actually would call her mother back or not.

She pressed the Receive button and answered Janine's call.

"Hey, J."

"Hey, how are you?"

"Not good, girl. I was going to call you as soon as I got off with Mom."

"Why, what's wrong?"

"Long story short, I pulled Curtis's cell phone records and found out he's been talking to some woman every day for months. He's been doing it for at least a whole year."

"No, girl."

"Yes. I also called the number, and that's how I know it belongs to a woman. Plus, he admitted it last night when I showed him the printouts, but he wouldn't tell me her name."

"Is he having an affair with her?"

"He says he's not, but even if he hasn't slept with her, that's still what he's been doing."

Janine was quiet.

"I know you don't wanna make me feel bad, but you know I'm right, J. I mean, how would you feel if Carl had been having phone conversations with a woman more often than he did with you?"

"I guess you have a point. But maybe he just needed someone to talk to because of what you and he have been going through."

"Then he should have confided in one of his guy friends or another minister. Not some woman."

"I'm sorry this is happening."

"So am I, and I'm really worried, J, because if Curtis has been talking to this woman every day, they must really have a connection. There has to be some very strong chemistry involved."

"Did he say he would stop talking to her?"

"Yes, but who's to say he will?"

"Maybe he'll stop because you know about it."

"Who knows? My mom says I should call her and tell her to stop talking to Curtis, but I'm not sure I wanna do that."

"Chances are that'll only make bad matters worse."

"It might, but I also feel like she deserves to hear from me."

"I think you should sit down and discuss this a little more with Curtis."

"For what? I mean, as far as I know, he's still divorcing me, anyway, so why would he feel the need to stop calling her? For all I know, she's the woman he's planning to marry."

"I don't believe that."

"Why?"

"I just don't. I know Curtis says your marriage is over, but he does still love you."

"I'm not so sure."

"Well, I am. No matter what he said to me on Sunday when I called him, I could tell he was still in love with you. He's just hurt."

Charlotte listened to Janine for a few more minutes, but soon her mind wandered back to this unidentified woman and whether she should contact her or not. Her mom was all for it, Janine was totally against it, and Charlotte fell somewhere in between. Either way, she knew she had to make a decision very soon, and she would before the day was over.

CHAPTER 26

It hadn't been more than five minutes since Curtis had spoken to Lana and the rest of the administrative staff, then moseyed into his office and closed the door behind him. Now he lifted the church phone from its base and couldn't dial Sharon fast enough. He hadn't thought about anything else all night long or even this morning, and he was ready to make his last call to her.

"Hey, baby," she said.

"Do you have a minute?"

"All the time in the world when it comes to you."

"Look, my wife pulled my phone records, so after today I can't talk to you anymore."

"So I guess that's who called me yesterday and held the phone. She did it twice."

"I'm sorry to have to end our friendship this way, but I was wrong for talking to you in the first place, and I certainly never should have come to your home."

"There's nothing to feel sorry about. Not when I know for a fact we're supposed to be together. So, all we have to do now is be more careful until you get your divorce."

Maybe she hadn't heard him correctly, so he said, "What I'm saying is that you and I can no longer communicate in any way, and we can never see each other again."

"You're just afraid she'll use our relationship against you in court and then the judge will rule in her favor, but it's like I said, all we have to do is be more careful. I'll add a second line onto my wireless account, and you can use that phone instead. That way, she'll never know about our conversations."

He wasn't getting through to Sharon, and he wasn't sure what he needed to say.

"The bottom line is this: I'm a married man. I won't be calling you anymore, and I won't be answering any calls from you."

"You're just upset about her finding out. You're worried about what this will mean for your court case, and I don't blame you. But, baby, this is all going to be okay. You'll see."

Curtis realized being nice wasn't working. "This has nothing to do with my divorce. This has everything to do with you and how I don't want you contacting me again. What I want is for you to go on with your life and completely forget about me."

"I can't do that," she said before he'd barely finished his sentence.

"Why?"

"Because I don't want to go against God's will."

Curtis lowered his eyebrows. "What are you talking about?"

"Baby, before I moved here, God spoke to me loudly and clearly. He told me that I was going to be your next wife. Remember when I first introduced myself to you, and I told you how I'd seen you on television a few times and how I packed up everything and transferred my job to Mitchell? Remember when I said I'd done it because I wanted to be close to you? Well, what I didn't tell you was that the real reason I never hesitated was because I didn't want to disobey God. He wants us together, Curtis. He wants us to be married."

"Are you crazy?"

"No, I couldn't be more serious if I tried. God planned our meeting and our destiny years and years ago, and now it's finally time for us to be together. I know you're in a tough situation and that Charlotte obviously doesn't want to let go of you, but you have to fight and keep pushing forward. You have to end things with her the way you planned."

Her tone was calm, and Curtis wondered if she believed what she was saying.

"I think you're a little confused, Sharon, and while I know you've been hoping we would eventually get together, I'm sorry to say it's never going to happen. Right now I have to focus on my children and on doing what's right for them."

"You're just a little overwhelmed with all that's going on, and you weren't expecting Charlotte to find out about us this way. But things'll get better as time goes on."

Trying to reason with her was a lost cause, so he said, "I have to go now, but you take care of yourself."

"Why are you acting this way?" she hurried to say. "Don't you want me?"

"No."

"You don't mean that?"

"I do mean it. I mean every word I've said to you over the last few minutes."

"Baby, just tell me what I need to do. I've tried to make changes so that when the time comes I'll be the perfect first lady. I've changed my hairstyle, the way I dress, but if there's something you don't like, just tell me. Tell me what you want me to do, and I will."

Curtis had dealt with some pretty interesting people over the years, namely Adrienne, his former mistress who had become the ultimate fatal attraction, and he had a feeling Sharon might be falling into the same category. But there was no way this was happening again, not when he hadn't even slept with the woman. Not when all he'd done was talk to her.

Curtis decided trying a different approach. "Sharon, you're a really nice woman, so I know you'll meet the right person very soon. He's out there, but you're never going to find him if you don't start looking."

"I found the right man when I connected with you."

Curtis was done with this. "I have to go now."

"You take care, and like I said, try not to worry. Everything will work itself out in no time."

"Good-bye, Sharon."

Curtis hung up the phone and exhaled. This woman had issues, and all he could hope was that she would eventually forget about him and that this would be the end of it. Still, he couldn't fathom anyone acting this obsessively over something that was nothing more than a friendship, but maybe he'd spent too much time on the phone with her. Maybe he'd given her false hope without even realizing it, and she had somehow taken his words the wrong way. He'd said it before but he couldn't help thinking how he never, ever should have gone to her house on Sunday evening and allowed things to escalate between them. They hadn't had sex, but they'd come extremely close, and maybe that had been far too much for her. Maybe this was the reason she was acting as though she'd lost her mind and couldn't imagine her life without him.

Curtis's cell phone rang, and Alicia's number displayed on the screen.

"Hey, sweetheart, what's goin' on?"

"Hey, Daddy. I have to prepare for a conference call, but I wanted to let you know that James is in the hospital."

"Oh no."

"Yeah, remember I was telling you last week about his finger and how it got infected? Over the weekend it got worse, and last night they admitted him so they could administer an antibiotic intravenously."

"How's your mom?"

"She was pretty worried because of how high his fever was, but it's finally come down quite a bit this morning. I just talked to her, but I thought I would call and let you know what was going on."

"I'm glad you did, and I'll give her a call right now."

"Please pray for him, Daddy, because James has been such a wonderful husband to Mom, and you know he's been the best stepdad to me."

"I know, sweetheart, and, of course, you know I will."

"Okay, well, I'd better get going, but I love you."

"Love you, too."

Curtis dialed Tanya's cell, but it rang a few times and went to her voice mail. But just as he was about to leave a message, she called him back.

"Hey, I just spoke to Alicia," he said. "How are you? And how's James?"

"I'm hanging in there, and James is finally doing better. We had a rough day yesterday, but his fever is finally down, and not long ago the doctor said the swelling in his hand has started to go down as well. So I think they finally found the right antibiotic."

"Praise God. Alicia told me last week that he cut his finger, but I had no idea he would end up in the hospital."

"Neither did I. They tried different oral antibiotics but nothing worked, so I'm glad they finally got him admitted."

"Well, I'll certainly be praying for a full

recovery."

"I really appreciate that, Curtis. That's very kind of you."

For the first time in years, their conversation seemed awkward and neither of them said a word. Of course, Curtis knew it was because the last time they'd spoken, he'd told Tanya how much he still loved her.

"So where are you now?" he said for lack of anything better to say.

"I spent the night at the hospital, so I'm on my way home to shower and change."

"Oh, okay."

There was dead silence again.

"Curtis, I need to say something."

"Go ahead."

"You really caught me off guard last week when you said the things you did, and of course, it really got me thinking. I thought about old times, and it wasn't long before I had to admit to myself that there's a part of me that does still love you. A part of me always will . . . but I also love James with all my soul, and the thought of losing him has only made me love and appreciate him more. James is my rock. He's treated me like a queen since the very beginning, and Alicia doesn't think there's a better stepfather in the world."

Curtis thought about the conversation

he'd just had with his daughter and how she'd basically said the same things.

"So you see," she continued, "I could never hurt him or leave him under any circumstances."

"I understand, and just so you know, I never should have come to you the way I did. I know you're happily married and that you love your husband, and I completely respect that. I think I was just at a point where I allowed my emotions to get the best of me, and the next thing I knew I found myself reflecting on you and what could have been had I been faithful to you. Even now, I'm very messed up emotionally, and to be honest, I'm not sure things will ever get better. Especially since I've done so many awful things in my life and made a ton of bad decisions. There are times when I wonder if I'll ever truly be happy again or even if I have the right to be."

"Of course you do. Everyone deserves to be happy, and if you would toss that huge chunk of pride of yours to the side when it comes to Charlotte, I think you'd feel a lot better. You need to truly forgive her, Curtis, because no matter what you say, I know you love her."

Curtis knew Tanya was right, but he wasn't sure giving Charlotte another chance was the right thing to do, not when there was the possibility of her sleeping around on him again. "I don't know."

"Well, I think you should, and just like you're going to keep James in your prayers, I'm going to pray for your and Charlotte's marriage."

Curtis glanced at the photo of him and Charlotte, sitting next to the one of his children, and picked it up. Despite all of the anger he'd felt toward her, he could no longer pretend he wasn't in love with Charlotte. And now after hearing Tanya's words, he realized it was time he stopped allowing his fury and pain to control him. It was time he stopped lying to himself and doing everything he could to mask his true feelings — time he stopped and reconsidered a few things because maybe divorce wasn't what he wanted after all. From here on out, what he would do was look at everything a lot more rationally and then make a final decision. Hopefully, this time it would be the right one.

CHAPTER 27

Talk about debating back and forth and trying to weigh one thing after another. That's what Charlotte had been doing ever since hanging up with Janine two hours ago, but now she'd decided to call Curtis's mystery woman to see who she was. While on the phone, Janine had insisted she shouldn't, but for some reason, Charlotte tended to agree with her mother. And why not? Why not confront the tramp who obviously saw nothing wrong with going after a married man?

Charlotte scrolled through her phone history, blocked her number, and dialed.

"Hello?" the woman said.

"Hi, this is Charlotte Black, Curtis's wife."

"Really, now. Well, what can I do for you on this fine day?" She was being sarcastic, and Charlotte wished she could yank this tramp through the phone.

"I'm not sure who you are, but I'd just

like to know why you feel the need to talk to my husband when you know he's married."

"I talk to a lot of people."

"Oh yeah, well, sweetheart, I'm not talking about a lot of people, I'm talking about my husband."

"Why are you calling me?"

"I just told you."

"I really don't have time for this."

"Well, you sure seem to have a lot of time when it comes to Curtis."

The woman ignored her comment and said, "What is it you want?"

"I wanna know why you've been talking to my husband for months now."

"Maybe you should ask *him* about that."

"Right now I'm asking you, and that's who I want answers from."

"You know, I really don't appreciate you calling me."

"And I don't appreciate you messing with my husband."

"I'm hanging up now."

"You'll never get him," Charlotte took a chance on saying.

"Humph. Yeah, okay."

"What's that supposed to mean?"

"You seem to have everything all figured out, so you tell me."

"Are you sleeping with him?"

"Now we're getting somewhere," the woman said.

Charlotte wished she could strangle her. "Are you?"

"You know, it's always interesting how some women have no problem sleeping around on their husbands but then they get upset when he goes looking elsewhere."

"Excuse me?"

The woman laughed. "You're pathetic."

"No, you are. As a matter of fact, it's pretty obvious that you're the one who's desperate, miserable, and willing to settle for a man you'll never be married to."

"Think what you want . . . Oh, and just for the record, do you really believe your husband could talk to me every single day and not be sleeping with me? I mean, come on now, let's be logical about this."

Charlotte's heart crumbled. She'd been thinking that same thing all along, but now that she was hearing the actual words from this whore's mouth, she was crushed. She would never let on how hurt she was, though. "No matter what you say, all I know is that Curtis doesn't want you. He won't be calling you or having anything else to do with you."

"We'll see about that."

"I guess we will, trick."

The woman hung up, but now Charlotte wondered if she was telling the truth or if she simply had been trying to torment her. Had she really slept with Curtis? Would Curtis look her straight in the face the way he had last night and still lie about it? He'd claimed all he'd done was talk to her and nothing else, but years ago when he'd messed around with Tabitha, he'd told more lies than Charlotte could count. So Charlotte didn't know what to think or who to believe and just wished none of this had happened. She wanted this nightmare to be over so she wouldn't have to deal with it.

Janine smiled and squeezed her hand, and Charlotte was glad she'd decided to attend Bible study. Actually, Janine came a lot more often than she did, and since Charlotte was the first lady, she knew that was pretty pitiful. But her lack of attendance was basically a result of the problems in her home life and of how troubled she was about it. She hadn't wanted to do much of anything because of how sad she'd been, but tonight she'd made the decision to come.

Curtis strutted across the front of the sanctuary with a microphone attached to the lapel of his blazer. He wore a round-neck knit shirt under it and jeans. Charlotte had always loved when he dressed a little casual. Funny how she still did after all these years. He looked good even in a T-shirt and also when he dressed in elegant suits, but it was the kind of outfit he wore now that took her breath away. Her feelings hadn't changed about that, regardless of how terrible their relationship was.

Curtis flipped through his Bible. "Tonight, I want us to take a look at the Book of James, chapter one, verses two through eight." Curtis waited a few seconds for everyone to turn to the appropriate page and then said, "The first chapter of James focuses on faith and endurance, and what I've come to realize more than ever before is that if you keep your faith strong, you can endure just about anything, if not everything." He looked at Charlotte and smiled and then said, "I'll be reading from the New Living Translation side of my Bible, and verses two through eight read as follows: 'Dear brothers and sisters, whenever trouble comes your way, let it be an opportunity for joy. For when your faith is tested, your endurance has a chance to grow. So let it grow, for when your endurance is fully developed, you will be strong in character and ready for anything. If you need wisdom — if you want to know what God wants you to do — ask him, and he will gladly tell you. He will not resent your asking. But when you ask Him, be sure that you really expect Him to answer, for a doubtful mind is as unsettled as a wave of the sea that is driven and tossed by the wind. People like that should not expect to receive anything from the Lord. They can't make up their minds. They waver back and forth in everything they do.' "

Charlotte watched Curtis walk to the other side and knew with everything in her that he was talking about himself. He was now trying to make up *his* mind about her, because he was no longer sure about a divorce. She just knew that's what he was thinking, and it was the reason he'd smiled at her before he'd begun reading, something he hadn't done while standing in the sanctuary for a long time now.

She was so excited and prayed things were finally going to turn around for them. She prayed he hadn't slept with that woman and that he truly wouldn't be talking to her again. But then Charlotte looked over to the next section of pews and saw a female parishioner staring at her. Charlotte had seen this particular woman a number of times at the church and knew she was a member, but for some reason she seemed familiar because of something else. Maybe it would come to her eventually.

"I love the entire passage," Curtis said. "But I especially love the part that says, 'Whenever trouble comes your way, let it be an opportunity for joy.' I love it because it says everything, but also because when I was a child, my mom used to say, 'From everything bad that happens, something good always comes out of it.' She would say that all the time, and as I look back over my life and all my many experiences, I realize she was right and not once have I seen her proven wrong."

A number of people nodded in agreement and offered *amens,* but the woman Charlotte had just looked at raised her hand. At first it seemed as though Curtis hadn't wanted to call on her, but then he said, "Yes, you have a question?"

The woman stood up, and Charlotte noticed they had the same hair color, and it was almost as long as hers, too. She also had on a beautiful spring leather jacket with three-quarter sleeves like the one Charlotte had worn to Bible study a month ago. The woman had good taste, and Charlotte wished she could remember where she knew her from. Other than there at the church, that was.

"Actually, I do, Pastor," the woman said. "The scripture talks about how when trouble comes our way, we should let it be an opportunity, so I was just wondering, does that apply to everything?"

"It absolutely does."

"So for example," she went on, and Charlotte was sure she'd heard her voice before, "if someone finds themself in a horrible marriage and it finally comes to an end, does that mean they'll likely find real joy with someone new?"

"Yes, that's certainly possible," Curtis answered, but then moved away from that section of pews and left the woman standing there.

It couldn't be, Charlotte thought. Could it? Was that the woman she'd spoken to on the phone today? Was this the woman Curtis had been consorting with? But just as Charlotte tried to gather her thoughts and figure things out, the woman glared at her, smirked, and took her seat, and Charlotte's question was answered. It was definitely her.

CHAPTER 28

Over the last three days, a lot had happened — a *whole* lot for that matter. Much had been said, and Charlotte and Curtis were on better terms than they had been in months. Wednesday night had proven to be a humdinger of an evening, what with Sharon Green audaciously standing amongst hundreds of members making sure Charlotte recognized her. It was a good thing that not as many members attended Bible study as they did on Sunday morning; otherwise there was no telling what Sharon might have done or said with a couple thousand people present. But the good news was that Curtis had sat Charlotte down as soon as they'd gotten home and explained everything in great detail. He'd told her the woman's name and that it had been Sharon who'd told him about her being at Chelsey's.

And now Charlotte realized why Sharon

had looked so familiar. She vaguely remembered seeing her there last Sunday afternoon but hadn't paid much attention to her. Curtis had then gone on to reiterate how he'd never slept with Sharon and how he also regretted ever talking to her by phone. He'd insisted his dealings with her were over and that Charlotte had nothing else to worry about when it came to her. He did, however, want to know more about Greg, and Charlotte told him the same thing she'd told him a few days ago, that she'd met him at the bar and had never seen him anywhere else and that she hadn't gone to bed with him. Thankfully, Curtis seemed to believe her — they believed each other, and that was a plus in itself.

The other great thing was that Curtis's heart had finally softened toward her. They'd even taken Curtina out to Chuck E. Cheese last night, and Matthew and Racquel had tagged along as well. They'd had a wonderful time, and Charlotte could barely stop smiling. It was as if God had seen fit to work a miracle in their marital life very quickly, and she was monumentally grateful.

Charlotte folded the last of Curtis's underwear and socks and slipped them inside one of the large mesh pockets in his garment bag. He hung his suit on the hook, zipped the flap, folded it, and zipped the bag up completely.

Then he slid on his silver watch and checked the time. "I'm sure the limo is already downstairs, so I guess I should get going."

"I wish I was going with you."

"So do I, but I'll be back before you know it."

"You're getting in at ten, right?"

"Yep."

Curtis set his bag on the floor and pulled up the handle. Charlotte stood to the side of him, ready to cry.

"What's wrong?"

"Nothing."

"Then why do you look so sad?"

"I guess I just hate to see you go. Especially when we just started trying to work things out three days ago . . . I mean, what if you change your mind while you're gone?"

Curtis took her in his arms. "Look, sweetheart. I meant everything I said, and this trip won't change that."

"I hope not."

"It won't. We agreed to give our marriage another try, and that's exactly what we're going to do."

"I really do love you, Curtis."

"And I love you."

They gazed into each other's eyes, and Curtis lifted her chin and kissed her. Charlotte held back tears for as long as she could but they fell, anyway. Curtis wiped them with his hand.

"Do you think this is the last time we'll have to do this?" she asked, sniffling.

"What?"

"Start over."

"I hope so, because God knows we've done that enough for one lifetime."

Charlotte nodded in agreement. "We have, but I promise you, I won't ever hurt you again. I really mean that."

"I'm glad to hear it."

They kissed again, and Curtis grabbed his bag and headed downstairs. Charlotte followed behind him and stood next to Matthew. Curtina waited at the front door wearing an unhappy face. "I don't like it when you have to go out of town, Daddy. And why can't I go with you?"

Curtis kneeled on the floor. "We already went over that, remember? Daddy has a conference to speak at for Christian women, and it's not for little girls. I'll be back in the morning, though, and we'll do something fun tomorrow afternoon, okay?"

"Okay."

Charlotte shook her head because some things never changed. Every time Curtis had to travel, Curtina made the same comment and asked the same question. But today, Charlotte felt the same as she did and wished Curtis didn't have to go.

"Now give me a big hug," he said. "Daddy loves you."

"See you later, Dad, and I love you, too," Matthew said, embracing his father when he stood up.

Charlotte smiled because on any normal day, Matt and his dad always fist-bumped before one of them left the house; she guessed because it was the cool thing to do. But no matter how old Matthew got, when his father went out of town, he always hugged him.

"I love you back, son. Okay, I guess this is it," he said, sliding on his sunglasses and kissing Charlotte one last time. "I love you."

"I love you more."

He opened the door, and Carlisle, the driver they always requested through the local car company, was already standing at the side of the sleek, black stretch limo. But now he walked up the steps to grab Curtis's bag.

"Good morning, Mr. Black. Beautiful day, isn't it?"

"Good morning, and yes, it's perfect flying weather."

"Good morning to you as well, Mrs. Black, and hey, kids."

Charlotte walked closer to the threshold of the doorway. "Good morning, Carlisle. Good to see you again."

When Carlisle closed the trunk and then Curtis's door, he went around to the driver's side, got in, and curved the limo around the water fountain. Curtina waved one last time, and Charlotte shut the door. Matthew went into the family room, and Curtina followed behind him. Charlotte went back upstairs, but as soon as she walked inside the bedroom, she noticed the stack of photos they'd taken on Curtina's birthday and flipped through them. She scanned through a number of them but stopped when she saw one that Matthew must have taken of just her and Curtis. They weren't posing in any particular way and certainly hadn't realized they were being photographed, but they stood side by side, laughing and applauding as they watched Curtina blowing out her birthday candles. Oh how very much Charlotte loved this man, her children, and the life they'd been blessed with, and suddenly she had an excellent idea. She hadn't thought about it before now, but why shouldn't she go to Detroit and spend the night there with Curtis? It was a little late for her to pack, book the same flight Curtis was on, and make it over to the airport in time, but she could certainly take a later one and surprise him. Yes, that's exactly what she would do.

So, she went into her office, signed on to one of the online reservation sites, and called Lana's cell number. She knew she was already at the conference, but she hoped maybe the first seminar hadn't started yet. Sure enough, Lana answered her phone.

"Good morning, Charlotte, everything okay?"

"Everything's fine. How are you and how's the conference going?"

"I'm wonderful, and, honey, when I tell you the speakers yesterday were dynamic and so profound that's exactly what I mean. Every one of them, and can you believe I finally got to hear and meet Dr. Betty Price? You know, she's the first lady of Crenshaw Christian Center out in Los Angeles."

"Of course I know her. Isn't she fabulous?" Actually, Charlotte would never forget Dr. Betty or her book, *Warning to Ministers, Their Wives, and Mistresses*, as it had been such a huge help to her and so many others she knew.

"Oh my goodness, talk about a true woman of God. It was a blessing just to be in her presence, and she made me feel so special. She made every woman here feel important, and I was tickled pink when I got a chance to say hi to her. I so wish you'd been here."

"Well, actually, that's why I'm calling you. I know I've missed most of the convention, but I still want to surprise Curtis this evening if I can. So, what time do you think he'll be finished with everything?"

"Well, he'll be speaking at four, probably for about an hour, and then he'll be signing books for maybe three or four more hours. So, I'm guessing he'll be back at the hotel around nine-thirty or ten."

"That's pretty late, but I still think it's worth coming."

"Of course it is! You and Pastor need some alone time away from home, and it does my heart such great joy just hearing you're going to surprise him."

"Thank you, Lana. You're always so supportive of our marriage, and I'll never be able to thank you enough for that."

"You know Pastor is like my son, and I love you like a daughter."

"We love you back."

"Okay, well you'd better get off the phone and make those reservations, and if you need anything, just call me."

"I will. See you soon."

CHAPTER 29

The COBO arena was filled to capacity, and it seemed all twenty thousand women were having the time of their lives. Curtis had arrived at the convention center right on schedule, and now the founder of the conference had finished reading his bio and was finalizing her introduction of him.

"So without further ado, I give you the man of the hour, this powerful man of God, the one, the only, Pastor Curtis Black!"

Curtis strutted onto the brightly lit stage, waving and then hugging the founder of the conference, a fiftysomething woman with lovely white hair, and went to the podium. The crowd of women gave him a standing ovation and joyfully applauded. This, of course, wasn't the first time Curtis had spoken before thousands of people, but every time he did, it felt like a new beginning. No matter how many times he spoke, he experienced a certain euphoria, and adrenaline rushed through his body. He'd certainly come a long way since childhood, growing up in a poverty-stricken neighborhood on the south side of Chicago and living with an alcoholic father who had cared nothing about his wife and children. But thank God for all His grace and mercy and for having a different plan for Curtis.

Thank God for all the ups and downs, all the good and bad, and all the struggles and triumphs, because after all that had happened, he was still alive and well, and doing God's work. He was delivering the Word every chance he got and trying his best to lead people down the proper path. It was true that he was still a work in progress himself, the same as every other human being, but he was proud of the fact that he'd made major improvements. He wasn't perfect, but he was a good man who now strived to do the right thing as much as he could, and he was never content when he didn't — he was never pleased when he did anything immoral. He was thrilled about his new philosophy, because it meant he finally had a conscience and didn't want to disappoint God.

Curtis waved to the crowd again with a huge smile. "Thank you so much. God bless you. Thank you so much."

The women applauded more and acted as though they were waiting to hear from a rock star instead of a pastor, and he appreciated such a warm welcome and all their love.

When the crowd finally settled down and took their seats, Curtis said, "Wow, you ladies really know how to boost a man's ego." Laughter could be heard throughout the entire building, and Curtis laughed with them. "As most of you know, my latest book is entitled *God's Favor and How to Accept It*," he said.

But before he could finish the rest of his sentence, there was more clapping, and Curtis laughed again. "Okay, now, I hope all this excitement means that at least a few of you have already read it." The women roared, and many of them held up their copies. "I really appreciate that. You're all so very kind. And since my book is about favor, I figured that's what I would talk to you about tonight — favor and how to accept it. If you haven't heard the song 'Favor Ain't Fair' by the very talented gospel artist Kim Stratton, then you're missing a treat. It's one of my all-time favorites, and part of the lyrics go something like, 'God doesn't choose those who are qualified, He qualifies those who He calls.' And you see, what that means is that you don't have to be on top; you don't have to be the best-looking; you don't have to be the most talented; you don't have to have a PhD, or any degree for that matter, yet if God calls you to do great things for Him, He'll give you all the skill and qualifications needed to get the job done. It was the same way when Jesus Christ chose His twelve disciples. These were common men who were uneducated, you know, plain, ordinary folks, but these very men were responsible for spreading the gospel throughout the Roman Empire, and they also wrote several books in the New Testament."

The arena was quiet. Women nodded or shook their heads in agreement, completely mesmerized, and Curtis went on with the rest of his message. He felt like God had lit a fire under him, because his heart overflowed with happiness. He knew a lot of it was because he loved, loved, loved delivering God's Word, but he also knew much of it had to do with Charlotte and their recent reconciliation. Life was good, and Curtis looked forward to getting back to his family tomorrow.

As soon as Curtis finished speaking and thanking everyone, four escorts and his publicist, Lisa, led him off the stage and down a long corridor toward his signing table. As they passed a line of people that wrapped as far as his eye could see, he smiled and spoke to as many as he could and even shook a few hands.

"We love you, Pastor Black," one woman said.

"You completely changed my life with your last book, Reverend Black," another said.

"Girl, did you see how gorgeous that man is?" yet another woman said.

"Your message was magnificent, son, so please keep doing what you do," a woman who looked to be in her seventies or eighties commented, and Curtis stopped and hugged her.

When he arrived at the table, he immediately shook hands with one woman after another and signed their books. Some shared major testimonies and thanked him for writing on specific topics, and one woman thanked him for taking time out of his schedule to come share with them tonight.

Curtis signed three copies for the next woman in line, and Lana walked up and placed her arm around him. "Guess who's here, Pastor?"

"Who? I wondered where you ran off to."

"I went down to the entrance to meet your surprise."

Curtis turned around. "What surprise?" But then he saw Charlotte and smiled. She winked at him and smiled back.

He signed another fifty or so books, all the while chatting and having his picture taken, but then a group of five women surrounded the table. "We're a small book club, Pastor Black, and it's so great to finally meet you," one of them said.

"It's great meeting all of you as well. So, where are you ladies from?"

"Dallas."

"Wonderful. My wife and I love Dallas."

One of the women looked behind him. "That's her right there, isn't it?"

"It sure is."

"Do you think she'd mind signing her name in our books, too?"

"Of course not," he said, turning around and beckoning for Charlotte. "Baby, these nice ladies would like for you to sign their books."

Charlotte took a few steps forward. "Wow, what an honor, and thank you for supporting my husband."

"We love him, Sister Black, and we love you, too."

"That's very sweet of you. Thank you."

Curtis signed each of their books and passed them on to Charlotte.

One of the women snapped a picture with her digital camera. "Thank you both so much."

Curtis smiled when the next woman approached the table because it was the same older woman he'd hugged when he'd been on his way to begin the signing.

"Baby, this nice lady said some very kind words to me," he said.

Charlotte smiled and shook the woman's hand. "It's very nice to meet you."

"Likewise, and while I don't know either of you personally, I just wanted to let you know that I've been praying for the two of you for years. I prayed for your marriage because I was married to a pastor myself, God rest his soul, for fifty years, and it wasn't always easy. We had a very large congregation, so we went through many of the same things as the two of you have — had a lot of the same problems I've heard you talk about in your books, Pastor Black. My husband and I were young when we first started out and still had a lot to learn, but we hung in there because no matter how many times we hurt each other, there was one thing that never changed, and that was the love we shared. So, I'm telling the two

of you to please hang in there. Stick together, let the past stay in the past, and go
on and live a happy life."

Curtis was touched and knew for sure
he'd met this woman for a reason. Her
words had come at the right time, and it
made him think. As it was, on Monday God
had allowed him to see that his relationship
with Sharon was wrong and he'd ended it
(even though she still wouldn't stop calling
him), on Tuesday Tanya had encouraged
him and insisted he needed to stay married
to Charlotte, and now here was the woman
standing right in front of him.

Curtis covered the woman's hand with
both of his. "Your words mean a lot, and
thank you for sharing your story. And please
excuse me for not asking before now, but
what is your name?"

"Iris Jackson."

"Well, it's very nice to meet you, Mrs.
Jackson."

Charlotte grabbed the woman's other
hand. "Yes, very much so."

Curtis looked over at Lisa. "Can you write
down Mrs. Jackson's phone number for me
and make sure she has Lana's direct number?" Then he looked back at Mrs. Jackson.
"If you ever need anything at all, please call
us."

"Just be happy," she said. "That's all I want."

Charlotte beamed and Curtis thanked God for opening his eyes before it had been too late. They'd been given another chance, and he was grateful.

CHAPTER 30

Charlotte nestled farther under Curtis's arm. They were inside the limo, heading down the highway and only minutes from the hotel. "After all these years, it's so great to still see so many people supporting you and the ministry."

Curtis stretched his legs out. "I know. I was thinking the same thing earlier and how it truly is a wonderful blessing. And then to meet that wonderful lady, Mrs. Jackson."

"She was such a sweetheart, and then to hear how she'd been praying for us all along, even though she'd never met us."

"It just goes to show that there truly are some very special people in this world. Men and women who genuinely care about others."

Charlotte leaned her head back, and while it was pretty dark inside the limousine, Curtis looked at her and kissed her. Their passion was intense, and it was a good thing the tinted partition that separated the driver from his passengers was closed, otherwise Charlotte wouldn't be able to look at the man when he dropped them off.

"I've really missed you," Curtis said. "I know it probably hasn't seemed like that, but I have."

"I've missed you, too, and thank you for changing your mind. I promise you won't regret it."

"No thanks needed. What I want us to do now is take Mrs. Jackson's advice."

"Which is?"

"Leaving the past in the past. I know we can't erase it, but we don't have to focus on it. What we have to do now is concentrate on the present."

"I agree, and I'm glad you feel that way."

Curtis and Charlotte held each other for the rest of the ride, and soon the limo pulled in front of the hotel.

One of the greeters opened their door. "Welcome back, sir."

"Thank you," Curtis said, stepping onto the pavement, taking Charlotte's hand and helping her out of the car, too.

The driver still walked around to where they were standing. "It's been a pleasure driving you today, Pastor Black, and I'll be here at eight a.m. for the airport."

Curtis pulled out his wallet and passed him a fifty. "Thanks again for everything, Chris. We'll see you then."

They went inside the ritzy hotel, adorned with exquisite marble flooring, and Curtis said, "Is your bag with the bellman?"

"Yes."

"Then we'll call for it later."

Charlotte smiled. "And why is that?"

"Because we've got business to take care of and can't be disturbed."

"Sounds good to me."

They strolled through the lobby and down to the elevators, and Curtis pushed the top button. The doors opened immediately, and when they stepped inside, Curtis inserted his key just above the floor selections, since this was the only way to access the VIP/ concierge floor. When they arrived at their destination, the doors slid open again and they proceeded to the end of the carpeted hallway. But before Curtis opened the double doors to his room, he took Charlotte into his arms, kissing her forcefully, and she could barely stand it. He was driving her wild, and now she believed he really had missed her as much as he'd said. Their being together felt like old times, and she was relieved that all her waiting — and yes, praying — had been worth it. She'd thought for sure that this time she'd lost Curtis for good, but here they were together, happy as could be.

Curtis slid the plastic card inside the slot and opened the door, and Charlotte couldn't believe her eyes. Candles lit the entire living room area, and one of Luther Vandross's beautiful love songs played softly from what must have been the bedroom.

Charlotte lovingly touched the side of his face. "You still never cease to amaze me. You still know how to romance me no matter what."

"I wish I could take credit, but I can't."

"Well, then who set out all the candles?"

Curtis paused for a minute and then smiled. "I'll bet it was Lana. She's the only one who knew you were coming, and I'll bet she asked someone to do this for us."

"Gosh, how thoughtful of her."

Charlotte dropped her handbag on the luxurious sofa, and Curtis led her into the bedroom, but as soon as they entered it, Charlotte almost fainted.

Curtis stopped in his tracks. "What in the world?"

"Well, I certainly didn't expect you to bring the little wifey with you," Sharon said, leaning against a stack of large pillows with her legs crossed, dressed only in a lacy negligee.

Curtis took a step closer to the bed. "Sharon, what are you doing here?"

She chuckled. "Oh, so now you wanna act like you're surprised to see me, huh? But you know you invited me."

"I did not."

"Of course you did. You invited me a month ago when you told me your wife wouldn't be coming on this trip. Plus, when I called you at the church yesterday, you said you couldn't wait to see me."

Charlotte was too stunned to speak or move.

Curtis was outraged. "Why are you lying like this, and how did you get in here?"

"Well, since you forgot to leave me a key at the front desk, I found a nice woman from housekeeping who had no problem letting me in — at least not after I told her I was your wife. She even helped me light all the candles so you'd be surprised."

"I want you out of here," Curtis said, but Sharon folded her arms and relaxed farther into the pillows. "I'm warning you, Sharon. Either get out or be put out."

Charlotte finally found the will to say something. "Curtis, why is this woman here? Did you really invite her the way she says?"

"Baby, no. I would never have done that,

and I haven't even spoken to her since Tuesday morning. And the only reason I called her then was to tell her our friendship was over."

"Liar, liar, liar," Sharon said. "Say what you want, baby, but you and I both know what the truth is."

Curtis went over to the nightstand and picked up the phone. "Either you get your things and get out or I'm calling the police."

"I don't think so. Not unless you want everyone at Deliverance Outreach to know you've been sleeping around on your wife."

Curtis lowered the phone back down. "What are you talking about? I never touched you."

Charlotte shook her head. "Oh my God."

Sharon gawked at her. "Yeah, that's right, sweetie. Your husband has been sleeping with me on and off for months, and since everything is now all out in the open, where do you think he was last year, that day your son was held hostage at his school? Why do you think he was ignoring all his phone calls? He did it because he was in bed with me."

Charlotte squinted at her husband. "Curtis, is this true? Were you with her that day?"

"Baby, look, I can explain."

Sharon laughed. "And while he's explaining, you might want to ask him where he was last Sunday. Ask him who he came running to right after you came home sloppy drunk. Ask him who he was with for hours."

"You know I've never slept with you, Sharon. So why are you doing this?"

"I'm doing it because it's time you stopped playing games and told her the truth."

"What truth?"

"That you and I are going to be married as soon as you divorce her."

Curtis picked up the phone again and this time he dialed zero. "Yes . . . we have an uninvited guest, so can you send security up here as soon as possible?"

Sharon scooted out of the bed and grabbed her pants and jacket. "Fine, I'll leave, but, Curtis, you know this had to be done. Actually, you should have told her a long time ago, so, sweetie," she said, glaring at Charlotte, "I'm glad you came. I'm glad Curtis and I now have all our cards on the table, and there's no reason for us to hide our relationship any longer."

Curtis tossed her overnight bag into the living room area. "You're sick."

"I know you're upset, baby," she said, pulling on her jeans, "and that you didn't want your wife to find out like this, but what's done is done, and now we can finally be together without hiding out at my place."

There was a knock at the door, and Sharon hurried to slip her shoes on, tossed her purse onto her shoulder, and went into the other room. Curtis followed behind her and opened the door.

"Is there a problem, Pastor Black?" Charlotte heard a man asking.

"Yes, we'd like this woman to leave."

"Ma'am, I'm sorry, but you're going to have to come with us."

"Gladly," she told the man, but then said to Curtis, "Call me later, baby, okay?"

Charlotte walked into the living room and saw that she was finally gone, and Curtis rushed over to her. "Baby, you have to believe me. I never invited that woman here. I don't know how she got in, and I've never once slept with her. As God is my witness, I —"

Charlotte held up her hands. "Just stop it, Curtis. Stop trying to cover up this game you've been playing, because I really don't want to hear it. You're such a liar and to think I actually started to believe you a few days ago when you swore you hadn't slept with her."

"I'm not lying."

"So you've never been to her house, then?"

Curtis covered his face and Charlotte's question was answered. "Baby, look. I only went there twice. That day Matthew's teacher held them hostage and then again on Sunday. But I didn't sleep with her."

"If that's true, why did you tell me the only thing you'd done with her was talk on the phone? Why didn't you tell me you'd been to her house?"

"Because I was afraid if you found out, you'd think I'd slept with her, just like you do now."

Charlotte picked up her handbag. "Wow, I can't believe I've been such a fool. I mean, here I've been begging you like a child to forgive me, and then I was dumb enough to believe all you'd done was talk to that woman. That was bad enough, but now to find out you've been sleeping with her and that you were with her the day our child could have been shot. . . . Oh my God."

Curtis stepped closer to her. "Baby, you have to listen to me. Sharon is lying."

"No, I'm outta here."

"Baby, please," he said, but Charlotte pushed the door open and stormed to the elevator. If she hadn't been so sure this was reality, she would have sworn she was dreaming. Or having the nightmare of her life.

CHAPTER 31

Thankfully, it was late in the evening, so not a lot of guests were in the lobby, which meant very few people saw how distraught Charlotte was. She was an emotional mess, and it was all she could do to get on the elevator and make her way down to the front desk without passing out. This thing with Curtis and Sharon had slashed her heart in two, and for a few moments, she'd felt as though she couldn't breathe. Curtis claimed he hadn't slept with this woman, but why would she lie? And what person in her right mind would fly all the way from Chicago to Detroit, finagle her way into his suite, and then pretend she'd been invited if she hadn't? It didn't make any sense, and just the fact that Curtis had so conveniently not told her about his visits to Sharon made her suspect he was lying even more. The other thing that unnerved Charlotte was the way Sharon looked — just like her in so many ways — so there was no doubt Curtis was attracted to her. This whole situation was very bizarre and so unnecessary, and Charlotte was tired of thinking about it.

"Here's your credit card and ID back. How many keys will you be needing?" the woman at the front desk asked. Charlotte had come straight down there so she could book another room for the night.

"Just one."

The woman programmed the key, slipped it into a tiny paper jacket, and passed it to her. "Is there anything else I can help you with? Do you have luggage?"

Charlotte pulled out the stub a bellman had given her earlier in the day when she'd first arrived and had checked her bag with him. She passed it across the counter.

"I'll have it brought right out."

Charlotte stood there waiting, and when she looked toward the entrance, she saw Sharon walking outside with her garment bag. Charlotte's blood boiled, and if she hadn't been the wife of a well-known pastor or thought fighting was totally beneath her, she would have beat Sharon down to the ground and waited to be arrested. Although, the more she thought about it, what good would that have done? It certainly wouldn't change anything, and it certainly wouldn't stop Curtis from continuing to sleep with her if he wanted to.

Charlotte turned back toward the desk but then turned around again when she heard a male voice saying, "Ma'am, is everything okay now? I'm with hotel security."

"Yes, I'm fine."

"Good, but please don't hesitate to contact us if you need to."

"Thank you."

Charlotte stood for only a few more seconds, and the bellman brought out her roller bag.

"Can I take this up to your room?"

Charlotte opened her purse. Normally, she always wanted help with her luggage, but right now she just wanted to be alone and didn't feel like having any small talk on the elevator with a young man she didn't know. Plus, she wasn't the best company for anyone at the moment. "No, I think I can handle it, but thank you," she said, passing him a ten-dollar bill.

The man smiled. "Thanks so much."

Charlotte started toward the elevator but stopped when she heard someone calling out to her. It was Lana, walking alongside her niece, Tracey.

"I thought you and Pastor were locked away in that big ole suite we booked him upstairs. So what are you doing down here?"

"It's a long story, Lana. You have no idea."

"Why? What happened?"

"Auntie," Tracey said, "I'm going to head up to my room so I can call home, but I'll see you in the morning, okay?"

"Sleep well."

"Take care, Charlotte," Tracey said.

"You, too."

When Tracey left, Charlotte and Lana walked farther away from the desk and down toward the elevators. It was a lot more private there.

Charlotte leaned against the wall. "Do you know Sharon Green?"

"Not personally, but I know she's a member of the church. As a matter of fact, we just saw her getting into a taxi, but when I spoke to her, she turned her head and didn't say anything. She seemed really upset about something."

"I'm sure she was."

"Why? Did you talk to her?"

"No, but she had a lot to say to Curtis as soon as we walked into the suite and found her in his bed."

"What? I know you're joking. You have to be."

"I wish I were."

"Wait a minute. She was actually in Curtis's bed?"

"Yeah."

"How? I mean, I knew she was probably going to book a room at this hotel because just two days ago, she called the church, saying she'd seen online that Pastor was speaking at a conference in Detroit, and she wanted to know if any women from the church were going. Then, when I told her my niece and I were, she said there were a lot of recommended hotels listed on the conference website, so she just wondered where the Deliverance members were staying. And that's when I told her I wasn't sure but that Pastor and my niece and I were staying here."

"Well, I don't know if she booked her own room or not, but she was lying in Curtis's bed wearing a negligee and swears he invited her."

"I don't believe that. And now that I think about it, it was sort of strange, anyway, that she called the church about a national conference at the last minute."

Charlotte's phone rang, but when she pulled it out and saw it was Curtis, she pressed Ignore and dropped it back inside her purse.

"Was that him?"

"Yep."

"Honey, you should go talk to him."

"For what? I've seen and heard all I need to for one night. Plus, if he really wanted to talk to me, he would have followed me down here."

"I know you feel that way, and I'm sure he wants to, but with how upset you are, if Curtis had come running behind you, there would have certainly been a scene. And you know people are just dying to publicize your business."

"Well, he should have thought about that before he slept with that whore."

"What do you mean?"

"I told you . . . it's a long story."

Lana sighed and shook her head. "Lord, what a mess."

Charlotte grasped the handle of her luggage. "I appreciate your concern, but there's not a lot you can do. This is all on Curtis."

"Why don't I walk up to your room with you so we can talk a while longer?"

At first Charlotte hesitated, but then she agreed because deep down, she did want to tell Lana everything. So they went up the elevator.

When they walked into the room, Charlotte turned on the lights, and Lana sat in one of the chairs. Charlotte sat down on the side of the bed, facing her. "Gosh, where do

I begin? I guess the first thing you need to know is that Curtis has been talking to this woman every single day for at least a full year, and then I find out tonight he's been going to her house."

"Did he admit that?"

"He didn't have a choice but to, because I finally pulled his cell phone records. Then, tonight, when Sharon said he'd been to her house, he admitted that he had but still claimed he hadn't slept with her."

"Why was he over there?"

"The same reason any man goes to visit a single woman."

"I know it may be hard to believe, but what if he's telling the truth? I know he was wrong for talking to her and for going anywhere near her house, but you never know about some of these women."

"But if he wasn't sleeping with her, why didn't he tell me last week that he'd gone over there? All he kept saying was that he'd never done anything more than talk to her on the phone."

"Maybe he was afraid you might think exactly what you're thinking now. I agree that he should have told you everything, but I'm sure he thought if he told you he'd been to her house, then you'd be even more suspicious."

Curtis had given that same explanation, but Charlotte still wasn't buying it. "I'm not sure what to think anymore, but I know I'm tired."

"The two of you have been to hell and back more than once, but I think you need to do a little more investigating on this one because your husband isn't the average man. He's exceptionally handsome, he's known by hundreds of thousands of people, and he's a prominent pastor. Your husband has money and power, and there are women out there who will sell their souls to the devil just to have one night with him. Some of them are willing to do worse than that, especially if they think they can replace you. I've seen and heard it all for years, and you'd be amazed at how devious, two-faced, and sneaky some of these women are. As it is, we've had to stop a few of them from sitting in the front row because of all the skintight dresses and skirts they wear. Some barely cover their little narrow-tail behinds, yet they're the first ones to go plopping down on the front pews so Pastor can see them."

"I hear you, and I know all that's true, but imagine how you would feel if you'd finally gotten things right with your husband, enjoyed your time at a conference with thousands of women, and then come back to the hotel and walked in on a woman who was half-naked?"

"I wouldn't like it at all, but don't you think if Pastor had invited her, he wouldn't have been so happy to see you? Do you think he would have taken you up to his suite?"

"I don't know."

"Well, I do. So something isn't adding up."

Charlotte didn't say anything.

"Honey, I know you're upset and now you're wondering who to believe, but why don't you call Pastor? Why don't you call him down here so you can talk to him?"

"I don't think so."

"Well, if you won't do it for yourself, then do it for me, okay?"

Charlotte could tell Lana wasn't going to take no for an answer, so she agreed. "Okay, I'll call him."

The two of them hugged.

"You guys are going to be fine, you hear me? I'll check on you in the morning."

"Thanks for listening."

"Of course.

"Good night, Lana," Charlotte said, shutting the door and eyeing the minibar. She'd gone almost a solid week without drinking, but now she needed something to calm her nerves. She knew vodka, gin, or brandy would do the trick, it didn't matter which one, so she pulled out the first tiny bottle she laid her hands on and opened it.

CHAPTER 32

Curtis plopped down onto his bed, wondering how this thing with Sharon could have happened. It was barely after six a.m., he hadn't slept a wink, and he was worried to death about Charlotte. He'd been calling her cell all night, and then when he'd called downstairs to see if she'd checked into a different room, he'd had them ring her hotel room several times. But she refused to answer. He knew this whole incident with Sharon didn't look good and that Charlotte had ample reason not to believe his side of the story, but what bothered him was that even though he was telling the truth, he honestly couldn't prove it. For the first time since he'd been married to Charlotte, he found himself in a his-word-against-her-word situation, and he had no idea how he was going to confirm his innocence. Sharon had insisted they'd slept together, he'd told Charlotte they hadn't, and now Charlotte wouldn't even talk to him. So there was no doubt who she believed. He also knew he couldn't blame anyone for this but himself, because he'd had no business driving out to Sharon's house in the first place. He'd known it was wrong both times he'd gone there, but he'd still carelessly allowed his pride and pain to override sound judgment and this was the result.

He dialed Charlotte's cell phone again, but the call went straight to voice mail. It had begun doing that around three this morning, which meant either her battery had died and she hadn't charged it, or she'd turned her phone off altogether. He wasn't sure what else to do at this point, so he dialed Lana. He'd tried his best not to involve her, but he was desperate and needed her help.

"Hey, Pastor," she said right away. "How are you this morning?"

"Not good."

"I hear you and Charlotte ran into a few problems last night."

"You talked to her?"

"I did. She was in the lobby when Tracey and I came in from a late dinner, and then I went up to her room with her. She said she was going to call you as soon as I left, though."

"Well, she never did. Not to mention, I've been calling her all night and she won't answer."

"I had no idea. I was so sure she was going to call you and that everything would be all right."

"I really messed up this time, Lana."

"You know I rarely get upset with you, but I have to say, I'm not happy about this whole Sharon madness. You never should have been talking to that woman, Pastor, and you certainly shouldn't have been spending time with her. I know you were upset about Charlotte's affairs and that you'd been planning to divorce her, but you're still a married man."

"I know, I know, I know, and if I could change what I did, I would. But I promise you, Lana, I absolutely did not sleep with that woman. Not once."

"I believe you, but you also have to realize how bad this looks to Charlotte. You know the old saying, 'If it walks like a duck and quacks like a duck . . .' "

"But I didn't sleep with her."

"Doesn't matter — you still look guilty."

Curtis paced back and forth. "Satan is busy."

"True. But we all have choices, and this time you made the wrong one. This time, it's your fault, and Satan has nothing to do with it."

"You're right."

"So what you need to do is fix this."

"I'm trying, but she won't talk to me."

"Let me try to call her, and if she still won't answer, I'll go to her room."

"Thank you, Lana . . . for everything."

There was loud pounding on someone's door, and Charlotte wished the guest in the room next to her would answer it.

"Charlotte, are you in there?"

Charlotte forced her eyes open and tried lifting her head off the pillow, but since it was too heavy, she dropped it back down.

"Charlotte, open up. I wanna make sure you're okay."

Was that Lana?

There was more knocking, so Charlotte got up and dragged herself over to the door.

"Lord have mercy," Lana said, but Charlotte went straight back to bed. "Honey, why are you doing this to yourself?"

"What?"

"Drinking like this."

It sounded as if Lana had picked up one of the little bottles Charlotte had guzzled down last night, but she wasn't sure. She also didn't care.

"You can't keep this up."

"What?"

"This whole getting drunk business. If you keep it up, the next thing you know, you'll be addicted to this stuff. I was once married to an alcoholic, and, honey, it's just not worth it."

"I'm fine."

"No, you're not, and what happened last night? I thought you were going to call your husband?"

"For what?"

"To talk. You need to sit down and let him explain things."

"I'm really not in the mood."

"But, honey, locking yourself away in a hotel room drinking isn't the answer."

Charlotte was tired of hearing all this hoopla and wished Lana would leave.

"So, why don't you get in the shower and get dressed, and I'll tell Curtis to come see you."

"No."

"Charlotte, please don't throw your marriage away because of some lying tramp. You've spent months trying to save it, and now you finally have another chance to work things out."

"All I want is to be left alone."

"Well, I can't do that. I care too much

about you and Pastor to leave things the way they are."

Charlotte was done tolerating this and sat up. "Lana, I know you mean well, but I'm going to have to ask you to leave now."

"But —"

"Please go. Please leave my room, and tell Curtis I said to stop calling my cell phone and my room number."

"If that's what you want."

"I do."

As soon as the door closed, Charlotte went over to the minibar and pulled out a miniature bottle of vodka and then walked over and dialed the front desk.

"Good morning, Mrs. Black, how may I assist you?"

"Good morning. I'm calling because I've decided to stay an extra day, so is it possible for you to extend my reservation?"

"I'm sure it'll be fine, but let me double-check the system to make sure there's availability."

Charlotte waited and wondered what Curtina and Matthew were doing. She missed both of them terribly and was sorry she wouldn't be going home today. But she just couldn't face Curtis right now and wanted nothing to do with him. Not when he'd broken her heart all over again. Plus, chances were Matthew was going to spend the day with Racquel, and Curtina was always thrilled about staying with Aunt Emma, so she knew they would be fine.

"Okay, yes," the desk clerk said. "I've made the change, and you're all set."

"I really appreciate it. Oh, and one more thing — can you have someone come restock my minibar?"

"Of course. Our staff members who handle that won't be in until around nine, though, but if there's a certain snack you're interested in, I can ask someone from room service to bring you up something."

Charlotte was so embarrassed. "Uh . . . no . . . there's no rush at all."

"You sure?"

"Yes, definitely. Thanks again."

Charlotte hated feeling like this and hated humiliating herself this way. Here it was not even seven a.m., and she was already trying to replenish her liquor supply. Then, adding insult to injury, the front desk woman had automatically assumed she needed more chips, cookies, or candy and hadn't even considered the little liquor bottles because of how early in the morning it was. Charlotte was sure that alcohol had been the last thing on the woman's mind. And the thing was, Charlotte wanted it to be the last thing on hers as well; however, lately she couldn't seem to help herself. She wasn't an alcoholic, but it was just that liquor really seemed to relax her. It eased her pain, lessened the impact of bad news, and stopped her heart from aching so terribly. So to her, drinking sort of served as her rescuer and made her feel much better almost instantly. She didn't necessarily like the hangover effects that overwhelmed her the next morning, but slowly but surely, she was getting used to that part of it. Not to mention, she didn't drink every day nor did she feel she *needed* to drink. She wasn't even sure she liked it, but again, it helped her, and that's why she wanted it sometimes.

It was the reason she opened the tiny bottle of vodka she'd pulled out of the minibar a few minutes ago and turned it up.

CHAPTER 33

"She's been at it again," Lana said.

Curtis repositioned the earpiece to his phone and placed the last item in his garment bag. "I'm not surprised."

"She wasn't happy to see me, and after I tried talking to her, she asked me to leave."

"You didn't deserve that, and I'm sorry I involved you in this."

"It's no problem at all. I want to help you guys in any way I can, but I've never seen Charlotte like this. She's so bitter and withdrawn. Says she just wants to be left alone."

"I know she's hurting, but this drinking thing is more than I can handle. My father used to drink, so I'm not very tolerant of people who abuse alcohol. I love Charlotte, and I'd made up my mind to stay with her, but I won't be able to deal with her under these kinds of conditions."

"Does her family have a history of alcoholism?"

"Not that I know of. She got drunk last year over at a jazz club in her old neighborhood, but as far as I know, she hadn't gotten drunk again until just recently."

"It's hard to believe that if she's an alcoholic she'd be able to turn it off like that for such a long period of time."

"Yeah, but many alcoholics start out drinking socially and then over a period of time, it gets worse and they can't stop."

"So what are you going to do?"

"Try to talk to her again, I guess."

"Are you still leaving on your ten o'clock flight?"

"That's the plan, but I also don't want to leave Charlotte behind."

"Maybe you should go down to her room to see if she'll let you in."

"I think I will. What room is it? For privacy reasons, the front desk wouldn't tell me."

"Five-eighteen."

"Thanks, Lana."

"You're welcome. Oh, and even though Tracey and I are going to run over to the mall around eleven, we won't be heading to the airport until around three-thirty. So please keep me posted."

"I will."

Curtis slipped on his shoes and left for

Charlotte's room. On the way to the elevator, he approached a group of five women.

"We really enjoyed you last night, Pastor Black," one of them commented.

"You ladies are very kind, and I'm so glad you enjoyed yourselves."

"Have a safe trip home," one of them said.

"You, too."

When the elevator chimed, he stepped inside and pressed 5. He had no idea how Charlotte was going to react when she saw him, but he hoped their conversation wouldn't evolve into some huge blowup. As it was, over the last couple of weeks, all they'd done was argue and say hurtful things to each other, and he didn't want to do that anymore. What he longed for was a new beginning and a house filled with peace.

Curtis stepped off the elevator, walked a few feet down the hallway, and knocked on the door.

"Who is it?"

"Me."

There was no response; needless to say, he'd anticipated this.

"Look, you may as well open the door because I'm not leaving until I talk to you."

There was more silence.

"I'm waiting," he said, but prayed Charlotte would open the door before this new group of women made it down to where he was standing. The last thing he wanted was to have them hear him begging his own wife to let him into a hotel room. Thankfully, she came to the door and unlocked it.

"Why are you doing this?" he asked.

"Doing what?"

Curtis went over to the curtains and drew them open. "Hiding out in a dark hotel room, drinking."

"What is with everybody? First Lana comes up here trying to tell me what to do, and now you barge in here like some prison guard."

"We're going home, so get dressed."

"I'm not going anywhere. I'll be home tomorrow."

"The car will be here in forty-five minutes for the airport."

"For you maybe."

"No, for both of us."

Charlotte got back into bed. "Like I said, I'll be home tomorrow."

"You do realize tomorrow is Memorial Day?"

She paused for too long, and Curtis knew it hadn't so much as crossed her mind.

"Of course I do."

"So, you know it's a holiday, and you're

still going to disappoint Matt and Curtina?"

She turned her back to him and curled up in a ball. Curtis could tell she was crying.

He sat down on the bed. "Baby, look. I'm sorry. I know you're hurting, and I know Sharon sounded very convincing, but look at me."

"Just leave me alone, Curtis."

"No, I want you to sit up and look straight into my eyes."

"Why?"

"Just do it, and then if you still want me to go, I will."

Charlotte sniffled and slowly sat up.

Curtis held her chin with his hand. "I never slept with that woman. I never even kissed her. I did go to her home once last year and then again last Sunday, but God knows that was it."

Charlotte broke into tears again. "I wanna believe you, but I'm so confused."

"I understand that, but I'm telling you the truth. I have no idea how she figured out what room I was in or when she got here, but I never invited her. She's called me every day this week, but I haven't spoken to her since last Tuesday. I've ignored every phone call."

"But why would she go to all this trouble if you told her you couldn't talk to her anymore?"

"I don't know, but since she hasn't called this morning, I'm hoping she's finally finished with this silly charade of hers."

"We were having such a good time yesterday, Curtis, and then this woman came here and ruined everything."

"I know, but let's just try to move on. I know it won't be easy, but let's not let a lie come between us like this." Charlotte wrapped her arms around his neck, and he rested his around her waist. "There is one other thing, though," he said.

"What's that?"

"Your drinking. This really does have to stop. It's not good for you, and it's certainly not good for our family."

"I know. I'm really sorry I started doing that, and it won't happen again."

Curtis prayed she was telling the truth and that this wouldn't be an ongoing problem. "I'm glad."

They gazed into each other's eyes, but then Curtis glanced at his watch. "At this point, I don't think we're going to make it to the airport in time. You still need to get dressed."

"Maybe we can take a later flight."

"I'm sure we can," he said, and then went over and dialed the bell stand.

"Hello?" a man said.

"Yes, this is Pastor Black. Can you let our driver know we're going to be staying until later this afternoon and that I'll call the car company to schedule a new pickup time?"

"Of course. No problem."

"I appreciate it," Curtis said, and laid the phone back on its base.

Charlotte smiled at him. "So now what?"

Curtis pulled his shirt over his head. "Well, for one thing we still have some unfinished business."

"From last night you mean?"

"Yep, and I say we take care of it."

"I say we take care of it, too. . . . as soon as possible."

CHAPTER 34

God was good all the time, and all the time God was good. Charlotte loved that saying, and oh how she finally recognized how true it was. She and Curtis had flown home late Sunday afternoon from Detroit and spent time at home with Curtina and Matthew, and then they'd all had the best Memorial Day at Aunt Emma's. Her parents had driven down as well, and Charlotte could still see the huge grin on her mother's face when she told her everything was going to be fine with her and Curtis. She'd hugged her like never before and did the same thing to Curtis, and she'd played in the yard with Curtina like she was a preschooler herself. But the best news of all was that after more than a year, Curtis had finally moved back into the master suite. He'd slept there right away on Sunday evening, but last night, he'd moved a few pieces of his clothing back into their walk-in closet, and Charlotte was comforted. She was also thankful Curtis hadn't given up on trying to talk to her while they'd been in Detroit and that he hadn't flown back home without her. If he had, there was a chance things might have turned out differently for them.

Curtis opened his eyes and stretched his arms. "Good morning."

Charlotte leaned over and pecked him on the lips. "Good morning, yourself."

"I can't believe it's Tuesday already."

"I know. Probably because we had a pretty eventful weekend."

"Isn't that the truth? But the holiday yesterday was a nice way to end it."

"It really was a great time, and as usual, Aunt Emma made way too much food, and I ate way too much of it."

They both laughed. "I think everyone did," he said.

"So do you have a lot to do at the church today?"

"Sort of. I have a quick meeting with our associate ministers and then a premarital counseling session with one of our new couples. After that, I need to work on tomorrow night's Bible study lesson."

"Are you continuing where you stopped last week?"

"I am."

There was a knock at the door, and Charlotte and Curtis shook their heads, smiling. There was no question who it was, and it was a good thing Charlotte had already slipped on a silk pajama set when she'd gone to the bathroom not long ago, and Curtis had on a pair of pajama bottoms.

"Yes, Curtina?" Charlotte sang.

"Can I come in?"

"You may."

Curtina pushed the door open, strolled over to the bed, and climbed on top of it. She sat with her back to the door, facing her parents. "Good morning, Mommy. Good morning, Daddy."

Curtis clasped his hands behind his head. "Good morning, pumpkin."

"So what are you doing up so early?" Charlotte asked.

"I'm always up at this time."

"Yeah, I guess you're right."

"You know what, though?"

"What?" Charlotte said.

"I'm so glad you and Daddy have the same bedroom again, because now I only have to go to one place to see both of you."

Charlotte and Curtis looked at each other, and then he said, "Well, we're glad, too, sweetie."

Curtina turned around when she heard

her brother walking in and humming to a song. "Matt's listening to his iTouch again. He always listens to that thing."

"Just like you always watch DVDs," Curtis reminded her, and Matthew sat on the bed next to his sister.

"When am *I* gonna get an iTouch?" she said.

Curtis reached forward and tickled the bottom of her foot. "When you're older, young lady."

Curtina squealed with laughter. "Stop it, Daddy." Then she squealed even louder when Matthew tickled her with no mercy. She laughed so hard she was out of breath.

Matthew pulled his headphones from his ears, letting them drape around his neck, but he didn't say anything. He sat contently and hadn't come in there for any particular reason, and Charlotte knew he was just as happy his dad had moved back into the master suite as Curtina was. He was eighteen and heading off to college, and of course had his own issues with his mother, but he was no different than any other child who wanted their parents to be happy. He'd claimed he didn't blame his dad for divorcing her, but the serene expression on his face told a different story. The son Charlotte saw now was glad his mom and dad were staying together.

Charlotte sat up in the bed a little farther. "You have finals tomorrow, Thursday, and Friday, right?"

"Yep, and Racquel and I are going to the library in a couple of hours so we can study."

"Good. Do you think you're ready?"

"For the most part. We studied most of Saturday and all of Sunday."

Charlotte knew it was wrong, but she hoped that's *all* they'd been doing. Especially, since Agnes didn't work on weekends, and Charlotte had dropped Curtina off at Aunt Emma's before heading to O'Hare. She knew Matthew was an adult now, but she still worried about him having sex too soon the same as any mother.

But she didn't want to think about that, so she got up and told Curtina, "It's time for you to get ready for school, so we'd better get busy."

Charlotte's mojo was back, and she felt wonderful. She hadn't been on the treadmill in over two weeks, but she still had no trouble striding along at her usual four-point-eight-miles-per-hour speed and couldn't get enough of it. For whatever reason, it seemed as though she hadn't missed a beat because she didn't feel exhausted the way she sometimes did whenever she missed too many days of working out. Normally she had to coax herself back into the groove at a slightly slower speed, but not today. Right now, she'd already been going for fifty minutes and saw no problem with finishing her final ten.

But she knew her stamina, determination, and bubbly attitude had everything to do with Curtis, her marriage, and their new commitment to each other. She was also happy to say she was done drinking and done wallowing in the effects of liquor whenever she had problems. She must have been completely out of her mind to ever have started down that path, anyway, and she was ashamed she'd allowed anyone to see her so inebriated. It would have been humiliating for any woman, she was sure, but somehow since she was a pastor's wife and first lady of a large congregation, it seemed worse. Maybe because, had their members found out about it, they wouldn't have appreciated it too much. So she was glad the lightbulb had flashed in her head, and she'd used some common sense.

When she finished her five-minute cooldown and wiped her face and neck with a towel, she realized there was someone else she was grateful for, too, and to whom she owed a huge apology. So, she drank half of her bottled water, grabbed her phone, and dialed the number.

"Pastor Black's office, this is Lana speaking."

"Hi, Lana."

"Hey, honey. How are you?"

"Embarrassed."

"For what?"

"The way I spoke to you and for the way I acted. I'm so sorry. Can you ever forgive me?"

"Don't think twice about it. We all have our moments, and we all say things we don't mean when we're troubled."

"Still, I know you were only trying to help, so I never should've asked you to leave my room."

"Well, the good news is that everything turned out great. I could tell that as soon as I saw your husband's happy face this morning."

"Yes, everything is wonderful, and we owe you a lot."

"You owe me nothing. I told you, the two of you are like family, and I would do anything for you."

"I know that, Lana, and I won't ever forget it."

"Hey, I have another call, so can you hold for a minute?"

"I'll let you go, but thanks again for everything."

"Anytime."

Charlotte ended the call and saw she had a new text. It was from Greg, so she called him.

"Hey, how are you?" he said.

"I'm good."

"So what's been up? Haven't seen you at Chelsey's lately."

"No, and you probably won't again."

"Why?"

"Well, as you know, I had just a little too much to drink when you saw me, so my drinking days are over."

"I can understand that, but they do serve more than alcohol you know."

"Yeah, but I think it's best I stay away."

"What about lunch somewhere else maybe?"

"No, and I may as well tell you, my husband and I have decided to stay married, so this will be my last conversation with you. I don't mean that in a rude way, but we're really trying to start over, and I don't want to do anything that might hinder that."

"Wow, well, good for you. I won't say I'm

happy about not seeing you again, but I'm glad you and your husband are working things out. To be honest, I'm a little jealous."

"Why is that?"

"My divorce was just finalized about six months ago, but had it been left up to me, my wife and I would still be together."

"I'm sorry to hear that."

"Divorce is tough, so my hat goes off to you and your husband for not giving up."

"Thank you for saying that."

There was a bit of silence, and then Greg said, "Okay, then, I guess I won't hold you."

"You take care of yourself."

"You, too, and all the best to both of you."

What a nice guy he is, Charlotte thought. His character was kind and sincere, and she could tell he truly wished her and Curtis well. Of course, that hadn't been the case when she'd ended things with Michael Porter last year, so it was good to know that some men weren't pushy. Although, maybe the difference between Greg and Michael was that Greg wished he was still with his wife, while Michael had wanted out of his marriage for good. Either way, Charlotte was thankful she hadn't gotten involved with another man, because it would have only meant more trouble for her and Curtis. She was pleased to have made the right decision about something.

CHAPTER 35

"Pastor, Tyler and Deanna are here to see you," Lana said.

"Sounds good. Send them right in."

Lana opened the door, and the couple walked over to Curtis's desk. He shook both their hands. "Please, have a seat."

Deanna, a tall, model-like young woman, scanned her surroundings. "You have a beautiful office."

"Why, thank you."

Tyler examined the room as well. "Yes, very nice." He was at least six-two and dressed with the utmost class.

Curtis looked down at his notes. "Well, first, let me just say how honored we are to have you as two of our newest members, and I hope you've both been enjoying the service."

"We really have," Deanna said. "You're a wonderful teacher and speaker, and we love that."

Tyler nodded. "We're not for all that screaming and hollering kind of preaching, so we were thrilled the first time we heard you. We knew this would be our church home right away."

"Glad to hear it, and thank you for your kind words."

Deanna crossed her legs. "We also love the couples' ministry as well."

"So you've already joined? Good."

"We have," Tyler said. "But we're also glad to have the opportunity to speak with you because we know you can't possibly counsel everyone. Not with so many members."

"True, but I try my best to handle most of the premarital sessions myself, because I think it's important. You're getting married in two months? Is this correct?"

"Yes," Deanna said. "We set our date at the beginning of the year, and our ceremony is taking place in the Caribbean."

"That's great, and I look forward to hearing all about it when you return," Curtis said, leaning forward. "Well, what I'd like to ask you first is if there's anything you have concerns about in particular?"

Deanna looked at Tyler, and he laughed and said, "Oh, here we go."

"What? You know that bothers me, and I told you I was going to bring it up."

"Let's hear it," Curtis said.

"Well, I just think as a Christian man, Tyler shouldn't drink alcohol."

He shook his head. "Baby, not even a beer every once in a while?"

"No. But what do you think, Pastor?"

Curtis was always amazed at how some of the problems he and Charlotte experienced usually paralleled those of the couples he counseled. Their problems were rarely identical, because if he had to guess, he doubted Tyler was hanging out at sports bars, getting drunk, but still the subject of drinking now resonated with Curtis more than usual.

"That's a question many Christians ask, and depending on who you talk to, you'll hear a different answer every time. But for me, I've always chosen not to drink alcohol. Not because I think it's a sin, but because it's not something I've ever wanted to do. My father was an alcoholic, and I have a lot of bad memories."

"See, I told you!" Tyler was proud to say. "Even Jesus drank wine, and the Bible clearly states Jesus *never* sinned."

Deanna smiled but rolled her eyes at him.

Curtis smiled, too. "That's correct. However, drinking does become a sin if a person drinks excessively and it alters their behavior in a negative fashion. Or let's just say, it harms your health or causes you to break the law, for example. That's when you know it's a problem."

"I don't even drink every day, Pastor," Tyler said. "And, actually, it's mainly only when my boys come over to watch football or basketball. But nobody ever gets drunk."

Curtis looked at Deanna. "Is that true?"

"I guess."

Tyler laughed. "She knows it is, but Deanna doesn't want me drinking period."

"It's not very Christian-like to me, but to each his own."

"Is this a problem for you?" Curtis asked.

"No," she said. "It doesn't really bother me, but I just wanted clarification on it, because my hope is that we can start our marriage out living as closely by God's Word as we can. My parents never went to church, never really believed in God, and they've been miserable for years, and I just don't want Tyler and I to end up like that. I also want our children to grow up in a safe, loving, Christian environment once we have them."

Tyler took her hand. "Baby, I want the same thing, and that's how it'll be."

Deanna beamed, and Curtis could tell how in love they were with each other. "So, is that the only concern the two of you have?"

"Yep," Tyler said. "Because I don't have any. I love this woman, and I don't want her to change a single thing about herself."

"I love him, too," she said. "More than anything."

"Well, if that's true, then you're way ahead of the game. Especially if you're best friends."

"We are."

"There are many things that help sustain a happy marriage, but I've always believed the top three are keeping God first, keeping each other second, and being best friends. If you're not best friends, that means you can't confide your deepest desires and dreams to one another, and you'll never have a reason to laugh. You'll never have fun, and without fun and laugher, you're doomed before you even get started."

Tyler agreed. "That makes a lot of sense, Pastor."

"It does," Deanna said.

Curtis asked them a few more questions and they discussed a few other items, and when they left, he got up to go talk to Lana. Until his phone rang. He cringed when he saw it was Sharon. He'd thought since he hadn't heard from her since Saturday night, maybe she'd never call him again, and he debated answering her call. Although, based on her actions, he realized it might be best to make things clear to her again.

Curtis pressed the Send button on his cell. "Hello?"

"I thought I'd give you a couple of days to calm down, but I guess you're still mad at me."

"If you're talking about Detroit, I'm over that."

"Well, I'm sorry things happened the way they did, but we didn't have a choice."

"What do you mean, *we?*"

"I could tell the last time we spoke that you were starting to feel guilty about divorcing your wife, so I knew it was time I stepped up to the plate. Of course, I wasn't counting on her flying to Detroit, but then I realized God allowed that to happen on purpose. He set things up so I could tell her everything. It was time she knew the truth, Curtis."

This woman was a bona fide lunatic. She lived in a world filled with fantasy, and he had no idea how to get through to her. "What truth are you talking about? Because for the most part, all you did was lie to Charlotte."

"Maybe a little, but it had to be done. I

had to embellish a few things because otherwise, she might have thought there was still a chance for you and her. I needed her to understand that her marriage to you is over and that you've already moved on."

"But that's just it, Sharon, I haven't moved on. I'm not going anywhere. I love my wife, I'm committed to her, and I'm not leaving her."

"I know this is a tough time," she said as if she hadn't heard any of what he'd just explained to her. "But it'll all be over soon. You'll finally be free, and we'll be able to marry the way God wants us to."

"No!" Curtis shouted a lot louder than he'd wanted to. "Listen to me, Sharon. I appreciate the friendship we had, but it's over. I never slept with you, and now you have to forget we ever met and go on."

"But I know you love me. You have for a long time now."

"No, Sharon, I don't. I liked you a lot, but I could never love you."

"You don't mean that."

"I mean every word. I love my wife, and it's time you accept that."

"So you used me?"

"How?"

"By coming to me when things were bad with your little wifey. You called me all the time, and I was always here for you. I gave you my undivided attention. Even worse, I gave up a six-figure salary and a house just so I could be near you. I told you that."

"You told me you moved here because you'd seen me on television, but you never said you gave up that kind of a job. I thought you said you transferred here with the same company you'd always been working for?"

"Well, I didn't. I gave up everything for you, and I've already used up half my savings on the house I live in and all my living expenses. I do a little contract work here and there, but I don't earn nearly what I used to. I sacrificed my career and everything else that mattered to me so I could do what God told me."

"I guess I don't know what to say."

"Say you're going to divorce your wife and be with me."

"I've already explained that to you. Charlotte and I are not breaking up, Sharon, and that's all there is to it."

"This really disappoints me. *You* disappoint me, and I'm not okay with it."

"I'm really sorry."

"You never should have led me on and played with my feelings, Curtis."

"Like I said, I'm really sorry. I truly am."

"Oh yeah? Well, not as sorry as you're going to be. That I can promise you."

CHAPTER 36

Today was a new day, and while Curtis had been sure he'd hear from Sharon again, he hadn't since yesterday. He'd also thought she might crash Bible study, but it was ten after seven, he'd already prayed and he was now ready to get started.

"I'm so glad to see so many of you back this week, because I'm very excited to continue the Book of James. Last Wednesday, we covered chapter one, verses two through eight, but this week, I want to move on to verses nine through eighteen. So if you'll open your Bibles with me, I'd like to begin with nine through eleven." Curtis paused and then recited the verses. " 'Believers who are poor have something to boast about, for God has honored them. And those who are rich should boast that God has humbled them. They will fade away like a little flower in the field. The hot sun rises and the grass withers; the little flower droops and falls, and its beauty fades away. In the same way, the rich will fade away with all of their achievements.' "

Curtis saw a young man standing up with his Bible in his hand. "Wow, I guess you had your question ready as soon as I finished reading."

The young man laughed and so did many of the members. "Well, actually, Pastor, I've sort of wondered about this scripture and a few others like it for a while. I get the part about those who are rich and how they should feel glad because it means God has humbled them, but then where it gets confusing is when it says, 'and the rich will fade away with all of their achievements.' So, does that mean it's a bad thing to be wealthy?"

"I can see how that passage could be a bit puzzling. What it means is that if you're wealthy and humble, meaning you give freely from your heart, you go out of your way to help those who are in need, and you're not just focused on hoarding and spending lots of money on yourself; then this is pleasing to God. But if you're rich, and you believe you're above everyone else, you look down on those who are less fortunate, and you never help others who are struggling financially, well, then that's a problem. Then the part about fading away, well, that's very true no matter what your situation is because when it's all said and done, when you die, you won't be able to take money, luxuries, or anything else with you. On Judgment Day, everything will in fact fade away, so your primary goal in this life should be to make sure you have things right with God. Make sure you're living in a way that pleases Him and also in a way that uplifts Him daily."

"Thank you," the young man said. "That helps a lot."

There were a couple of other questions, but just as Curtis was ready to move on to the next section, Sharon waltzed in. He'd so been hoping this wouldn't happen, and only God knew what she might say or do before the evening was over. But he couldn't let her presence stop the teaching of the lesson, so he went on. "If you will, let's take a look at verses twelve through sixteen. And it reads, 'God blesses those who patiently endure testing and temptation. Afterward they will receive the crown of life that God has promised to those who love him. And remember, when you are being tempted, do not say, "God is tempting me." God is never tempted to do wrong, and he never tempts anyone else. Temptation comes from our own desires, which entice us and drag us away. These desires give birth to sinful actions. And when sin is allowed to grow, it gives birth to death. So don't be misled, my dear brothers and sisters.' "

No sooner than Curtis had finished reading, Sharon stood with her Bible. "If you don't mind, Pastor, I have a question about a part of this particular passage."

Curtis glanced over at Charlotte, who discreetly shook her head in amazement, and then he said, "Okay."

"What I'd like to know is why do people place themselves in tempting situations if they know they don't want to commit sin?"

Curtis had a bad feeling about this. "We all do it because we're human."

"I understand that part, but maybe I should give an example. If a man is married, and he knows committing adultery is a sin, then why would he spend time with another woman? Why would he tempt himself that way when he knows, as the scripture says, that these desires give birth to sinful actions?"

"Because we all make mistakes, but the good news is that we're all gifted with the ability to learn from them."

"I see. Then what about the part that says when sin is allowed to grow, it gives birth to

death? Does that mean when people know-
ingly enter into temptation and commit sin,
the result will be death? Does that mean
they'll end up reaping what they've sown?"

Curtis knew she was indirectly threatening him, but he kept a straight face. "Yes,
we all reap what we sow, no matter what."

"Okay, I get it now, and thank you for
answering. Oh, and one more thing: If a
person has lustful desires, how does he or
she control them? I know you said we're all
human and that's why we sometimes give
in to temptation, but how do we stop ourselves?"

"Through prayer and by reading the
Word. We should all do that regularly."

Sharon smiled. "Thank you. And if you
don't mind, just one last question. I'm sorry
to keep asking so many, but tonight's passage really has me excited, and I'm learning
so, so much. I was reading ahead after last
week's lesson, and since I walked in a little
late this evening, I don't know if you said
whether you'd be covering verses nineteen
on. That section talks about listening, obey-
ing, and doing."

"No, we'll get to that next week."

"Sounds good. I can't wait because I think
many times, we don't listen to God or obey
Him, and that's when we're forced to deal

with consequences . . . anyway, I'll wait until next Wednesday. Sorry, everyone."

The congregation laughed, clearly thinking her questions and comments were genuine — thanks to the honest look plastered across her face and the well-feigned sincerity in her voice. They had no clue she was obsessed with their pastor or that she wasn't dealing with reality very well, and this worried Curtis. He wasn't sure what this woman was planning to do next, but he knew this wasn't the end of her.

CHAPTER 37

Charlotte hadn't been sitting more than five minutes when her longtime stylist, Robin, walked over and greeted her. "Hey, how are you?" she said, hugging Charlotte the same as always.

"Good, and you?"

"Couldn't be better. How was your holiday?"

"It was great."

Charlotte had been a customer of Robin's Hair Creations for years, and unless Robin retired or moved to a different city, she would likely continue coming to her every Thursday forever. Charlotte kept a standing appointment, and she wasn't sure anyone in the city of Mitchell was more talented, dependable, and kind. Sometimes they could talk for hours on end about God, life, politics, clothing, and everything else one could think of, so Charlotte had long since stopped seeing her as just her stylist and mostly saw her as her friend.

Charlotte took a seat in Robin's chair, and Robin wrapped a cape around her.

"Are we still doing a relaxer today?" Robin asked. "I know we sort of talked about it last week."

"Yes, definitely."

Robin parted Charlotte's hair with her hands, examining it. "It doesn't look all that ready to me, but I guess you do have a little new growth."

"I do, and you know I don't like it when it gets too thick. It makes combing it every day a little unmanageable."

Robin rubbed a petroleum base at the beginning of her edges, so no chemical would damage her skin, and then she added some to the inside sections of her hair as well. "So what's new in the Black household?"

"Well, Matt's taking finals this week and gearing up for graduation, so we're all pretty thrilled about that," she said. She wished she could tell Robin about her personal problems, how she and Curtis were dealing with some loony woman named Sharon, but too many people were around.

"Still can't believe he's eighteen and preparing to head off to college. Time sure does fly."

"Tell me about it. I still remember when he was just a newborn, and now he's grown."

"Amazing."

"Oh, and Curtis and I went to a women's conference in Detroit last weekend, and it was huge. One of the largest ones I've been to in a while."

"You didn't tell me you were going anywhere."

"I know. Curtis was the speaker on Saturday evening, and I decided to surprise him at the last minute."

"How nice."

"It was. We enjoyed ourselves and then flew back on Sunday. So what's going on with you?"

"Well, a few friends and I went to a birthday party, and I met a new guy."

"Really?"

"Yes, girl, and he seems so nice. He's also a very handsome attorney, so that doesn't hurt either."

"I guess not. Good for you, and I hope it works out."

Robin applied a bit of relaxer near Charlotte's scalp. "You never know, but so far so good."

"I'm glad, and I would love to meet him sometime."

"If we keep seeing each other, you will. Oh, and I have some other great news as well. I've decided to expand the salon."

"Really? That's great, Robin."

"I found a wonderful building a little farther north of here, and I'm so excited."

"So when do you plan on moving in?"

"The building is already nice inside and out, but I'm having some remodeling done to make it a little more contemporary. They should be finished in about three or four months, and at the very latest, I'll be able to move in by November or December."

"I can't wait."

"Neither can I, and while you know I don't like imposing, do you think Pastor would be willing to say a few words at my grand opening?"

"Of course. He'll be glad to, I'm sure."

"That would make such a huge difference with the media if I'm able to include his name on the press release."

"We'll do whatever we can to help you."

Over the next twenty minutes, Robin added more relaxer to Charlotte's new growth near her scalp and then applied it to her edges. "I'll let you sit for maybe ten minutes, and then we can rinse this out."

Charlotte heard Robin talking, but she wasn't sure what more she'd just said because it was all she could do not to scream with irritation. Sharon had just walked into the salon, and Charlotte was fascinated by the nerve of her. As long as Charlotte had been a customer, not once had she ever seen Sharon there before.

"You guys are busy today, huh?" Charlotte asked, hoping Robin would elaborate on what Sharon was doing there.

"I guess we are. She's not my client, though. Sheba, one of the new stylists, started doing her hair about a month ago. I think I've seen her at church before, too, so do you want me to introduce you?"

"No, girl, that's okay," Charlotte hurried to say. "You know I like my quiet time, and for all I know, she might wanna do a little chatting. You know how it is, once people find out I'm married to Curtis, they usually have a ton of questions."

"Yeah, I forgot about that. Sorry."

"No problem."

"Actually, she normally comes on Fridays, but maybe she had to switch days this time."

Yeah, right, Charlotte thought. With the way this woman had been acting, chances were she'd been following Charlotte and had discovered that late Thursday mornings was when she got her hair done. It certainly wasn't beyond her, not after seeing her in action last night at Bible study. And Curtis had also told Charlotte about Sharon's phone call to him and how she wasn't willing to take no for an answer. Charlotte then thought about Tabitha, Curtina's biological mother, and how she'd suddenly begun frequenting Robin's salon as well. She had no idea why these women who became obsessed with Curtis always became infatuated with her, too.

Two and a half hours passed, and Robin was just about finished styling Charlotte's hair. She'd washed out the relaxer, placed her under the dryer with a deep conditioner, rinsed that out as well, and then dried her hair and gave her huge curls with a flat iron. She did this because Charlotte had never liked tight curls and preferred wearing her hair long and wavy.

When Charlotte looked up, Sharon walked out of the salon, and Charlotte thought it interesting how she'd purposely never made eye contact with her. When she left, though, Sheba came over and said, "You know, I hadn't really thought about it until now, but your hair is the exact style and color of my client I just finished with. It's beautiful."

"Thank you."

"I remember the first time she came in, she showed me a photo of the back of a woman's head so I could cut it the same way toward the bottom and so I could see the color. She said she wanted it pretty exact, and then I sort of matched up the color as best I could. The color she was already using was very close to what was in the photo, anyway, but when I switched to the current one, she said it was perfect. I remember I laughed at her, too, when she said something like 'every man has a certain look he's attracted to' and that the guy she was interested in liked his women with that hair color. She said he also liked it long."

Charlotte held her tongue but wondered if Sharon had maybe had the audacity to somehow snap a picture of the back of her head at church. If so, how eerie.

When Robin finished, Charlotte paid her and went outside to her car. She was so relieved to get out of there, given what she'd just experienced with Sharon, let alone what Sheba had just told her and Robin. But as soon as she unlocked her door and grabbed the handle, a car pulled up next to her, and she turned around. The vehicle was identical to hers and had seemingly come out of nowhere, and she was stunned to see Sharon driving it.

The woman rolled down her window and tossed Charlotte a dirty look. "Just a word to the wise. If you know what's good for you, you'll move on so Curtis and I can start our life together."

Charlotte lowered her sunglasses farther down her nose. "And if you know what's good for you, you'll leave this parking lot as fast as you drove in here."

Sharon shook her head like Charlotte was a big joke. "Consider yourself warned," she said, and sped off.

CHAPTER 38

"Curtis, this woman is nuts, and you have to do something." Charlotte had phoned Curtis and come straight to the church after leaving the hair salon. She was outraged.

"I know. I realized that last night at Bible study, and I've thought about little else most of today. I'd been hoping she would go away quietly, but now I know that's not going to happen."

Charlotte folded her arms. "Maybe we should call the police."

"I thought about that, too, but I'm trying my best not to because as soon as we report something like this, the media will be all over it. They'll tear us apart, and I just don't wanna subject Curtina to the same kind of public scandal we subjected Matthew and Alicia to — let alone humiliate Matthew right when he's finishing up finals and getting ready for graduation next week. Imagine what it would be like on a campus such as Harvard to have his family's private business flooding through national news outlets. So, unfortunately, we're going to have to handle this situation a little differently. We also can't push Sharon so far that she'll end up going to the media herself. You know this is what usually happens when people can't get what they want from us. It's the price we have to pay because of what I do as a minister and writer . . . and sadly, because I made a stupid and very selfish mistake. I never should have gotten mixed up with this woman, and this is all my fault."

"I agree about not wanting to cause more pain for Matthew and Curtina, but, baby, I have a bad feeling about this woman. I'm worried about our safety because who knows what Sharon might do? To us or to our children."

"At this point, we only have one option," Curtis said, picking up his cell phone and searching through his contact numbers.

Charlotte wondered what he was doing. "Who are you calling?"

Curtis raised his hand, silently asking her to give him a minute, and then he said, "D.C., hey, this is Pastor Black. I hate bothering you, but remember last week when you said if I ever need you for anything, you had my back? Well, I'm gonna have to take you up on your offer."

D.C. drove his black Cadillac Escalade, the extended version with tinted windows, across the gravel lot and parked directly behind Curtis. They'd agreed to meet at a location on the outskirts of town, because Curtis knew he'd be dealing with an even bigger scandal if folks learned that D.C. had suddenly begun meeting him at the church. Running into him at a sandwich shop was one thing, but having regular contact was off-limits. Being a pastor and joining forces with the city's most notorious loan shark wasn't suitable by any means, and as it was, Curtis was ashamed of having to ask him for help. He was uncomfortable with the whole idea of it, but if he couldn't go to the police, he knew D.C. was his only hope.

D.C. shook Curtis's hand. "This must be pretty serious."

"It could be."

"What's up?"

"Well, a lot has happened since the last time I saw you. My wife and I worked things out, and we're no longer getting a divorce."

"Well, that's a good thing, ain't it?"

"It is, but over the last year, I sort of started this little friendship on the side with this woman named Sharon, and now it's become a problem."

D.C. laughed. "Uh-oh, you musta hit that pretty good."

"No, actually, I didn't. I never touched her, but she won't go away. She's talking crazy and claiming God told her to pack up and leave her job so she could be near me. She used to live outside of Chicago, and now she's upset because I won't leave Charlotte and marry her."

"Wow, Pastor, this is deep. So is she threatenin' you?"

"Sort of. Let's just say she's obsessed with my wife and me for different reasons. She wants me to be her husband, and she seems to have gone out of her way trying to mimic Charlotte. She wears her hair the same way, she drives the exact same car, she wears similar clothing, and she's almost the same height and weight. The resemblance is so close that from a distance, you'd swear you were looking at my wife and not her."

"Sounds like you're dealing with a nut-case."

"It gets worse. Last weekend, I had a speaking engagement in Detroit, so Charlotte flew in and surprised me. But when we arrived back at the hotel and went up to my suite, who do you think we found in my bed . . . with hardly anything on?"

"Get outta here. This Sharon chick was in your hotel room?"

"Can you believe it? And I still don't have a clue how she got in there. She claimed she paid someone from housekeeping, but who knows."

"Well, it does happen. I mean, you'd be amazed at what people will do for money nowadays, especially with the economy being so out of control. But she was actually half naked when you walked in with your wife?"

"It was a nightmare. And then she claimed I'd invited her and proceeded to tell my wife we'd been sleeping together. But of course everything she said was a lie. And then the killing part was when she called me yesterday expecting me to say everything was good between us and that I was divorcing Charlotte. I keep telling her that's not going to happen and that I can't talk to her anymore, but she's not hearing it."

"This *is* serious, and it sounds to me like you're going to have to put some fear into this trick. Let her know you're not playin' games."

"I don't want to hurt her physically, if that's what you mean, but I really need this problem to go away. I can't have my wife and children walking around in danger."

"I hear you, and there are a lot of ways to send a message without killin' somebody."

See, this was the sort of thing Curtis had been a little concerned about. He couldn't say he'd ever heard about D.C. killing anyone, but word on the street was that he'd ordered quite a few beatdowns and broken bones in his time. It was also common knowledge that D.C. wasn't the kind of man you wanted to cross for any reason. He was as nice and as gentle as could be but not when you betrayed him or cheated him out of money. He also wasn't lenient on people who stole from him either, such as some of the deputy loan sharks who worked for him. Although, there was last year when Curtis had asked him to go easy on Raven, the church's former CFO, when she'd stolen money from D.C. to pay off gambling debts, and he'd chosen to be merciful.

Curtis leaned against his own SUV. "Right now, all I want is for you to have a couple of guys watch my house at night, have someone monitor my daughter's school, and of course have someone follow Matthew and Charlotte."

"I can do that."

"You have enough men?"

D.C. grinned. "More than enough. In my

line of work, you have to have folks watchin' out twenty-four-seven. Plus, my uncle manages a security company, so I can ask him to handle this situation, too."

"Will he keep all of this confidential?"

"Definitely."

"What about the men who'll be assigned to my family?"

"We'll just tell them you finally decided it was time you had full-time protection. No one will be shocked to hear that because of who you are. I'm surprised you don't have a couple of full-time bodyguards, anyway, since you're so well known."

"I just don't wanna live that way. Every now and then, we hire heavy security for certain events, and I have two other men I hire on an as-needed basis, but that's it."

"I can understand that. But gettin' back to this Sharon chick, you sure you don't want me to have someone pay her a visit? Or at least let a couple of my associates have a conversation with her?"

"No."

"Okay, but if she keeps trippin', then I won't have a choice but to take this to the next level."

Curtis didn't like the sound of that and said, "But you'll let me know what you're planning beforehand, right?"

"Well, actually, my associates don't usually roll like that. Normally they handle what needs to be handled and that's the end of it."

"I hear that, but even though this woman is causing serious problems for me, I still don't want any crimes committed. I don't want any violence taking place."

"Trust me, they'll start at the bare minimum of things and then work their way up. But I will tell you this — they don't believe in spendin' a lot of time babyin' troublemakers, so if she knows what's good for her, she'll leave you alone and go on about her business."

"Hopefully she will."

"Let's just see how things go, but just in case, I'd better get her address."

Curtis recited the information, and D.C. wrote it down.

"Where does she work?"

"From home. She's self-employed."

"So she's there most of the day?"

"As far as I know."

"Is she a member of the church?"

"Yeah, I forgot to mention that. She is, and last night she got up asking multiple questions during Bible study. She did all she could, trying to ridicule me."

"She's gotta be stopped, Pastor."

"I know. I really wish I could call the police, but it's like I told my wife — we can't take our children through another scandal. So I'd really like to handle this privately if I can."

"I don't blame you, but don't worry, we'll get this taken care of. Believe that."

"Again, I appreciate this, and let me know what I owe you."

"Are you kiddin'?"

"No, I wanna pay you for your services."

"You can pay the bill I'll be gettin' from the security company, but my part in this is pro bono. Not to mention, my associates owe me a few favors, anyway. Also, to tell you the truth, just hearin' about some skank tryin' to punk you like this pisses me off. And all because you want nothin' to do with her. So just let me do this for you because I want to."

"You're sure?"

"Positive."

Curtis and D.C. shook on their agreement, and Curtis hoped things wouldn't escalate. In a perfect world, Sharon would pack up her bags and move to another state, and D.C. wouldn't have to do anything. But somehow, he knew Sharon wasn't going anywhere without being forced.

Chapter 39

Curtis sat at the busy intersection and thought, *What a day.* It had been one thing for Sharon to show up at Bible study last night, but now she was stalking Charlotte at her hair salon. She was taking things a lot further than Curtis had expected, and while he hadn't wanted to disclose what was happening to anyone at the church, he realized it was time to at least alert his two right-hand men, Elder Jamison and Elder Dixon, just in case Sharon involved the church in some way. They were meeting him for an impromptu meeting in about a half hour, and he knew they weren't going to be happy. They would support him, he was sure, but they wouldn't be thrilled about the possibility of more negative publicity.

When the light changed, Curtis turned the corner and dialed Charlotte.

"Hey," she said. "So what happened with D.C.?"

"Our meeting went well, and I've asked him to get a few bodyguards in place. A couple to monitor our house and also someone who can follow you and Matt whenever you're out and about."

"This is crazy."

"I'm sorry, but we really need to do this."

"I know. I just hate having to watch my back all the time and live in fear."

"I'm praying this will all be over soon, but in the meantime, I think this is best. I don't think we should worry Matt with this, though."

"I agree, because if he finds out someone is following him, he'll be worried to death. But what about Agnes?"

"Yes, definitely. Especially since she picks up Curtina from time to time. We can tell her tomorrow morning when the children leave for school."

"Actually, since I wanted to work out a few details for the marriage seminar, I asked Agnes if she could pick up Curtina for me, so she'll still be at the house when we get home."

"We'll tell her then. Are you almost finished?"

"Pretty much. I just wanted to get a seminar update over to one of Lana's assistants because they'll be printing Sunday's programs tomorrow."

"I'll be home in about an hour. I've decided to tell Elder Jamison and Elder Dixon what's going on, and they should be at the church shortly."

"I know you're not looking forward to that."

"No, but I don't want them to be caught off guard either."

"You're doing the right thing."

"And, baby," he said, sighing, "I'm very sorry about all of this. I'm sorry for causing so much trouble for us."

"We've both made a lot of bad decisions, but we'll get through this."

Curtis braked at the next red light. "I hope so."

"We will. It won't be easy, but we'll be fine."

"Okay, well, if you leave the church before I get there, I'll see you at home."

"Love you."

Curtis waited for the light to change, but frowned when he looked over at his ringing phone. It was Sharon, of course, and while he debated answering, he didn't think it was a good idea to ignore her or infuriate her — not when she seemed capable of almost anything.

"Hello?"

"I'm sure you already know, but I saw your little wifey today."

If Curtis had been a cursing man, there was no telling what he might've yelled at her, but then he realized maybe it was best to remain calm and cordial. It was probably a good idea to go along with whatever she said.

"Look, baby," she went on. "I just want to say how sorry I am about Saturday. I've had a lot of time to think about it, and I truly regret showing up at your hotel the way I did."

Curtis wondered if maybe God had answered his prayers, and Sharon had come to her senses, but then she said, "I should have let you end things with your wife in your own way. I should have been more patient, because just a few minutes ago, I saw a minister on TBN discussing 1 Corinthians 13:4 . . . You know the scripture that says love is patient and kind? It also talks about how love doesn't envy or boast and how it isn't proud or arrogant, so, sweetheart, I was wrong. I should have let you be the strong man you are, and I should have waited. Can you forgive me?"

Curtis knew that scripture like the back of his hand, but not once had he heard someone relate it to breaking up another person's marriage. He listened and heard everything Sharon had said, but he was flabbergasted and unable to speak. There were no words to say to a person who believed this kind of philosophy and who used scripture to suit their own evil desires.

"Baby, why aren't you saying anything? Please talk to me. Please don't shut me out, because I really am sorry for the way I've been acting."

"It's fine," he forced himself to say. "We all make mistakes, and what's done is done."

"So you forgive me?"

"Yes."

"Oh God . . . I'm so glad and so relieved," she said, sniffling. "I was so worried that I'd ruined everything. I was afraid I'd lost you for good and that you didn't love me anymore."

Curtis opened his mouth by reflex, preparing to tell her that he could never love her, but he didn't want to agitate her and send her into a tailspin. "I think what we have to do now is move forward."

"I agree, so now what?"

"What do you mean?"

"When can I see you again, and when is Charlotte moving out?"

Curtis went along with the show. "We have to let things die down for a while, and wait for my son to leave for college."

"In August?"

"Yes."

"That's over two months from now!"

"I know, but —"

"But nothing, Curtis! I'm not waiting that long, and how dare you try to patronize me. I'm not stupid."

She'd turned on him again, and from the sound of her heated voice, the whole premise of 1 Corinthians 13:4 had vanished. It was as if she hadn't even heard the minister on television or brought this up to him.

"I know you're not stupid," he tried saying, "but —"

She cut him off again. "Look, I'm getting tired of this whole situation, and I'm almost at my wits end, John."

"Who's John?" Curtis wanted to know.

"What are you talking about?"

"You called me John."

"No, I didn't."

"Yes, you —"

"Like I said," she interrupted him again. "I'm tired, and I wanna see you."

"I can't."

"Can't or won't?"

"Can't."

"You just wanna run home to that little

wifey of yours, but that's okay. When it's all said and done, I'll be the last one laughing."

"Why do you keep threatening me?"

"Because you deserve it," she said, and hung up.

Unbelievable, Curtis thought, arriving at the church, stepping out of his SUV, and heading toward the building. Sharon was a piece of work, but now there was something new he couldn't stop wondering about, too. Who the heck was John?

CHAPTER 40

Charlotte stuck her head inside Curtis's office, spoke to the two elders, and then said, "Okay, I'm outta here. See you at home."

"I'll be there soon."

When she shut the door, Elder Dixon said, "This must be extremely important 'cause it's been years since you called sayin' you need to see us as soon as possible."

"It is, and I'm sad to say it isn't good news."

Elder Jamison leaned forward in his chair. "How do you mean?"

"For a good while now, I've been communicating with a woman who's a member of the church, and now things are turning ugly."

Elder Dixon shook his head. "Lord have mercy, boy. When are you ever gonna learn to be more careful with your personal business? I mean, don't get me wrong, I wasn't always in my late sixties. Once upon a time,

I was a young man, too, but you just can't mess with all these different women. Some of 'em are just plain crazy."

Curtis felt horrible and couldn't respond. He felt like a child who should have known better, and he couldn't blame Elder Dixon for chastising him.

"So what is she threatening to do?" Elder Jamison asked.

"Nothing specifically, but she showed up at my hotel in Detroit unannounced and then at the place Charlotte gets her hair done today."

Now Elder Dixon leaned forward. "So let me get this thing straight. She's havin' an affair with you, but now she's harassin' your wife?"

"I never slept with her, but yes, she's harassing Charlotte."

"She's doing all this, and you never even touched her?" Elder Jamison asked.

"Yes. I know it doesn't make sense, but she's lost it, and she doesn't wanna hear anything I have to say when it comes to ending our friendship."

"Why you even start seein' her?" Elder Dixon asked.

"I hadn't told you and Elder Jamison, but I'd been planning for a while now to divorce Charlotte. Still, though, I only saw this woman twice. I see her on Sundays here at church and I spoke with her on the phone, but I promise you, I only went to her house two times over the last year."

Elder Dixon laughed. "This is sad, son. Not good at all."

"No, it's not, and that's why I wanted to inform the two of you."

Elder Jamison leaned back in his chair. "So why were you going to divorce your wife? I don't mean to pry, but I had no idea."

"We've had a very rough time lately, and there were some things that happened that I didn't think I could live with. The last thing I wanted was to break up my family, but I just couldn't see us staying together."

"And now?"

"We're working things out, and we're not separating."

"Well, I'm at least glad to hear that," Elder Dixon said.

Elder Jamison nodded. "Me, too. I am a little concerned, though, because if this woman spins further out of control, the ministry will definitely be affected."

"I'm praying that doesn't happen, and I couldn't be more sorry about placing the church in such a vulnerable position."

"When did you try to end things with

her?" Elder Dixon asked.

"About a week and a half ago, but she's still calling me and saying she wants to see me. She's still under the impression that I'm gonna leave Charlotte."

"Maybe she'll finally get the message," Elder Jamison said.

Elder Dixon wasn't so sure. "Hmm, let's hope that happens, but when these women don't get what they want, they never walk away like ladies. They always have to act a complete fool."

"Gosh," Elder Jamison said. "You know I'm behind you no matter what, Pastor, but I can't even imagine the kind of damage control we'll have to do if this woman goes public. You remember what it was like when we had to deal with that last scandal a few years ago. Some folks weren't very happy. They slowly but surely started coming back to service, but now we have a lot more members and the entire community behind us, and it would be a shame to ruin that."

"I think the police should be called," Elder Dixon said.

"I thought about that, but if we do, the media will be on us like vultures."

Elder Jamison agreed. "They'll definitely start calling for comments. They'll want to know why you need an order of protection or why some member of the church is harassing you. Then, next thing you know, they'll be contacting her . . . By the way, what's her name?"

"Sharon Green."

"I don't think I've met her."

"She pretty much stays to herself."

"She should," Elder Dixon said matter-of-factly.

"You've both seen her, though. She was the woman who asked all the questions at Bible study last night. Her hair was about the same length as Charlotte's and the same color."

"Her?" Elder Jamison said.

Elder Dixon shook his head again. "So now she's tryin' to look like your wife, too? Tryin' to take her husband isn't enough?"

"I never thought she was like this," Curtis confessed. "Never saw this side of her until now, and I'm baffled over it."

Elder Dixon didn't seem shocked. "Sometimes crazy don't show up until there's a reason. Although, I bet if you think back, you'd recall a few interestin' signs."

Curtis *had* thought back. He'd remembered a lot of things about Sharon and his relationship with her, and there was no doubt that her packing up and moving to a brand-new town just for him wasn't normal.

She'd told him this right from the start, but he hadn't paid much attention to it. He guessed it hadn't actually mattered, because when it came to the women who'd come after him throughout the years, he'd heard and seen much worse. "I just wish this would go away."

"We all do," Elder Jamison said, "but you definitely did the right thing by telling us."

"Son, we're here for you, but I hope you learned somethin' from this."

"Trust me, I have."

Curtis's cell rang, and he hoped it wasn't Sharon again. He relaxed when he saw it was Charlotte.

"Hey, baby, what is it?"

"Oh my God, Curtis, this woman is trailing me bumper to bumper!"

"Who?"

"Sharon! She's practically chasing behind me."

Curtis grabbed his keys and got up. "Where are you?"

"Almost home. Maybe three blocks away."

"Just keep driving and try to stay calm. We're on our way."

Elder Jamison stood up, too. "Pastor what's wrong?"

"It's Charlotte. Sharon is following her."

Now Elder Dixon got up. "Lord have mercy."

Curtis headed out of his office and the elders followed him. "Is she still behind you?" he asked Charlotte.

"Yes."

"She's not trying to run you off the road or anything, is she?"

"No, but if I stopped, she would literally slam right into me."

"Just keep focusing on the road."

"I'm trying, I'm trying!"

"I'll drive," Elder Jamison said when they walked outside, and Curtis went around to the passenger side of Elder Jamison's car. Elder Dixon slid into the backseat, and Elder Jamison drove out of the parking lot as fast as he could.

Curtis tried to comfort Charlotte. He would never forgive himself if something happened to her. "How close are you now?"

"Almost in front of the house."

"Good. Hopefully when you turn in, she'll keep going."

"The only thing, though, is that the gate will be closed, and I'll need to wait for it to open."

Curtis hadn't thought of that. "I still think you should turn into the beginning of the driveway, but start pushing the remote now because normally it'll work a few feet away."

"Okay, I'm here," she announced.

"Did she keep going?"

"No, she slowed down and now she's just sitting there, but I'm already driving through the gate and just pressed the button to shut it."

Curtis leaned his head against the backrest. "Good."

"Is she safe?" Elder Dixon asked.

"Yes."

"Did the gate close?"

"Yes, I'm good."

"Can you still see her?"

"She just eased in front of the driveway."

"We'll be there shortly."

"Curtis, what are we going to do? What if Curtina had been in the car with me?"

"Thank God she wasn't."

"Okay, she just sped off."

Charlotte finally sounded somewhat relieved and Curtis exhaled. "Good. We'll be there in a few minutes, but you go straight in the house just in case she comes back."

"I will."

"Are you okay?"

"I'm shaken up, but I'm fine."

"See you in a few."

Curtis looked straight ahead, knowing this

wouldn't likely end in his favor. At the rate things were going, how could it?

Chapter 41

Once Elder Jamison had driven back to the church, Curtis had run inside, grabbed a few items, stuck them in his briefcase, and headed home. Thankfully, Sharon hadn't tried calling him, and when he'd arrived, there hadn't been any sign of her, but he still worried. So, after spending a little time with Curtina and sending her up to her room to watch television, he and Charlotte had explained everything to Agnes. Now he and Charlotte were in his study with the door closed. He'd also just dialed D.C.

"This Sharon trick deserves whatever she gets," he said. "Is your wife okay?"

"She's fine, but I really need that security detail in place."

"I'm on it. My uncle can't get his men assigned until early tomorrow afternoon, but my boys will have you covered until then. I'm sendin' two of them to your house tonight, and then I'll have another one follow your son to school in the mornin' and stay there."

"And my daughter?"

"There'll be someone in front of her school all day, too. I do need both addresses, though."

Curtis looked them up and gave them to him.

"Pastor, are you sure you don't want a couple of my associates to pay this woman a visit?"

"No, that's not necessary."

"Well, if I was dealin' with this kinda skank, I would at least have someone put a gun to her head. That always gets people's attention. You never even have to pull the trigger, but you get results."

"We already talked about this, D.C. No violence, remember?"

"Okay, it's your call, but I'm tellin' you now, any woman who shows up in another state uninvited and then stalks your wife like this is a clear-cut psycho . . . and when you're dealin' with a psycho, you have to respond accordingly."

Curtis knew he was right, and the old Curtis from twenty years ago — even fifteen years ago — wouldn't have thought twice about sending a hostile message to someone if his family was being threatened. But today, he was a better man who knew violence wasn't God's way of doing things.

"All I want is to make sure my wife and children are safe."

"Okay, we'll do it your way, but I think it's a mistake."

"I appreciate that, and just keep me posted on the security status."

"I will."

Curtis laid his phone down and Charlotte came around to the side of the desk where he was sitting and leaned her bottom against it. At that moment, however, his phone rang, and he looked at it.

"It's her."

Charlotte winced. "Good grief, when is this going to stop?"

The phone rang again.

"Answer it," she said.

Curtis finally picked his phone back up. "Hello?"

"How's your wife?"

"Look, Sharon, you're going to have to stop this."

"Stop what? Fighting for what's mine?"

"You could've caused a major accident, and this isn't funny."

"I never said it was, and I told your little wifey earlier that if she knows what's good for her, she'll move on."

"I'm not sure what you want me to say."

"That you're leaving her!" she screamed. "I want you to get her out of there so we can get on with our lives. I want you to obey God's instructions."

"You need help, Sharon."

"Excuse me?"

"There's something very wrong with you, and you can't keep going like this."

"I'm as sane as anyone else. The only difference is that I know what I want, and I know what God has for me."

"I'm ending this conversation."

"I'll bet she's standing right there, isn't she? Breathing all down your neck, trying to hear what I'm saying."

"Good-bye, Sharon."

"You belong to me, John, so why can't you accept that? Why won't you do what God is telling you?"

There she was calling him John again, and he wondered again who that was. "What did you call me?"

"What do you mean?" she yelled.

"You called me John again."

"Don't try to confuse me, Curtis."

Charlotte sat quietly, but Curtis could tell from the look on her face that she heard how loudly Sharon was talking.

"Please don't call me anymore, Sharon,

and stay away from my wife."

"You're wrong for this, Curtis. You used me, and now you're trying to act as though I never meant anything to you. Well, I don't like it. You're stealing my joy, and I just wonder how you would feel if I stole yours. Huh? How would you feel if I went to your elder board and then told all your members that we've been sleeping together? Or better yet, how would you feel if something happened to your children?"

"If you even think about touching my children or coming near my wife again, you'll regret it for the rest of your life."

"Yeah, well, you just keep pushing me and see what happens."

"I'm not playing with you, Sharon," he said, but she was gone.

Charlotte turned toward him. "Why was she calling you someone else?"

"I don't know. She did the same thing earlier."

"What else was she saying? Was she threatening to do something to our children?"

"Yes."

"Oh my God."

"Baby, you know I won't stand for that."

He pressed the Contacts icon on his phone. "We have to end this. I'm calling D.C. back."

With a solemn face, Charlotte gently slipped his cell way from him. "No."

"Then what do you expect us to do?"

"Go to the police and file for an order of protection. I know you don't want to hear that, but I've been thinking about this a lot, and it's the only way."

"But you know what's going to happen once the local media gets wind of it. They'll contact Sharon, and she'll say we've been seeing each other. She'll tell all kinds of lies just like she told you. Then it'll only be a matter of time before the national media comes at us, and all the gossip will begin."

"I don't want you, me, or the children to experience that again, either, but what choice do we have?"

Curtis stroked his hair from front to back with both hands.

"She's never going to leave us alone, Curtis, and I think you know that."

"But what about Matt and Curtina and even Alicia? What about all those wonderful members at our church? They're going to be so disappointed," he said, and it was funny how Alexis, D.C.'s sister, fell on his mind. As it was, she was already leery of pastors and hesitant about joining Deliverance Outreach, so this news about Sharon would certainly validate her thinking.

"Not if we tell them the truth beforehand. Not if we stand together and tell them what's been going on with our marriage for the past year."

"I don't know."

"Let's just go before the congregation on Sunday and then contact the police. D.C. has us covered security-wise, anyway, right?"

"Yeah."

"Well, then all we have to do is lie low until Sunday. Matt's last day of finals is tomorrow, and we'll just ask him to hang around here on Saturday."

"Are you sure you wanna do this?"

"I'm positive. It's the only way, and it's the right thing to do. Plus, when you think about it, all Sharon has are phone records, so the rest of what she says will be her word against yours."

"I guess, but this still won't be good."

"It's better than living in fear and wondering what she'll do next."

Curtis hesitated but then said, "Fine, but I think we need to inform Matt because if this does go public, he'll be deeply affected by it."

"I agree. We'll have to wait until tomorrow evening, though, because he and Racquel are at her house studying. I also don't want him upset while he's taking his last

376

two exams tomorrow."

"I'll also alert Lana, the elder board, and the assistant pastors in the morning so they'll know what to expect on Sunday."

"That's a good idea, and, hey," she said, caressing his face, "we'll be okay. We'll make it through this storm the same as we have all the others, and I'm praying this will be the last one."

"That's my prayer, too, and I believe it will be. It's time we stop all the madness and just be happy. Just be faithful to each other and take our vows more seriously," he said, standing and hugging her. He held her close, and while he dreaded having to admit his indiscretions yet again to his congregation, he knew Charlotte was right: Sharon would never leave them alone. She'd proven that on a number of occasions already, and it was time they brought things to a halt — not violently, the way D.C. kept suggesting, but legally and morally. At the same time, though, he wondered if maybe there was something incriminating he could find on Sharon, some terrible thing she'd done in her past and was trying to keep a secret. Everyone had skeletons, so maybe what he needed to do was a little digging. It was certainly worth trying.

CHAPTER 42

"Do you want your dad and me to drive over for morning service?" Noreen asked.

"I really would, Mom," Charlotte said. "I know Curtis and I will be okay, but I would feel even better if you and Daddy were here with us."

"Of course, honey. Maybe we'll just come on Saturday evening and spend the night with you all."

Charlotte smiled with tears in her eyes. "Matt and Curtina will love that."

"I really hate you're going to have to tell your business to everyone, but I guess if there's no other way . . ."

"There isn't, Mom. We've thought about this a lot, but given the situation, we have to go to the police. And if we go to the police, we have to prepare the congregation so there won't be any surprises."

"I understand, but it just seems to me your personal life should be off-limits. You shouldn't have to tell anybody anything if you don't want to."

"It's different, though, when you have a couple thousand people supporting your ministry, not to mention the thousands upon thousands of readers Curtis has nationwide. They become your family, and you feel like you owe them an explanation when things aren't right. Years ago, I used to feel the same as you, that our business was nobody else's. But not anymore. What I realized was that there are so many people who look up to us, that it's time we become much better examples."

"You've come a long way, sweetie, and I'm really proud of you."

"Thanks, Mom. But you know what's interesting?"

"What's that?"

"I almost had to lose everything to get to this point. The idea of losing Curtis and Curtina and then having Matt lose faith in me, too, really made me take a long look at myself. It made me recognize how self-centered I was and how I had hurt so many people."

"That's all behind you now, though, so don't even look back."

Charlotte's phone beeped, and Janine's name and number displayed on her screen.

"Mom, this is J, so I'll call you tomorrow, okay?"

"Tell Janine I said hello. Love you."

Charlotte pressed the Send button. "Hey, how are you?"

"I'm good, but how are you?"

"Hanging in there."

"How's Curtis?"

Charlotte had called Janine early this morning and filled her in. "He's okay. He's not happy about what we have to do, but he's still in agreement about it."

"It's not going to be easy, but we'll all be there for you."

"Thank you for that."

"Have you guys spoken to Matt yet? I know you said you were planning to."

"No, but I think he just got home."

"How do you think he's going to feel about this?"

"I don't know, hard to say."

"Maybe it'll be different for him this time because he's so much older."

"Or it could be worse because he's tired of all the drama we've caused him. Matt has been a wonderful child all his life, and it's hard to believe he made it this far without any issues. He's never gotten into trouble, he's always treated people the way he wants to be treated, and he has a kind spirit."

"You and Curtis are very blessed to have him as a son."

"Don't I know it. But we haven't been the best parents, and that bothers me."

"Things will be so much better now, though."

"I hope so."

"It will," Janine said.

"Well, hey, I'd better get going so we can sit down with him."

"I'll be praying for the best, and I'll speak to you tomorrow."

"Kiss my little goddaughter for me."

Charlotte left the bedroom and went downstairs. She passed by the family room and went into the kitchen and wondered where Curtis and Matthew were. She was sure she'd heard Matthew talking while she was on the phone with Janine. But then she walked down the other hall and heard Matthew and Curtis chatting. They were discussing his finals.

She walked into Curtis's study. "So you're all finished?" she asked her son.

"Yep."

For some reason, he didn't look too happy, so Charlotte hugged him. "I'm so proud of you, Matt. You're actually graduating next week. What an accomplishment."

"Where's Curtina?" he asked.

Curtis sat on the edge of his desk. "She's playing with her little friend next door. We sort of sent her over there so we could talk to you about something."

Matt already seemed uncomfortable, as if he didn't want to hear what they had to say. He seemed sad, even, and Charlotte hated this.

"Son, your mom and I are going to address the congregation on Sunday."

"Why?"

"There's this woman who's been threatening us."

"What woman?"

"A woman at the church who I sort of became friends with."

Matthew put his hands in his pockets. "So what's wrong with having friends?"

"Nothing when it's the right kind of friendship, but as a pastor, I never should have started communicating with this woman."

"Did something happen between you?"

Charlotte was a little shocked that Matthew was asking his father such a bold question, but then again, she had to remember he was eighteen.

"If you mean sexually, no. I never touched

her in that way, but she thinks she's in love with me and that I'm going to marry her."

Matthew didn't respond to that, so Charlotte said, "This is all very complicated, Matt, but she's really become a problem, and we're going to have to go to the police. We need to get an order of protection against her."

"Oh."

Charlotte looked at Curtis, and since it was obvious Matthew hadn't considered the repercussions or the possibility of another scandal, she said, "The reason we wanted to tell you now is because you may end up seeing it on the news or posted on various websites." Charlotte thought about the whole Tabitha disaster and how by the time Charlotte and Curtis had decided to inform the congregation about his affair with her back then, Reverend Tolson, the pastor who'd been filling in for Curtis while he traveled, had gone on a national news channel and disclosed everything. From that point on, the news about Curtis having a baby with another woman had gone viral on the Internet and had been reported through all other media sources.

Curtis tried reassuring him. "We know how embarrassing this kind of thing can be, and we're really sorry, Matt. We're sorry that we haven't done right by you and Alicia and now Curtina. But I promise you, things are going to be different from here on out. I know it's a little late, but we won't ever disappoint you like this again."

Matthew looked at both of them and burst into tears.

Charlotte felt so sorry for their son and took him into her arms. "We really are sorry, Matt."

"I know, Mom, but I'm sorry, too."

"For what, sweetie? You didn't do anything."

"I did, Mom. You and Dad are gonna be so upset."

Curtis walked closer, placing his hand on his back. "Son, what is it?"

Matthew sniffled, wiped his face, and said, "Racquel is pregnant."

CHAPTER 43

The church choir sang beautifully, but Charlotte focused on something else. No matter how many times she replayed Matthew's words in her head, she still couldn't accept or believe them. Racquel was pregnant. Six weeks to be exact, and there was nothing anyone could do about it. What had Matt been thinking? He was a straight-A student who'd won a full four-year academic scholarship, to Harvard no less, yet he hadn't been smart enough to use protection? It was bad enough he and Racquel were having sex, period, but the very least he could have done was wear a condom, and Racquel could have used some sort of birth control as well. And what about all the diseases going around? She knew Matthew truly liked Racquel and maybe even loved her, but how did he really know he could trust her? How did Racquel know she could trust him for that matter? Charlotte just wished they hadn't been so careless. From the very beginning, as soon as Matthew had started bringing Racquel around on a regular basis, Charlotte had worried she might end up pregnant — she'd worried that she or some other girl would realize what a gold mine they'd tapped into and would do all they could to trap him. Curtis, of course, didn't feel the same and thought Racquel's feelings were genuine, but Charlotte wasn't so sure. She hoped they were for Matthew's sake, of course; however, she also knew that lots of women allowed this kind of thing to happen whenever there was major money involved.

But that was all pretty irrelevant now, because it was too late to do anything except be there for Matt and his child. She did wonder, though, what this was going to mean for Racquel, since she'd won a four-year scholarship, too, and was preparing to begin classes at MIT. Charlotte couldn't imagine she'd still be able to go, considering her condition, so it would be interesting to see how things eventually turned out. It would also be interesting to hear what her parents had to say, because she doubted they approved of this regrettable pregnancy either. Although, as Charlotte sat thinking, something else dawned on her. She'd stopped taking her own birth control pills nearly three weeks ago, so what if she was pregnant, too? With all that had been going on — her drinking episodes and now this new problem with Sharon — she'd completely forgotten about it. She did want to have another baby, and she'd thought getting pregnant might change Curtis's mind about divorcing her, but now that things were good between them, she would never want this happening without discussing it with him. She wouldn't want him thinking she'd purposely done something this huge behind his back, as that might mean more bad feelings and animosity on his part.

The choir sang another selection, but a wave of panic overshadowed Charlotte's spirit, and she closed her eyes, praying she wasn't pregnant. Not now, anyway. At least not until Curtis had confirmed he wanted another baby, which she knew wouldn't be for a while since they were dealing with so many other delicate issues.

Charlotte squeezed Curtis's hand, and he turned and smiled at her. He was sitting next to her on the front pew, something he hadn't done in a long time, and it gave her calm. To her right were her mom, dad, Aunt Emma, Anise, Janine, and Carl. They'd all graciously assembled together for the big announcement, and Charlotte welcomed all their love and support. Of course, even with all of them standing by her and Curtis, getting up a few minutes from now, looking out at the entire congregation, was going to be one of the most difficult things she and Curtis had ever had to do, but she still believed it was necessary. Charlotte had hoped, though, that maybe there would be some strange turn of events and that maybe Sharon wouldn't show up, but sadly, she'd arrived well before service had started. She'd even smirked at Charlotte, and that's when Charlotte had known for sure that if they didn't tell their side of the story first, Sharon would take the floor and do irreparable damage. She would twist and turn things, making her version of what happened seem believable, and they couldn't allow that.

When the choir took their seat, Elder Jamison went to the podium. "Good morning, Church."

"Good morning," everyone said.

"As Pastor would say, this is the day the Lord hath made, so let us rejoice and be glad in it."

"Amen," various members agreed.

"I know all of you have come to hear God's Word, but Pastor and Mrs. Black have something very important to say to you, so one of our assistant pastors, Reverend Morgan, will be delivering the message. That way, once Pastor and Mrs. Black have spoken, they can go spend the rest of the afternoon with their family."

People whispered and all eyes landed on Charlotte and Curtis. It was obvious that most folks were dying to find out what this was all about.

"I also want to say that, as of today, I don't know a braver couple than our pastor and first lady," he said, glancing over at Curtis and Charlotte. "I want you both to know how proud I am of you and that I'm here for you always." Then Elder Jamison looked back at the audience. "Thank you all for being here today, and if you would, let's please offer our pastor and first lady a huge welcome."

There was much applause and the majority of people stood to receive them. Curtis held her hand, and while Charlotte was very thankful for everyone's devotion to them, she couldn't recall ever feeling so nervous when walking to the podium. But she took a deep breath and prayed for this to go quickly.

Curtis waited for everyone to be seated, released her hand, and pulled the mic from its holder. "I would first like to say that you are by far the most loving congregation I have ever known, and I really appreciate that. You go out of your way to support me as your pastor, and you support my wife as your first lady and my family as a whole, and we are both extremely grateful. But, of course, there comes a time when mistakes are made, bad decisions enter the equation, and as human beings, we sometimes don't do the right thing . . . and unfortunately, that's what we're here to talk to you about."

Charlotte watched how attentive everyone was and hoped she'd be able to get her words out when it was time for her to speak.

"A little over a year ago, my wife and I went through some very trying times with our marriage, and I'd made the decision to divorce her."

There was more whispering, people nodded in disbelief, and most everyone was shocked.

"I know this must come as a surprise, but it's true. We basically went our separate ways, and I was pretty much sitting back waiting for my son to leave for college so I could begin the dissolution process. But in the meantime, I started having phone conversations with a woman who is a member of this church, and I spoke to her almost daily. I did this for more than a year, until last week. I also visited her twice during this same period of time, and while I never touched her, not once, it was still very wrong. I had no business talking to or going to see her, and I'm very sorry for that. I've apologized to God, and now I'm apologizing to all of you because you deserve so much better than this."

Charlotte looked around, and interestingly enough, no one seemed incensed by any of what Curtis was saying, and she knew it was because he'd said he hadn't slept with this woman. They could hear the sincerity in his voice, and they could tell he was being truthful with them.

"You deserve better than this, and I'm ashamed of my actions," he continued. "Not to mention, it was only a few years ago that I disappointed many of you with another mistake I made, so you can only imagine how much I regret having to stand before you today. To be honest, I tried looking for other ways to handle this so I wouldn't have to face you, but it was my wonderful wife here who said the best thing for us to do was speak to you directly. She thought it was better to tell you everything before you started hearing rumors and lies from someone else, and now I'm glad I listened. And finally, before I pass the mic over to her, there's something else I want you to know. She and I have worked things out, and if it's left up to me, we'll be married until I take my last breath."

The congregation stood and applauded, and Charlotte wanted to burst with joy. Everything was going so well . . . until she saw Sharon getting up, sliding out of her row, and walking into the aisle.

"I don't believe you people! You're actually going to sit here clapping and giving this man a standing ovation? And don't get me started on this tramp you call your first lady. Are you people insane? Didn't you hear him say he's had a relationship with me for months now?"

Charlotte watched her slowly turning in a circle, making sure she addressed members in every direction, but she wondered why Lana had just walked into the sanctuary, giving Curtis what looked to be an everything-has-been-taken-care-of sort of look. Charlotte had thought it strange that she hadn't seen Lana yet this morning, and suddenly Curtis appeared calm and unworried about what Sharon would say or do next. Then, in a matter of seconds, six police officers entered through the double doors, quickly making their way down the aisle to where Sharon was standing.

"Sharon Green," one of them said, "we're going to need you to come with us."

"Why?"

"You're under arrest for five counts of tax evasion, fraud, and the illegal use of three aliases."

Loud gasps and noisy conversation resonated throughout the sanctuary. Everyone was clearly stunned — including Charlotte.

"Let me go!"

An officer handcuffed her and recited the Miranda warning. As two of the officers dragged her out of the church, Sharon kicked and struggled, shouting, "I hate you, Curtis, and if it's the last thing I do, I'm paying you back for this." She kicked and fought and yelled a few obscenities, but finally, she was gone. Charlotte wasn't sure how and why this had occurred, but she was thrilled. Sharon was actually out of their lives. She was history, and Charlotte would have done a happy dance if it wouldn't have looked so silly. Nonetheless, she smiled and thought proudly, *Good-bye, good riddance, and thank God.* Still, she couldn't wait to hear how this had happened.

EPILOGUE

Five Days Later

Charlotte was still in awe of the way things had turned out. Who would have imagined Sharon was a criminal? A white-collar criminal but still a criminal who'd committed crimes for many years. She was certainly crazy enough — that much had been confirmed over the last month — but not even Curtis had suspected she was a pro at cheating the government and stealing the identities of deceased women. She'd gotten away with a ton of misdeeds, and while she'd lived well in at least five different states, she hadn't worked for anyone in over a decade. She also wasn't self-employed the way she'd claimed, nor had she transferred from some Chicago company before moving to Mitchell. Everything she'd told Curtis had been a lie.

They now knew who "John" was, too. Curtis had wondered why she'd made the mistake of calling him that on two different occasions. It seemed John had been Sharon's last love interest and victim. She'd met him while living in Atlanta, Georgia, the last place she'd resided before moving to Mitchell, and things had turned quite ugly. She'd baited him, seduced him, and even purchased a wedding gown for their intended nuptials, but after a few months, John had announced that he wasn't leaving his wife and told her their affair was over. Needless to say, Sharon hadn't taken the news very well and had begun stalking him and his wife the same as she'd done with Charlotte and Curtis. However, unlike them, John and his wife were the kind of people who didn't have to worry about public scandal, and John had reported her to the police. And it was then that Sharon had high-tailed it out of town and set up shop locally.

But besides all that, what fascinated Charlotte even more was the way Sharon had been caught. As fate would have it, D.C. had ended up having more contacts than Curtis had counted on, and even Lana had done a little investigating of her own after she returned from Detroit. Well, actually, it had been her niece, Tracey, who'd decided to see what she could find out about

Sharon's background through a couple of websites that specialized in this area. Lana hadn't told Curtis about it because, one, she'd broken his and Charlotte's confidence by telling Tracey what was going on, and, two, Tracey had said finding anything relevant was probably a long shot. But then Tracey had discovered some conflicting information about Sharon when it came to names, birthdays, and Social Security numbers.

That was when Curtis had phoned D.C., and he'd called a man he insisted was the best private investigator in New York — someone who big law firms used regularly. How D.C. even knew someone on that level, let alone how he'd met someone working in the Big Apple, was a mystery, but D.C.'s contact had come through brilliantly, and Curtis owed him. Of course, the catch was that by the time D.C. had contacted the investigator, it had been only two days before Curtis and Charlotte were to address the congregation, so Curtis had been forced to pay a large sum of money to make this happen. The investigator, along with some of his staff members, had worked all day and all night, both Friday and Saturday, and it hadn't been until Sunday morning that they'd secured enough information to give to the police. It had been a close call, and since Curtis hadn't seen Lana come into the sanctuary before he and Charlotte had gone to the podium, he'd known she hadn't heard anything from D.C. yet. It was then that Curtis had decided they would have to go through with confessing everything to the congregation as planned.

But thankfully, D.C. had gotten everything to Lana in the nick of time, and she'd contacted the police, letting them know there was a deranged woman in their congregation who had been threatening the pastor and his family. She had also given them copies of each of the arrest warrants that had been filed in the name of Sharon's aliases, and this had sealed the deal. This was the real reason the police had been able to storm into the church with just cause and escort her out of there — this was also the reason they wouldn't need to file an order of protection, and unless Sharon told lies from her prison cell, the news about Curtis's relationship with her wouldn't likely be newsworthy.

But in spite of it all, life was still good, and today was one of the happiest days the Black family had experienced. Matthew was finally graduating and he was waiting on the top step of the stage, listening for his name to be called. Charlotte squeezed Curtis's hand on one side of her and did the same with Curtina's on the other. Alicia was up toward the front taking photos, and Charlotte wasn't sure she'd ever seen her parents more excited. She knew her son had a baby on the way and that this was surely a worry for all of them, but after sitting down and speaking with Racquel's parents, Charlotte and Curtis did feel a little better about things. They were very nice people, disappointed parents no less, but still wonderful people who expected Matt to leave for Harvard as planned. They wanted nothing to stand in the way of his education, and they'd already agreed to raise the baby until both he and Racquel graduated from college — of course, Curtis and Charlotte would do everything they could for their grandchild as well. This way, Racquel would still be able to enroll at MIT the semester after the baby arrived. She would definitely lose her scholarship, just as Charlotte had been thinking, but her parents were more than willing to pay her tuition.

This certainly wasn't the kind of life Curtis and Charlotte had envisioned for Matthew, nor was this anything close to the life Racquel's parents had wanted for her, but as parents, the four of them loved their children and would support them completely. Yes, Matthew and Racquel had made a dire mistake and no one thought it was okay, but after all Curtis and Charlotte had subjected Matthew to for so many years, they knew the least they could do was see him through until the end.

So again, life was good. It wasn't perfect by any means, but they were truly a happy family. She and Curtis had finally gotten it right, and Charlotte knew their struggles had made them stronger, wiser, and more committed to each other. It was the reason she wouldn't change a thing, not when they'd learned so much. She'd also taken a pregnancy test and learned she wasn't expecting, but she wouldn't give up hope on that either. For now, though, she was just happy existing and being Curtis's wife.

"Matthew Curtis Black," the announcer read aloud.

Charlotte beamed, Curtis looked as though he were about to burst, and Curtina yelled out her brother's name as loudly as she could.

Yes, life was good — great, even — and Charlotte thanked God for everything she could think of. Most of all, though, she thanked Him for giving her another chance — and for saving her . . . from herself.

ACKNOWLEDGMENTS

To God for guiding my direction, for protecting me and for blessing me with so much mercy, grace, and unconditional love.

To my husband, Will. I love you from the bottom of my heart and soul, and thank you for still making me laugh every single day without fail. I thank God for the amazing twenty-one years we've shared together and that we're still counting

To my entire family — my brothers, Willie Jr., Michael, and Dennis; my sister, Nancy; my mother-in-law, Lillie; my brothers-in-law and sisters-in-law (Gloria, Ronald, Terry, Robert, James, Tammy, and Karen); my stepson and daughter-in-law, Trenod and LaTasha and their children; my nieces, nephews, aunts, uncles, and cousins (Lawsons, Stapletons, Haleys, Beasleys, Romes, Youngs, Garys, and the rest of the Robys); also my cousin, Patricia Haley-Glass, whom I grew up with, whom I love like a sister, and who is also an author — there is nothing comparable to family, and I love all of you so, so very much.

Then, a huge amount of love to my girls: Kelli, Lori, and Janell who are also like sisters and who encourage me, love me, and support me no matter what. And, of course, I could never say enough about my spiritual mother, Dr. Betty Price — I love you dearly.

To my incredible assistant, Connie Dettman; my editor/editor-in-chief, Beth de Guzman; my manuscript editor, Selina McLemore; my publicity director, Linda Duggins; my assistant editor, Latoya Smith; and everyone else at my outstanding publishing house Hachette/Grand Central Publishing — thank you all for absolutely everything! Then, to three other very talented and wonderful people: my freelance publicist, Shandra Hill Smith; my web designer, Luke Lefevre; and my online newsletter programmer, Pamela Walker-Williams — thank you all for everything.

To three amazing literary marketing gurus who promote my work in such a wonderful way: Ella Curry of EDC Creations, Radiah Hubbert of Urban Reviews, and Troy Johnson of AALBC.com. To each of my author friends and colleagues, every bookseller and retailer that sells my books; and to all the people in radio, TV, and print and online who publicize my work to the masses, including Andy Gannon, Aaron Wilson, Stone and Double T, Dean Ervin, Alex Wehrle, Rebecca Rose, Patrik Henry Bass, Julee Jonez, Maggie Linton, Dr. Avin Augustus Jones, Condace Pressley, Kimberly Kaye, Twanda Black, and so many others. Thank you for all that you've done for me for so many years now.

Then, last but certainly not least, to **my fabulous readers** — thank you for all your love and support, because I certainly couldn't do any of what I do without you. Your loyalty means everything in the world to me, and I am forever grateful.

Much love and God bless you always,
Kimberla Lawson Roby
(E-mail: kim@kimroby.com)

Discussion Questions for *The Reverend's Wife*

1. The difference between forgiving and forgetting is discussed throughout the story. Curtis tries to explain to Charlotte that while he has forgiven her for her past infidelity, he can't forget that it happened. Do you agree that "forgiving" and "forgetting" can be separated this way? Or to truly forgive a person for a wrong they have committed against us, do we have to wipe the slate clean and act as if it never happened?

2. Unlike he has with his father, Matthew seems to be unable to forgive his mother for her affairs. Does Matthew have a right to be angry at Charlotte, or should he remain neutral where his parents are concerned? Is infidelity a problem that a family must face, or just a husband and

wife? Does a child's age make any difference?

3. Do you think Curtis is justified in feeling
that Charlotte's affairs are more severe
than his own? Is it simply a numbers game
— she had more affairs than he did;
therefore, her behavior is worse? Does the
motivation for the affair make any difference?

4. Instead of turning to his wife for comfort
and support, Curtis slowly but surely
develops a secret friendship with Sharon.
This kind of friendship between a married
person and someone who is not his or her
spouse is often described as an emotional
affair. Do you think an emotional affair is
less serious, more serious, or equivalent to
a physical affair? Why?

5. Is it okay for a married man or woman to
have a close friend of the opposite sex?
Why or why not? Are there certain conditions that must be maintained or rules that
must be followed? Where is the line between a close friendship and an emotional
affair?

6. What do you think about Curtis's phone
call to Tanya? Are the feelings he expressed
normal, given their history? Was he right
to share those feelings, or should he have
kept them to himself out of respect for

Tanya's husband? Do Curtis's feelings for Tanya mean they can't have a friendship going forward? Have you ever had a spouse or significant other who maintained a close friendship with an ex? If so, how did you feel about their relationship? Do you maintain close friendships with any of your exes? If so, why do you feel it's important to do so? Would you continue the friendship if it bothered your current partner?

7. Sharon is clearly a disturbed individual who lied about her background. However, given that she was very open with Curtis about her feelings for him and that he continued to see her, speak with her, and confide in her about his marital problems, could Curtis be seen as leading her on? Does he hold any responsibility for her actions?

8. Divorce can be a difficult issue for a family to face, especially when children are involved. Curtis is very open with Matthew about his plans to divorce Charlotte, but he shelters Curtina from the situation. Do you think he was right to do so, or should he have been preparing his daughter for the changes to come? Would you have handled the situation the same way? If not, what might you have done

differently?

9. Deciding to end a marriage is never easy. Charlotte wants to continue to work on their relationship, but Curtis is resolved to end it. His assistant suggests counseling, but Curtis resists this idea. What might you have advised Curtis to do to save his marriage? What might you have advised Charlotte to do? Are there certain circumstances when divorce is absolutely necessary? Give examples and discuss why.

10. Everyone has different ways of dealing with stress, some healthier than others. When the stress of her situation becomes too much, Charlotte turns to alcohol. Do you think Charlotte is an alcoholic? Why or why not? This is not the first time Charlotte has had a problem with drinking. Considering her past experiences, do you think Charlotte's vow to not drink again is enough, or does she need professional help? Instead of going out for a drink, what would you advise someone to do to alleviate their stress? What helps you cope with stressful situations in your own life?

11. Matthew and his girlfriend are lucky to have supportive families, but that doesn't necessarily mean the road ahead will be easy for them. What do you imagine their future holds? Describe what their life

might be like in one year, four years, ten years.